NEWCOMERS

BROOKSIDE, OREGON TERRITORY BOOK TWO

JOHNNY GUNN

WOLFPACK PUBLISHING
— EST 2013 —

Wolfpack Publishing
9850 S. Maryland Parkway, Suite A-5 #323
Las Vegas, Nevada 89183

wolfpackpublishing.com

Paperback ISBN 978-1-63977-133-2
eBook ISBN 978-1-63977-132-5
LCCN 2023932590

NEWCOMERS

NEWCOMERS

CHAPTER 1

"If that ain't the most sad thing I've ever seen. Don't look like that man's had a full meal in a month or more." Thaddeus Younger was standing on the landing to his grocery store on a bleak fall morning watching a man lead two oxen yoked to a miserable wagon down Center Street in Brookside, Oregon Territory. There were two mules tethered to the back of the wagon. It was November 5, 1848 according to the calendar inside the store.

Younger was a rotund man, believed that a man should be well fed at all times. The man leading the wagon had just ridden and walked across the continent, that is, from Missouri to Oregon Territory. It was true, there wasn't a spare ounce on the man, but he was well fed and in fine physical shape.

Thaddeus's wife, Sarah Sprague Younger was just the opposite and was the one who did most of the work around their active store. She maintained the garden, bought what they couldn't grow, saw to it the shelves were stocked, and did the cleaning. Thaddeus was usually at the cash drawer or the kitchen.

"They just seem to straggle in but the numbers are frightening, Younger. Not bad for business, mind you, but soon there'll be more of them than us." Murphy O'Reilly and his wife owned O'Reilly's Tavern and Inn, one of Brookside's original businesses. "Well, in my opinion, Mr. Younger, as long as they're willing to work and be good citizens, let 'em come. It is good for business."

"It's the good citizens part that bothers me, Murph." They watched the wagon go on down the road. At one time it had had a fine canvas covering but that was shredded, some parts of it dragging on the ground. A gaunt woman holding a child sat on the seat with another child sitting next to her.

"Shore as I'm standing here, Murph, either the man or the woman will ask to put some food on a tab to be paid as soon as they're settled. Bet you a dram of that rum you like to pawn off on us."

"Ha!" Murphy laughed. "No, I'll not take the bet but looking at that man, I'd say he's not a bit afraid of a good day's labor, and, Younger, my friend, we do have jobs available in this fine little valley of ours." Murphy gave the immigrants another look. "He won't be looking for work, Younger. He's a farmer if I've ever seen one. He'll be selling you produce for your store next season."

There was considerable talk in the little village of Brookside about all the new people moving in. Great tracts of good farming land was being offered and taken up. For some, the immigrants were a threat while to others they were more than welcome. Younger looked at them as a threat to his way of life but Murphy thought of them as added income and beneficial to his way of life.

Some, and Younger was among these as well, were afraid that there was a decided criminal element among the new arrivals. There had been an increase in robberies, in attacks on travelers, and some blamed the newcomers.

————

FROM THE TIME OF MACKENZIE AND LEWIS AND CLARK, word of Oregon's wonders spread as a plague through the civilized eastern states and the rumbling of wagon wheels were heard from the Atlantic to the Pacific. It was the mountain men and the fur trade that gave the initial impetus to the movement, and it was the indigenous who fought back first. The Kalapuya tribe threatened open warfare and it was the fine work of the governor's representative that ended the threat. Rumblings of discontent were heard regularly from many of the tribes.

The threat of open warfare wasn't heard as often but it was always in the backs of the minds. For the newcomers, they had just come through what many considered hostile territory and weren't swayed much by the talk.

The fur trade brought people from the eastern United States and Canada, and fishing brought the Russians. It was timber that settled them all. Vast forests of fir, redwood, cedar, spruce and other fine wood seemed to cover mountains that reached well into the clouds. Some of those mountains belched smoke and fire, but all of them brought clouds in to dump feet of snow, which transformed the valleys into emerald jewels just waiting for the farmer's plow.

Now, those who were among the first to take up residence were looking with jaded eyes at the newcomers. Just as the Indians had looked at them? Why is that? What is it about these newcomers that brings this on?

The firsters at one time were those being seen as newcomers by those already there. Is it human nature to not take delight in others enjoying what you enjoy?

"How many of these immigrants are outlaws fleeing the wrath of eastern law, Murphy? After all, that belligerent Sam Bassett and his gang of ruffians sure ain't good citizens." Thaddeus Younger was going to make his point. "I'm worried that our way of life is going to change and not for the better, Murph. Our constable doesn't seem up to the chore of keeping us safe, either."

Murphy watched Younger's jowls do a little dance, saw anger in his eyes, and wondered just how it was that the two men, both in business in the town for several years, came to look upon the immigrants so differently. *He's afraid. Some people are afraid of the unknown, some people want to know more about the unknown. I'm looking forward to these people. They're simply new business. It's change that makes the difference. I've never been afraid of change. It's just another word for opportunity in my mind.*

"Tobias Kennedy is a fine lawman, Younger. It's the county that's giving him problems. Won't fund his office. When there were a couple of hundred of us, and mostly law-abiding citizens, one man could do the job. He needs a deputy or two."

Younger just shook his head back and forth. "I don't like it, Murph, and that's all there is to it. Sam Bassett's gang is just the start. Mark my words. You'll see."

Sam Bassett had fled in panic from Boston to St. Louis after a murder and robbery spree and then committed more crimes along the river front in St. Louis. Bassett was literally chased out of town. He found passage on a boat going into the wilderness, hitched up with a wagon train, and found three other men with his own love of wickedness and arrived as a gang in Brookside.

"Just ask Constable Kennedy about Bassett or some of the other recent arrivals," Younger said.

"In any barrel there's bound to be one rotting apple, Younger. I believe Oregon will build its way to statehood, my friend, and many of these new people will be looked on with pride. And, my friend, as I've said, they are good for business."

Murphy waved his goodbye and strolled down the muddy street, almost keeping pace with the oxen being led by the newcomer. *I think I will have a talk with Constable Kennedy, and maybe invite Ben Thorndyke to the table, too. And commissioner Hoagland. We have some of the most beautiful agricultural land, we have ample water, and for those long evenings after a day's work, the wonderful scenery. No, sir, I'm glad to share this with others.*

CHAPTER 2

The economic base that produced the hamlet of Brookside was strong, made up of timber interests and farming, with local businesses to support the two. Local businesses were always in need of workers as were the farming and ranching families. Men and boys could make more money going to work for the timber and mill companies than doing labor in the fields or behind a counter.

Other than the lumber businesses, the town's largest employer was Thorndyke Industries. Ben Thorndyke manufactured heavy equipment for farming and ranching as well as for the timber industry including the mills. He instituted the concept of young boys learning a trade by signing a contract for a number of years in which they worked at Thorndyke's factories for a specific number of hours per day and were required to also attend classes in reading and writing, arithmetic, and what Thorndyke's wife, Beverly, called life science.

"These boys need to know how to get along in this old world of ours. There should be more to life than just work, work, work," Beverly was heard to say often. With a lack of single young women on the frontier, boys were taught to cook, sew, and clean. Fighting came naturally.

The boys learned metal and wood working, at hot forges and massive band and circular saws, and lathes. There was a complete section of the compound set aside for leather and canvas sewing. All the machinery was driven by belts, which were, in turn, driven by a steam engine. When the boys were finished with their terms many were offered full time jobs at a good salary. Only a few refused the offer and those that did probably did so because their family needed them on the farm or ranch. What they learned was always needed on the farm.

County Attorney Claude Atkins was sitting at his desk with county commissioners Jacob Hoagland and Amos Dudley. Atkins was the owner of the largest of the timber operations in the county. That included harvesting and milling. Dudley was the manager and an owner of the Territorial Bank of Brookside.

The office walls were made of thin slabs of redwood and fir, with the lone window outlined in pine. Everything was highly polished and the light from oil lamps created a deep and warm glow in the room. The Brookside courthouse was a grand advertisement for what the county could offer, economically.

"I'm going to be opening a new mill on Trout Creek soon and I'm worried about being able to find enough men to operate it," Atkins said.

"We're seeing new families move into the valley regularly, Claude," banker Dudley said. "I wouldn't think finding workers would be that difficult."

"Most of those coming in are like I was," Hoagland said. "I came to Oregon Territory because of the stories we heard about fine land to farm. They aren't coming hoping to get a job. The land law is such that a man and wife can own three hundred and twenty acres after proving it up. That's the incentive."

"You're right," Atkins said. Claude Atkins was a sickly man, wracked by consumption, often laid up at home instead of being active in his business and his county duties. His wife, Sybil, and half the community had begged him to move south and get his health better but he said his trees were his life and he'd never leave them.

"There are young and single men coming along with the families, but some of them I'd just as soon not hire," Atkins said. "Rowdy, no respect for anything. There is a criminal element in those moving to the territory."

"So I've heard," Dudley said. "I'm like Thorndyke. I hire young people and train them up. Some of the youngsters in the community, raised on the farms and ranches, don't want that life and find they enjoy the banking business." He did as he said, hiring young people at rock bottom wage and demanding almost fealty in exchange. Dudley was a bully, contemptuous of those who got their hands dirty, and a lecher to boot.

Any number of young women in Brookside could attest to that. Married, single, widowed, it mattered not to the man. Many a woman walked on the other side of the street if they saw Amos Dudley coming their way. As far as the banking business was concerned, the man could be vicious in seeing to it that loans were repaid. Foreclosures were a regular occurrence.

"What has Constable Kennedy said about any of this?" Dudley asked. "I'm not sure the man is up to the work his job calls for."

There was just a moment of stunned silence in the room. "He's insistent about getting some help," Hoagland said. "He needs a deputy and there's no doubt. It's on the agenda for the next meeting. Personally, I'm in favor of hiring at least one or maybe two more for him. Just last week a wagon filled with a family of four were attacked and two of the children were murdered. The husband was brutalized to the point he'll never work again."

The attack was in a meadow just off the main road north out of Brookside, about at the halfway point between Brookside and the small village called Jasper, five miles to the north.

"It doesn't happen regularly," Atkins said, "but it does happen often enough that Kennedy can't keep up. Our county's population has grown considerably. We have a criminal element in the valley and that's new for us as well. It needs to be stopped. Not all these newcomers are the best we could hope for."

Hoagland took a long look at Amos Dudley. *Why would Dudley question Kennedy's ability? The man works harder at keeping the peace than anyone could imagine. Dudley isn't a deep thinking man, just reacts. This is strange.*

"If he can't do the job, maybe we should look for someone who can," Dudley said. Many in Brookside considered Amos Dudley a cruel man in his dealings with those who have loans through the bank. He's never been known to give a man a second chance and foreclosure sales come up often. Hoagland was sure that Dudley was being cruel for some reason not related to his job performance.

Jacob Hoagland was astounded by the comment. "My God, man, Kennedy's been doing an outstanding job. He's a fine officer. It's a case of increased crime by way of increased population. The man needs help."

Atkins sat back and looked a long time at the two commissioners before saying anything. "As the county attorney I can assure you that Tobias Kennedy has been doing a fine job. He's an outstanding officer of the law.

His arrests keep me busy prosecuting. We are seeing a large increase in our population and there are those taking advantage of the fact that Kennedy is alone in the office."

The village of Brookside was also the county seat of Brookside County, which included the village of Jasper. Neither community had its own law enforcement, rather, both depended on the County Constable. That office was just the single man, Tobias Kennedy.

"We'll discuss that at our next meeting," Dudley said. "His expenses have increased already. I'm not in favor of spending a lot of money on his needs. We'll talk about that, too." Dudley got up and walked out, snorting something under his breath, and not saying goodbye. Hoagland shook his head and followed the banker after shaking hands with Atkins.

———

"WELL, COMMISSIONER HOAGLAND, WHAT A NICE surprise. Come in. I just made a fresh pot of coffee. Join me?" Tobias Kennedy was a large and heavy man, carried virtually no body fat, and kept himself in excellent condition. His demeanor was robust and open. It was a long journey he made from his native Ireland to Oregon territory.

Kennedy rarely carried a firearm, relied instead on a long oak walking stick, more a staff, with a knot at the top end that had crushed more than one head and broken more than one limb. As many in the community, he walked from his cabin just a few blocks from the courthouse and only rode his horse or hitched a buggy if he was visiting an outlying farm or one of the other small communities. He was well liked by the law-abiding population and roundly damned by the rowdy.

"Got time to talk about some of our newcomers, constable?" The constable's office was almost tiny compared to that of the county attorney. There was a desk, a pot-belly stove, and two chairs. A door off to the side led into the jail area, which featured two cells, their iron bars sunk in cement, the back wall being the court-house wall. There was one oil lamp hanging from the ceiling but well out of reach from either cell.

"I'll always make time for you, Jacob. Sit, please." he poured two cups and produced a little flask. "A touch of rum, sir?"

"No, but go right ahead," Jacob chuckled. "How bad is the increase in crime?"

"I don't keep statistical records as such but I can assure you that compared to last year at this time we have had a considerable increase. Some is from stealing, robbing, thieving, if you will, while others are rougher, meaner. Most of the crime being committed is simply opportunistic, Jacob. Finding a door unlocked, a window open. And then there are those that are well planned."

"How would an extra hand in your office help?" Hoagland asked.

"We would have an officer on the job twenty-four hours a day. That alone would end much of the crime that I call opportunistic. The murders and armed robberies are another matter. A force of ten might have an effect," he said, adding, "maybe."

"It's those vicious crimes that scare most people," Hoagland said. "Some in the community fear that continual stories of murder and rape in the territory will keep others from coming. Personally, I think there is more than enough room for people looking for good land or a better life, but I wonder, looking back, would I have been so willing to bring my family here if I'd heard some of these stories?"

"Questions that can't be answered are the hardest, eh, Jacob? I don't have an answer and I fully understand the question," Kennedy said. "At the moment, I know of three different groups of men who may be behind a lot of the serious crimes. They prey on immigrant wagons coming into the valley, prey on the people trying to establish their new homes, and don't actually have residence in the village."

"What does that mean, exactly, Kennedy?"

"It means, sir, that they live in rough camps anywhere they want. These mountains we see every day are alive, Jacob. Bears and deer and every forest specie live as they would have ten thousand years ago. Some of these criminals that prey on our citizens are as primal as the other animals. They range down into our communities just as the bears and deer do." He took a long drink of his well-laced coffee.

"From day to day I am in no position to tell you where any of those outlaws might be. There is also the little village of Jasper, just a few miles north. It's a timber community, filled with single men, saloons, and sporting houses. A definite criminal element lives there as well. That's why they are able to swoop down on an immigrant family, wreak havoc, and get away clean. I have no means of keeping an eye on suspicious activity."

Jacob Hoagland accepted a second cup of Kennedy's coffee, even gave thought to a taste of his rum, and tried to put an answer to Kennedy's problem. "You, my friend, need the services of more than just one deputy."

"I do," Kennedy said. "In the larger communities back east, or, let's say, on the frontier, the county would have a sheriff and deputies, while the town would have a marshal and maybe one or two deputies. Right now, in Brookside and the county, including our little neighbor village of Jasper the entire law presence is one person, to keep order in the county and the villages. The criminal element is also aware of that, Jacob. They know where I am while I don't know where they are, or more often, who they are."

Hoagland shook his head and drained his cup. "There are those who want to demand action on the crime problem and there are others who want to blame the problem on you, constable. Our little village has grown considerably and that growth will continue well into the next many years. The tax base has increased and will continue to increase, and of course our expenses will increase."

Hoagland stood up and shook hands with Kennedy. "Put together a realistic plan for your department. Something I can bring to the next commissioner's meeting, something I can speak in favor of, something I can willingly defend. And be prepared for some opposition," he chuckled.

"I have already made the notes I will need, Jacob. I'll have it ready for you well before your meeting. How's that lovely wife of yours doing. Such a nice lady."

"She's due to bring us a new life in just a couple of months, constable. I'll tell her hello for you."

CHAPTER 3

"**H**ow much further to our property, Kenny?" Sandra Boyington yelled down to her husband. She and the children hadn't been down from that hard wagon seat since leaving camp just after sunrise. "Maybe we could walk with you for a spell."

"Another three miles or so," Kenneth called up. He was along the left rump of the left ox, prodding the tired animal along. He had a saddle horse tied to the back of the wagon along with two strong mules. It had been a long trail they were on, first across the vast plains, being attacked by roaming bands of Indians, then crossing those monstrous Rocky Mountains, wending their way across mostly open land along the Snake, and across Oregon Territory. Almost to the Pacific Ocean. Boyington couldn't hold in the smile as he thought about their crossing. He knew he had just a few miles to go before turning south to find their new home.

Ken Boyington was just as anxious as his wife to find their property and drive that first stake in the ground proclaiming it theirs. As he walked, he looked around at the vastness of the territory, mountains reaching, not to the clouds, but through the clouds, the ultimate height lost to view. Pastures so green the color burst into the eyes, and the ground, black with possibility.

There was that one mountain, capped by snow even this late in the season, and belching smoke and steam. Sandra was sure it would blow up. Kenny tried to assure her it wouldn't but she countered his thoughts by saying, "But how can you be sure?"

Such magnificent country and we will have our own place, not be farming for somebody else, not working myself to the bone over hard packed ground for another man. When what had been called Oregon Country became Oregon Territory, earlier in 1848, the territory put into effect a land acquisition law that Boyington found out about and signed up for immediately. On arriving in the new territory he signed the papers and now he was about to lead his family onto their own land.

I claimed one hundred and sixty acres and Sandra did too. Three hundred and twenty acres, and all I have to do is make it our home. This ground I'm seeing will grow anything and there's water everywhere. Prove up the land and build a house, and do it in just a few years? I'll do it this year.

He was almost laughing when he called up to Sandra. "Through town, they said, take the first left, up and away from the river, follow to the first creek on the right and that 320 acres sprawled across the mountainside is ours."

Boyington's voice was soft but the pride could be heard in every word. He and his wife were land owners in Oregon Territory and would be farming some of the richest soil west of the Rocky Mountains. "I'll know it the moment I see it," he called back. After all, he'd seen it in his dreams almost every night since leaving Missouri.

How many acres of wheat and corn had he planted during that crossing? How many head of cattle had he nurtured? Just how big an apple orchard was he growing? Every night his dreams were on this magnificent land he was now walking through. He dug his toe in and came up with the kind of ground that farmers around the world dream of.

Sandra had her doubts when Ken told her his plans for the family. They were in the hills of western Virginia fighting rocks, rocks, and more rocks for a man named Skelter who Ken had become indebted to by way of his father's death. When the elder Boyington died, he owed Skelter money, Ken couldn't pay it back, and Skelter forced him to work his farm to pay off the debt.

"I've heard nothing but good about this Oregon country, Sandra. I'm a fine farmer, would be better working something other than rocks." She held her infant girl, Sonja, tight, closed her eyes, thought about her parents, and whispered yes. Their little boy, Harold, was born somewhere along the Snake River. *It's taken us months to get here but it seems like a day or two ago that we were looking at another failed crop in a field of rocks. Home, he said. We'll have a home that we own, where we can raise our babies and have more, too.* She couldn't hold in the smile and squeezed little Sonja tight.

That was then, and she was almost laughing when she hollered out, "Take us home, Ken."

"I'll have to build us a quick shelter," Ken called up, switching the ox lightly. We're just weeks from winter, but I promise you, you'll be living in a fine home by this time next year. And eating food that we grew and raised."

She could almost feel his enthusiasm but contained her anxieties, cuddling the infant boy and smiling at her little girl. *Please lord, make this right for us. He's so thin but so strong. He's good with the ground, I know, and good with animals, but he's been through so much. Make this happen for us.*

It wasn't a steep climb at all out of the Brookside valley when they turned from the creek and into the rolling hills filled with grass and huge trees. It was late in the day when Kenneth Boyington found the monument that declared that land in front of him belonged to the Boyington family. "Home!" He hollered it out, loud and long, almost dancing as he turned the oxen from the roadway into tall grass, over a hillside and into a flat piece of what Boyington knew to be as close as he's ever been to heaven.

Ain't never seen anything quite this pretty. He dropped down to his knees and ripped some grass out, digging his hand down into the moist, rich dirt, letting it spill through his fingers. He brought his hand to his face, sniffing at the loam and laughing. "I'll grow the finest corn and wheat you've ever tasted, Sandra. Potatoes by the bushel. Our cattle and sheep will have the finest flavor in the world, and our children will play in this grass every day."

He had to fight to get control back, knew it would be dark soon and he had to make sure they would be comfortable on this first night in their new home. "Let's set up over by those cottonwoods, Sandra. We can sleep under the wagon for one more night, can't we?"

"For a week if we have to, Ken. I love where you've brought us. I can almost see you driving an ox plowing up this fine ground." She looked around from her high seat. "Ain't it wonderful? Cain't see a rock nowhere."

While he was undressing the yoked oxen Sandra pulled what was necessary from the wagon for the night.

Ken spotted a movement in the trees, grabbed his long flint-lock rifle, and walked slowly through the cotton-wood copse. *Thank you lord*, he murmured, took aim, and dropped a nicely fattened buck deer.

"Fresh meat tonight, Sandra. I'm gonna like this place."

CHAPTER 4

S am Bassett was thirty years in the making and the product was not a pretty one. He stood about five feet and eight inches, weighed almost one hundred and forty pounds, had a long, thin face, a beak of a nose, scarred from many fists, knives, and cudgels, and was not capable of telling the truth. He, Loren Ames, Michael Ambrose, and Randy Porter were making their way through a grove of tall fir trees, ferns, and ragged boulders. The grasses were thick but the pathway was almost not existent.

Broken trees, wind-fall, hampered their way and also concealed them as they followed the tracks of a single wagon. "You sure this wagon is a single, Ames?" Bassett asked. "Don't want to be ridin' up on a bunch of men with rifles."

After arriving in the territory, families would know the location of their new land and would venture out to find it, often alone. They may have arrived in a wagon train but the families dispersed from it alone and vulnerable. They were open, prey if you will, to outlaws of every sort. Some wanted what they had and didn't care whether they hurt or killed to get it. Others were sadistic and took advantage of the women and tortured the men. Those arriving were exploited from many angles.

"Left the main group yesterday and pulled in here last night. One man and a woman is all I saw. The wagon was pulled by four horses and the man rode a horse as well." Ames was smiling. "That woman is a looker, Bassett. I'm claiming her now."

"What you're claiming is a hot blade in the gut, Ames. Don't be claimin' nothing until I lay my claim." His eyes narrowed to slits and he let his hand drift toward the big knife at his belt. He carried a pistol but it was a single shot flintlock, not one of the new types. He always said he could throw his knife faster than a man could prime his flintlock.

Loren Ames got a sheepish look on his face and stepped a bit backwards. "Didn't mean I was claiming before you, Sam. You always get first claim, I know that." Bassett smiled an ugly, sarcastic smile and nodded, easing his hand away from the knife.

During the crossing, one man had stood up to Sam Bassett, called him a sadistic bastard in front of the gang, and dared Bassett to pull that knife of his. Bassett spit on the ground, turned his back on the man and walked away. The next morning, the man was found with his own knife stuck deep in his chest. Sam Bassett spit on the body as it was buried.

"Horses bring almost as much money as oxen," Randy Porter said, which quickly changed the subject. "Easier to sell, too. Was they a prosperous type family?"

"Couldn't see in the wagon," Loren Ames said. He had been prospecting for immigrant wagons, something Bassett and company were good at plundering. They searched for single wagons that often did not have a guide to help with protection. They would take only the finest of goods and sell them in near-by Jasper. They always took the animals and leather work, which always brought a good price. The market for working animals was a good one.

"Their little camp is just over that knoll, Sam," Ames said. "They don't got no dog or nothing, either. The man carried a long rifle and had a knife on his belt. Don't think that pretty little woman had any kind of weapon."

"All right, then, let's be quiet and sneak up as close as we can. Don't want no screaming or gun shots to bring snoopers around. Nice and quiet now," Sam Bassett said.

———

Tobias Kennedy was sitting in the constable's office in the courthouse nursing a tin cup of Virginia rum. The weather was blustery, not cold yet for November, and he was talking with Murphy O'Reilly, who just happened to arrive with a fresh bottle of rum. "Is it the Virginia sugar that's different, Murphy? Or is it the way they distill this stuff? Barbados rum is still the best, though."

That argument was a continuing one between the thirst parlor owner and the constable. Murphy favored Virginia rum and Kennedy the Barbados. The door to the office flew open and Skinny Doten rushed in. "Been a murder, Constable. Better hurry."

Skinny was more than a name for the man. He stood close to six feet tall but weighed in at less than one hundred fifty pounds. Even his face was long and skinny, but he was the friendliest man in the village. He was a hunter and his wife, short and plump, operated a meat market along with kitchen vegetables. They were a sight walking along the boardwalks or out on the levee.

"Where, Skinny?" Kennedy was on his feet reaching for his bear-skin coat and Murphy was trying to get out of the way of the big man.

"North of town. Looks like an immigrant family. I'll take you there."

"Why were you there?" Kennedy asked.

"Following some deer. Three lonely does looking for a buck and I wanted what they wanted. There's a glen filled with good grass and browse. There's always deer in there."

Skinny Doten was nearing fifty years, lived with his wife in a ramshackle cabin behind their little store. The store and cabin were just off a creek and they lived off the land. He only took work during the deep winter when game wasn't easily available and even so only worked a day or two in a week's time. He knew the valleys, ranges, creeks, and canyons in the area better than any man in Brookside.

It was a relatively easy hike of about three miles to the meadow that held the grizzly remains of Albert and Eudora Cringle. Eudora's body was tied with her hands behind her back, her clothing ripped away and there were obvious signs she had been horribly abused. Albert's throat was slashed.

"Weren't Indians, for sure," Skinny said.

The wagon that brought the young couple west stood alone, no sign of horses, mules, or oxen. Its contents were spread out from torn canvas sides and it looked like those responsible had only taken small or light objects that could be easily sold. Kennedy knelt down next to Eudora's mutilated body and slowly shook his head.

"Aye, Skinny, you did right calling me out here. Do you know these people?"

"They were here yesterday, Constable. I thought they'd be gone today." He looked around at the tall grass, the tree leaves low enough for good browsing, and shook his head, gently. "They said they were sure their land was just half a day's ride from here. Albert and Eudora Cringle late of Pennsylvania, they said."

"I'll be here for a while, Skinny. Would you run back to town and bring Shorty Salinski out. He'll need to take care of these bodies soon. Might be chilly right now, but that won't last." Salinski was Brookside's undertaker. "Then see if you can round up a team and we'll get this wagon into the courthouse yard. You'll be paid, Skinny."

Doten nodded, smiled at the idea of being paid for something he would have done anyway, and trotted off for the village. Kennedy started making notes of what he saw, drew little pictures of the scene, and growled out some nasty words about whoever was responsible. The drawings were in detail with direction noted, full descriptions, and his thoughts as he drew. All might end up being presented in court.

Who do I know would be capable of this? The criminal element before the newcomers started arriving weren't killers. Thieves, burglars, strong-arm robbers—but not killers. Some of these immigrants are of the worst kind.

Kennedy had Sam Bassett high on his list of trouble-makers, criminals, and ne'er do wells, but who else needs to be on that list? He thought of the Kinsey twins, sixteen-years-old and moving from obnoxious kids to violent young men. He knew for sure but couldn't prove they were the ones who tormented and robbed old Mr. Parker and may have been involved in the robbery of Stevenson's bakery.

Then, too, Seamus O'Leary had been seen sporting a new shotgun just a few days after Parker reported his missing. O'Leary was twenty something, came in with a wagon-load of heavy machinery for Ben Thorndyke's factory and never left. Hasn't been known to have a job in all that time either.

How do I keep track of all these people and still see to it that people's persons and property are safe? I need help and I need it now. The criminal element is well aware of my limitations. Why isn't Amos Dudley?

———

"IT'S NOT GOING TO BE GOOD WHEN WORD OF THIS GETS out. We become a territory, we make land available, and we seem to invite a criminal element that will put fear in those who might also want to come out our way." Murphy was behind the long oaken plank at Murphy's Tavern and Inn, talking with Ben Thorndyke.

"You're dead right," Thorndyke said. His business included manufacturing farm implements, timber industry implements, and he sold feed and animal tack. His was the largest business in the small frontier village and was the first business to use a steam engine. "Oregon is the richest territory in the west and criminal activity like this will certainly keep people from wanting to live and work here."

County Constable Tobias Kennedy had come in for his evening snort and joined the two men. "An ugly business, this of mine," he said. He pounded his walking stick to make his point. The gnarly old oaken limb had bruised far more heads than Kennedy could remember, brought men to understand that telling the truth didn't really hurt at all, and made other men cringe just seeing it.

"Such a lovely girl she must have been, and her

husband, strong as a good blue mule. Wasted, Murph, just wasted. Whoever is responsible is injured, though. Don't be passing that around, but there was a distinct blood trail leading out from the scene." Kennedy smiled to himself knowing full well that Murphy would spread the word before he even left the building.

He didn't say so but Kennedy also knew that there were four men involved in the attack and massacre. He'd let Murphy spread the word about the wounded one, even though he asked him not to. *I'm a devilish sort, ain't I?*

"Were there any other signs you can use?" Thorndyke asked. "It would be nice if someone witnessed that crime."

"It would, indeed," Kennedy said. "Skinny Doten met the two the day before but no one was around this morning except the criminals." Kennedy thought of something, drained his glass, said his goodbyes, and headed out the door.

"Something's got his dander up," Murphy said.

CHAPTER 5

Back at the courthouse complex, Kennedy was inside the Cringle's wagon going through some of the goods the killers left behind. *What was it that I saw? What was it that made me leave the warmth of Murphy's Inn?* He plowed his way through some of what Eudora would have worn, some of Albert's thread bare clothing. *So sad. All of those dreams gone in the flash of a knife's swipe, in the bash to the head by rotten men. I'm so glad those young people had no children. I'll do the bashin' when I find them.*

Kennedy had no doubt he would find them but how long would that take? So much to do and limited by the fact that he was alone in trying to do it. The county wasn't that big, only had the two villages, Brookside, the largest, and Jasper, mostly saloons and whore houses. He tossed a worn jacket aside. *What is there of such value that a man would kill these seemingly harmless young people? She was young and attractive but there are young and attractive women living in Brookside. What did she have that they didn't?*

Kennedy shook his head, his long locks swaying in the movement, his eyes, sad, and his mind burdened with questions he simply couldn't answer. "Availability," he said, right out loud. "They were out here, in the forest, alone, having made the trek from the eastern civilization to ours in the far west. And they found out that we are not civilized after all. Had they driven their wagon into town for the night they would still be with us."

Kennedy didn't ask himself why the Cringle's hadn't come into town to be safe. The word was spread from Oregon City, don't try to spend nights inside villages. The people don't want you, don't trust you, are afraid of you. It wasn't true. Those rumors were established by roving gangs of men who preyed on immigrants. And like most rumors, spread as wildfire and believed as gospel.

Kennedy was talking a mile a minute as he went through the remnants of the Cringle family. The men who made the fearsome attack, he thought, knew they were safe and the Cringles were not aware that they were not safe. "They made themselves available to attack. A young and attractive woman would not go walking alone after dark in a town but might feel safe deep in the forest." He was sure there was more to it than that but it was a good place for him to start thinking about ways to protect these newcomers.

Ah, here we are. I was right, it's silver. He held what looked like the domed top of a teapot. *No one would travel the breadth of this continent with the top of a teapot.* He chuckled at the thought. *If the Cringle's had a silver teapot, then they probably had a complete set. And possibly other silver ware. Serving dishes, gravy bowls, soup tureens, tableware.*

He had a smile on his face as he climbed down from the wagon. *All of that is missing but whoever murdered that couple left me the tea-pot lid. Where would I sell those valu-*

ables? Kennedy knew the answer. *Jasper. The horses were missing and would sell faster than gold.*

Deep in thought and Kennedy came up face to face with County Commissioner Jacob Hoagland, one of the valley's successful farmers and county commissioner. "Jacob, I didn't hear you. Good evening."

"Constable Kennedy, it's a good evening to you, too." Hoagland had his son Lucas with him. Lucas was ten, growing fast, and was a spitting image of his father. "Just heard about the horrible events. Was this their wagon?" Hoagland asked.

"Yes, it is, Commissioner. Hello Luke. These people were the kinds of families we have been hoping would come to our fine valley. Word of this terror will spread, I'm afraid. To rob our new neighbors is one thing but to kill and savage their remains is what people will hear about." He looked around to make sure no one was close.

"Indians have been known to do those kinds of things. Was it an Indian raid? Some of the tribes are upset with all these newcomers." Hoagland asked before Kennedy could continue.

"No, I'm sure this was not an Indian incursion. I'm sure it was a white man's doing." He didn't mention that he was also sure there were four men involved in the killing and that one was wounded. "Have you heard anything about someone selling goods on the quiet? This is the third immigrant wagon to be plundered recently, Jacob, and what they've taken have been valuables such as silver utensils and tableware, jewelry, and guns and knives. They must be selling their plunder somewhere, eh?"

"I would agree with that." Hoagland said. "Certainly wouldn't want to be too obvious about it, though. I remember back east people would joke about a thieves' market on the weekends where people would gather in an open field with items for sale. Haven't heard of such in Brookside, though." He nodded to the constable and walked off with his son.

Thieves' market, eh? I'll have to check on that. Kennedy chuckled, gave his tea pot top a quick look and headed in to his office. He smiled at the term and knew the closest to a thieves' den would be Jasper. *Thieves' market. Murphy would know about one if one is around.*

———

SAM BASSETT WAS STANDING, WEAVING, IF YOU WILL, NEXT to the fire, wearing a long pearl necklace and drinking whiskey from a silver gravy boat, laughing, trying to dance a little jig, and fell to his knees, protecting the contents of the vessel. "I'm gonna hate having to sell all this fine silver, boys."

The rag tied around his arm was still wet with his blood. Albert Cringle was fast and almost deadly with the big knife he carried. When Bassett pulled him from the wagon, Cringle whipped the knife out and sliced a long and deep cut to Bassett's arm. It was Michael Ambrose who killed Cringle, coming up behind and slicing the man's neck.

Bassett was furious at Cringle for wounding him and attacked the dead body, over and over. Cringle's wife was forced to watch the atrocity and Bassett didn't stop the attack until he became disoriented by the loss of blood.

Bassett sat by the fire almost hugging that gravy boat. Loren Ames chuckled. He was stretched out by the fire, a mug of whiskey in hand. "Another raid like this one and I'm going to retire to California and buy a saloon on the waterfront in San Francisco. Damn shame we had to kill that woman. She was a looker."

Randy Porter was stone sober as he walked around the fire looking at the others. "We got to start thinking, boys. We ain't got time to be gettin' drunk and stupid. They gonna be looking for us real soon. Gotta sell this stuff and move on."

"They ain't gonna be nobody looking for us," Bassett said. "How would anyone know it was us? But you're right about selling off all this silver and jewelry. I'm keeping that man's rifle. It was one fine piece of work."

"When are we gonna sell this stuff?" Ames asked. "Don't think we could do it in Brookside. That Kennedy feller would be on us in a minute. It's too heavy to just shove in our saddle bags."

"We'll just go on up to Jasper and let it be known we have some good stuff. Just like we've done before. Women will flock to get their hands on it. Jasper ain't got a constable." Bassett looked around the fire. "Mr. Porter. Think you could find us a small wagon or buggy to haul this stuff in?" He grimaced as he tried to get to his feet. Besides being half drunk, he was weak from loss of blood and just gave up, sitting back down in the dirt. The bloody rag was filthy but none of the bandits ever considered infection.

"Gonna have to have someone look at this arm. One of the working girls in Jasper might be able to make it feel better." He tried to chuckle but the pain was stronger. The whiskey had eased the pain and the anger but was wearing off.

"I'll have us a wagon before morning, Sam." Randy Porter got slowly to his feet, took a last drink of his coffee and wandered off toward the little village of Brookside. Porter was always first to volunteer for something and was always the least qualified for whatever the chore might be. He was a slow learner, had difficulty remembering what he might have learned, and the concept of thought process before action never came to mind.

It was a quick two mile walk through open forest land. Porter roamed over a rounded hillock, through a vale that had a creek running through its bottom, and skirted around some cabins as he reached town and made his way to the Ben Thorndyke property. *Rich old bastard's probably got two or three wagons parked around. After all, he makes 'em right here.* He tried to hold back his chuckles, looked around to make sure no one heard him.

The complex featured a large barn-like building where most of the manufacturing took place, another big building open to the public showing all the wares, the Thorndyke home, and a small cabin, Thorndyke's private office, near the banks of a small stream. The night was dark, clouds hanging heavy, waiting for just the right time to let the rain fall heavy and hard, and Porter made his way behind the retail building.

Just as I figured. Gettin' a horse ain't gonna be easy. Porter was looking at a small wagon that would be pulled by a single horse. It was a display wagon and the harness was already there so all he had to do was find a horse and fit the leather. Thorndyke had a small carriage house and hay barn near the house and Porter worked his way through the shadows and slipped inside.

Two fine carriages were parked inside the big doors and in the back he heard horses milling about. *Got to be quiet now. Get those horses riled and sure as all get out they'll bring people this way.* He found four large horses each in its own stall and connected a lead rope to one's halter.

"Shush now, big boy. We don't want to wake nobody. Follow me now."

As he neared the open doors of the carriage house, two of the horses left behind started to raise hell, neighing, stomping their feet, running back and forth in their stalls. *Herd sour.* Porter's thought screamed in his head. The ruckus was heard in the Thorndyke home, lanterns were lit, and Randy Porter knew he was in a bad place at a bad time. He started running across a broad lawn toward the log cabin and the creek behind it. He would never be able to tell anyone why he still had hold of the horse's lead rope.

He and the horse splashed across the creek and up the other side, darted through the trees lining the creek, and found himself in open country filled with stands of trees, scattered brush, and rolling countryside. He was a good two miles from the Bassett camp, got his bearings, and he and the horse started off at a fast walk.

Porter looked back and saw many lamps lit in the Thorndyke house, and saw a man running toward the carriage house, holding what looked like a shotgun. "Better make some time, horse," Porter said. He trotted through the brush, around rock formations, and into a copse of fir and spruce. He needed to catch his breath, thought about jumping on the horse and second thoughts told him that wouldn't be his best bet.

Had the horse ever been ridden? Why was he leading the horse when he didn't steal a wagon for it to pull? Questions his mind should have been working on but wasn't. His only thought was to get back to the Bassett camp. He started off again, not hearing noises behind him, not seeing groups of men with rifles and dogs following, and made for Bassett's camp.

"What the hell good is a horse, Porter?" Sam Bassett was furious. "We have horses. Where's the wagon?"

Porter stood silent for just a moment, shaking off the early morning chill. "The other horses woke everyone up. I had to run."

The sky was lightening some and Ames got a fire and coffee going. "We got the horses from the raid, and now this horse, we can load our stuff," old Michael Ambrose said. "Just one more horse for us to sell, Sam. Don't get your knickers in a bunch. Looks like this horse would bring top dollar, too."

Bassett didn't want to but saw the logic in what Ambrose said and calmed down. "All right, we'll make up packs for the horses and leave out for Jasper after we eat. Mostly loggers and timber workers in Jasper. Knives and guns we can sell but I'm not sure of all this fine silver."

"There's two whore houses, Sam. Them women'll buy for sure. And the men will buy to offer the women. You'll see." Ames poured some coffee, didn't offer the pot around, and ambled back to his bedroll. "I'm sure of it."

Bassett wondered about that. *Old man Ambrose don't never say nothing until the last minute and then he's usually right. But Ames here, he's a thinkin' man, too. Ain't much good in a fight, but when we're plannin' something, I'll listen to him first. Damn Porter's all talk but good in a fight. The two together make one man.* Bassett almost chuckled at the thought but the pain in his arm wasn't going to let that happen.

"I gotta get this re-wrapped," he said. "Somebody bring me a pan of hot water and some clean rags. Damn but it does hurt."

Ambrose got slowly to his feet, could almost see the pain in Bassett's eyes and filled a pan with hot water. "You swing on me or do something rash, Sam Bassett, I don't care how much your arm hurts, you swing on me and you'll regret it. Now lay back and let me look at it." Bassett made some strange noises but did as he was told.

Might be a good time to let the skinny little bastard die. Ambrose smiled at the thought. *Split the profits three ways instead of four. Might want to let Porter get all riled and take him out, too.*

Ambrose pulled the bloody rags from the wound and Basset groaned, gritted his teeth, and cussed a good streak of fine words, but didn't swing on Ambrose. "Got some infection going, Sam." He looked at the almost greenish ooze coming from the arm and cleaned the wound the best he could. "Like to pour some whiskey in this mess. You okay with that?"

He didn't wait for an answer, just poured and Sam Bassett erupted, swinging his good arm, kicking with both feet, and Ambrose jumped back, just the slightest hint of a grin on his face. "Best to calm down now so's I can get a fresh wrapping on the arm, Sam."

Between howls of pain, streams of ugly words and threats, Michael Ambrose got Bassett's arm wrapped in clean rags. He knew what he was looking at was gangrene but didn't say anything. "I don't think you'll die for at least another day, Sam. Unless you take another swing at me. Don't much care for that."

"I'm gonna kill you, Ambrose," Bassett said.'

"Not with that arm, you ain't." Ambrose wasn't worried about the threat, almost wished the ugly little fool would try and turned his attention to the other two. "Let's start making packs, boys. We got a short ride to Jasper so's we can sell this silver at high prices."

It wasn't noticed by the others but Ambrose had just taken control of what had been the Sam Bassett gang. Ambrose already considered Sam Bassett a dead man.

CHAPTER 6

"Damnedest thing I've ever seen," Ben Thorndyke said, following hoof prints across the lawn toward the creek. "Some fool breaks into my barn and steals a horse but don't ride him off. Just runs across the creek and into the wilderness. We'll follow as soon as it gets light, boys."

His oldest son, Peter, nearing thirteen years and growing big and strong like his father, stood next to his little brother, Gerald, coming eleven, and smiled. "That ground on the other side of the creek is soft as can be, Papa. I've talked to mama about plowing up a few acres and planting corn and wheat. Won't be hard following that heavy horse."

"I don't think I'll be much help," Gerald said. He was born with a misshaped foot and walked with a distinct limp. He wasn't up to heavy physical work but was a strong reader and was self-educated far beyond his eleven years. His mother provided him with every kind of book she could find. He's even fully designed a steam boat, as he says, yet to be built.

"That's fine, Gerald," Ben Thorndyke said. "Why

don't you go get Tobias Kennedy for us. Horse thieving's a mean offense and I'll want the constable with us when we catch that fool. That horse is a classic, Gerald. A classic, and I want him back."

The last man to be caught stealing a horse was put in the stocks in the center of town and given twenty lashes to his bare back with a cat-o-nine whip. All the time he was being whipped, and screaming in pain, the women in town were flinging rotten fruit and vegetables at him. Some say there may have been some throwing of animal excrement, but that's never been proved. He left town immediately after and it's been some time since another horse was stolen.

"Can't for the life of me think of why a man would sneak into our barn and take one horse when four were available," Thorndyke murmured. "And why didn't he ride off instead of leading that big bruiser?"

Thorndyke had two Belgians that he kept as wheelers for his large family carriage, and two leaders, smaller but strong Morgan studs to run out in front. The heavy carriage was fitted out with some of the finest wood available in Oregon Territory and touches of silver here and there always shone brightly.

"To take a wheeler instead of one of the fleet leaders wasn't the smartest thing to do, Peter. Of course it wouldn't be a smart man who would steal a horse in the first place, would it?" He chuckled and walked up to the creek. "Let's see which way those foot prints might lead while we're waiting for Kennedy."

Peter was a smaller image of his father. Ben Thorndyke was a big man, tall, heavy with muscle, had a large, square head covered in wavy blondish hair. His blue eyes sparkled with humor most of the time and were known to blaze when the man was angered. He was a logger before starting this business years ago and his shoulders told anyone interested that he could swing a double bladed ax as well as the best could.

"Most criminals, son, aren't deep thinkers," he chuckled. Thorndyke was close to both his sons and had long discussions with both often. They were called on to work in the factories, to know what it is that makes Thorndyke's products safe and reliable, why the business is a success. They were called on to clean the floors in the general store, the feed store, even the factory floor, to understand that every job on the place has its purpose in the overall picture.

"This man stole one horse when he could have had four. Did he steal it to sell? Or is it, he just wanted one big horse? Why?" Thorndyke walked right through the stream and found the trail left by his horse and Mr. Porter. "Looks like they're heading northerly, Peter. Another few miles that way and he would connect with the route most of the immigrants use to come into our valley. What's between here and there?"

"Lots of good forest, Papa," Peter said. "Our creek drains into a bigger river which then drains into the mighty Willamette River. Between here and there are some of the finest stands of timber around. Several operations are working their claims, have their own mills set up."

"In other words, son, ain't no good reason for a man to steal one horse and walk off in that direction. Right?" Thorndyke liked to let his sons develop their reasoning powers, make them think not just react.

"Not unless he was meeting up with someone already up that way, papa."

"There you go, son. And that's why we're going to wait for the constable. We don't know what we'd be walking into. A den of thieves? A gang of murderers? Or just some stupid men trying to make a buck stealing from others? Good thinking, son."

———

GERALD FOUND CONSTABLE KENNEDY AT THE BAKERY having a sweet roll and coffee. Kennedy was loved and somewhat feared by many of the children of Brookside. He caught them and punished them in their pranks, and was always available for a quick game of catch or to teach someone the art of fishing. Gerald thought he was wonderful when he read to children from old worn books.

"So, Gerald Thorndyke, my favorite young poet. Have you written a new verse for me?"

"No, Constable, papa sent me. Someone stole one of our horses and he wants you to come and lead us on the thief's trail."

"Ah, and it will be my pleasure to do so," Kennedy said. He stuffed the rest of the sweet roll in his mouth and washed it down with the last of the coffee. "Excellent timing, young squire. Excellent."

For the most part Kennedy did his patrolling around the village on foot but if he was going to be following a horse thief he stopped at his cabin and saddled a horse. "Here, Gerald, grab my hand, boy. Up you come," he laughed as Gerald plopped down behind him. He was at the Thorndyke compound in minutes and crossed the creek to where Ben and Peter stood.

"Morning, Ben," Kennedy said, easing Gerald to the ground before stepping down himself. "Gerald tells me this miscreant stole one of your fine Belgians. Can't have that, now, can we." Kennedy was looking at the trail through the grass and brush. "On foot? Well now. Best if you stay here, Ben. With your anger I might not be bringing the man in alive."

Ben Thorndyke didn't laugh or chuckle but the little gleam in his eye told the constable he was probably right on. "Those that take from those that have need to be set straight in their ways, constable. I'll be more than pleased to let you be the one setting them straight."

Kennedy nodded, with a smile, and mounted up. He rode off at a good trot following the well-marked trail and Ben Thorndyke snorted, glared at the constable's back, and then chuckled softly. "Man knows me too well, boys. Let's go make some breakfast and get on with the day. Peter, check in the barn to see if any damage was done."

———

THE TRAIL WAS AN EASY ONE TO FOLLOW AND SINCE THE man was walking, it went around steep inclines. A man on a horse would simply have ridden up or down the hillside. A man walking wouldn't. *I don't understand why the man isn't sitting up high on the back of that fine horse. Too small or weak to get up there? Afraid of the horse?*

Kennedy saw that the thief was not making for the nearest roadway but staying deep in the forest. Was he making for a camp? To meet with friends? Kennedy worked his way through several possibilities and wondered if maybe he should have brought a firearm with him. "Ah, no," he muttered. "I've got me cudgel. This old walking stick has bashed in more than one outlaw's head."

Making headway through deep forest while riding a horse or leading a horse is difficult at best and even worse when there is no trail to follow. Trying to keep a heading while moving around stands of trees, mounds of rock and debris such as storm downed or fallen trees is most difficult. The trail left by Porter and his stolen horse moved deeper into the forest, further back from any roadway, and Kennedy was positive the man was heading toward a spot known to him. Probably to meet with others.

"Best start thinking 'bout what lies in front of me more than watching this man's trail." It was the smell of smoke that alerted him and he pulled his horse to a stop and climbed down.

"I'll walk a spell now," he murmured. He tied his horse off, had a firm grip on his walking stick with its knotty knob, worn some from being used on other's heads, and checked his belt to make sure his knife was handy. He had a flintlock pistol, a couple of good flint-lock shotguns, and a flintlock rifle, but they were at his cabin. They were fine weapons but were for gathering food, not criminals. He thumped the end of the walking stick onto the ground and set off to follow the trail.

The source of the smoke was soon found. "So, this horse thief was meeting with others," he said right out loud. There was the smoldering leftovers of a cook fire, flat spots showing where four bedrolls had been, and horse prints by the score.

One of these men has been hurt. Haven't seen this much blood for some time. He remembered that one of the men who killed the Cringle family had been seriously wounded in the fray. Kennedy went back to get his horse and took up the trail once again, and this time it moved in a direct line to the main north-south roadway. *Four men, one wounded, and a large array of animals. These are the men who killed the Cringles and they are mine.*

"Heading for Jasper or I don't know my criminals," Kennedy said to his horse. "There are four men on horseback trailing at least five other horses. These have to be the men who attacked those young newcomers. The number of horses is strange, but there were horses stolen from the Cringle's. Too many people for me to take on." The conversation of the day before about a thieves' market brought the hint of a smile to Kennedy's face as he turned back toward Brookside.

Jasper was a town filled with saloons and whore houses, filled with single men making fair wages in the timber industry, and women selling their wares. It was a sort of haven for those who pushed the limits of acceptable behavior, where a thief just might be able to sell what was stolen. The horses would go fast, Kennedy was sure, but the silver? A single man might not be in the market for beautiful silver table ware. Prostitutes might be. Those running the house surely would be.

"I'll need a little help on this, I think." The thought was a constant. *Somehow I've got to convince the county board that I need help in this office. Our population is growing, almost daily it seems, and I need help.*

CHAPTER 7

Often, when Kennedy needed someone to be with him on a project, he would stop at Murphy's Tavern and Inn and find a body or two. Mostly they would be workers from the timber industry, seldom from the farming and ranching community. In the dining area of the tavern there were tables set up for four people and one long table referred to as the family table. It would seat eight comfortably and ten or twelve if needed.

Today, Kennedy found it empty. "Not one of our fine woodsmen not working today Murphy?"

"Sun's shining, winds are calm, and we're within just a few weeks of Christmas, Laddie Buck. Every man's putting as much silver as is available in his pocket. What is it you need besides a fine cup of rum?"

"We'll start with the rum, Murph. I need a man or two to take a short ride with me and be prepared for a nice bit of rough-housing if it comes to that. Seems that someone walked off with one of Ben Thorndyke's horses last night and he's in a fit. There were four horses to take and he took one. Worst yet, he walked off with it. Didn't even get on the beast, Murphy. What kind of man would do that?"

"Foolish, I'll say, Toby. Foolish. And you followed him? Have you asked Skinny Dolton to ride with you?"

"Aye, I followed and he has friends. Several friends with several horses. I'm thinking there is more than Thorndyke's horse missing this morning. The others with that bunch may have been the Cringle's horses. Skinny's off hunting somewhere. Couldn't find him."

Two men walked into the tavern and up to the bar. "Murphy," Joe Clausen said, "I want you to meet my cousin, Jack McGee, just arrived by way of the Missouri route. Jack, this is the finest man in Brookside if you have a bit of thirst."

"Welcome to Murphy's," Murph said. "Not working today, Joe?"

"No, need to help get Jack set up. He'll be working for old man Atkins starting as soon as he has a place open. Probably next week." Clausen turned to Kennedy. "Constable, meet one of our newcomers, and my cousin to boot. This is Jack McGee."

"Morning, Joe. Hello Jack. What exactly is it you're doing to get Jack set up?"

"We put up his tent, tied off a rope corral for his mules, cut enough wood for a day or two, and came to town for a cold beer," Clausen laughed.

Joe Clausen was a blow-hard of the first order, went out of his way not to work as often as possible, and expected everyone to understand that it was just his way. Kennedy was sure Jack cut and split the wood, not Joe. Joes wife worked at the bakery and was far more responsible than Joe would ever be. Kennedy wondered about his cousin, though. He looked fit, tough, had the hands of a man who never quit early.

"I'll find a place, I'm sure," Jack McGee said. "It's just me, no family. Shouldn't be too hard to find a place."

"Might not be as easy as you're thinking," Kennedy said. "We've had a number of families move into the valley recently, and single men, too." He nodded to Murphy. "Murphy, didn't you tell me yesterday that you don't have any rooms to rent here?"

"That's right. Full up, boys. Some two to a room."

Kennedy eyed McGee for a couple of long moments before he said anything. "Atkins hasn't actually hired you?"

"No," Clausen said.

"I was talking to Mr. McGee," Kennedy said and Joe Clausen scowled but didn't say anything. He's never been fully introduced to that walking stick of Kennedy's, but he's heard tales told about it.

"Uh, no," McGee said. "We went to the office and Mr. Atkins said he would let me know when there was an opening. Cousin Joe seems to think it will just be a day or two. It was a miserable trek getting here. Our group of wagons was attacked several times. The wagon boss didn't believe in giving the Indians a head of stock or two to keep from being attacked. I can use a day or two of rest. I've worked timber before, In Vermont and Maine. Mr. Atkins knows that."

"Have you considered taking up a homestead and farming?" Kennedy liked what he was hearing from McGee even if Joe Clausen was his cousin.

"If I knew anything at all about farming I sure would," McGee said. The humor crinkled his eyes and the smile was generous. "I've worked whale and cod boats for years before going to work in the forests a couple of years ago. No, I'm afraid I wouldn't even know where to begin as a farmer."

Kennedy looked at the man and wondered if maybe he was jesting, just a bit. "Are you sure you've never worked a hoe or shovel? You're joshin' us, eh?"

McGee chuckled. "Just a bit, sir. I've done a bit in those New England rock fields. Ground is different here, though."

"Ain't no money in farming anyway," Joe Clausen said. "The missus and I tried it. Didn't work out."

Kennedy didn't say anything but could well remember Mrs. Clausen doing everything in her power to make their little farm work out. She was the one driving the mule to plow the ground. She was the one digging irrigation lines and planting the crops. Clausen complained of a bad back, sore legs, wrenched knees, even bad headaches from being near the mules. "No, cousin, you're better off to stay in the timber business."

They finished their beers and left, saying their good-byes. "You're a cold one, Tobias Kennedy," Murphy said. "You're here looking to get some help and let those two walk right out the door."

"Only one of them would have taken me up and he hasn't been here long enough to know where he is. No, I think Jack McGee will turn out fine but Joe will never amount to anything. You did notice that it was McGee who paid for the beer."

Murphy laughed and poured another bit of rum in Kennedy's cup. "So, what's your next move?"

"Don't want to, but I'll take a little ride to Jasper and see if I can learn anything. The county commissioners are meeting Monday and I'm going to demand help. This stealing of Thorndyke's horse is exactly why I need help." He drained the cup and walked out the door., grumbling, thumping that walking stick.

AMOS DUDLEY WAS SITTING BEHIND AN OAK DESK, MAPLE paneling covered the walls, and brocade curtains were at the high windows in an elegant office at the Brookside Bank. Dudley built the bank with his father's and grandfather's money, and, with help from local investors, has created a viable business. His answer to most problems was simple. "Do whatever needs to be done as long as it doesn't cost any money."

The family moved across the Atlantic Ocean in the early 1700s having found themselves in opposition to the king's banking laws and managed to open banks in the Boston and Philadelphia colonies and stay on the good side of the law. Amos Dudley is not willing to discuss family history with anyone but family, and after moving to Santa Barbara, in northern Mexico, Dudley moved north to Oregon Country. Mexican banking laws were not to his liking.

The bank was established in Brookside and has been a big factor in Brookside's growth over the last few years. Dudley has had a seat at the county commission table for two terms and is looking to run again when his third term comes up. He runs on a simple platform. "No new taxes. No new spending."

The man was not particularly well liked by many in the valley. He was vicious when foreclosing on a loan gone bad, did not understand the word empathy, and some said, would evict his own mother if she was a day late with her payment. There were many who claimed he was also sadistic in his treatment of those who owed him money.

His visitor was Jacob Hoagland who, at the insistence of Dudley, was named to the commission. Hoagland is one of the successful farmers in the valley and is looked up to by many. His thoughts on money matters are somewhat different from Dudley's.

"I don't believe this is a case of saving money, Mr. Dudley." Hoagland was dressed in rough wool pants, heavy boots, and a wool shirt covered by a bearskin jacket. He had come straight from the barn to the bank for this meeting.

Dudley was dressed in a fine business suit, cut-away coat, and shiny black shoes. "I'm looking on the proposal as a case of possibly saving lives and property," Jacob said.

"That's where we differ, Hoagland," Dudley said. "We've gotten along just fine with the services of a single constable. After all, we're a tiny little village. Not more than three hundred residents at best. To put another person on the county payroll would be a complete waste of taxpayer money."

"Inside the confines of the village, there has been little growth over the last year, Mr. Dudley. You're right. But you're not taking into account the tremendous number of people who have come into the county and taken up homesteads. Hundreds of people are now farming and ranching in the valley and all along the rolling foothills of the mountains." Hoagland enjoyed discussions like these because, he said, they allowed his mind to expand. He was a good debater.

"As you know, commissioner, the timber companies are expanding as well, bringing many new jobs and land owners to our county. The little village of Jasper has grown considerably. The problem with all this is, along with these fine newcomers have come a criminal element as well, and the office of constable needs to be expanded."

"I will say it again. If Kennedy is unable to quell all this criminal activity, then he needs to be replaced. He is incompetent if he can't fulfill his responsibility."

Jacob Hoagland wasn't going to listen to that kind of talk again and stood up, an angry look on his face. "You're wrong, sir. Kennedy is a fine officer, a fine lawman, he's done fine work in his office. We have grown past the point where one man can protect the entire county. Good day, sir."

Hoagland was not a drinking man, it wasn't that he disapproved of drinking, he just didn't much care for the taste or the results. He did, however, enjoy the company of Murphy O'Reilly and those that drank there. Hot coffee was his usual.

"Well, I gave it my all, Murphy, and I got nowhere. We simply have to expand the constable's office and Amos Dudley will stand in the way." Hoagland took a long drink of coffee. "That bank has a lot of power in this community, but it's the people who are going to suffer from a lack of protection."

"You give a good speech, commissioner," Murphy said. "So, what are you going to do about it? Rile up the people?"

Hoagland took another long drink of Murphy's good coffee and stood back some. "That may not be a bad idea, old man. Not a bad idea at all."

At the supper table that night, Jacob Hoagland brought up the subject. "I think the idea of letting the people of Brookside make the decision is the right one. Even Dudley won't be able to argue that point. He's always talking about spending the taxpayer's money. Let's let the taxpayers make the decision."

"You are very definitely the right man to be a commissioner," Martha Hoagland said. "And you almost talked yourself out of the job. Did you make the order with Ben Thorndyke for next year?"

"Oh, yes. That's what led to the meeting with Amos Dudley. Someone stole one of Thorndyke's horses last night just a day after that family was murdered and robbed coming into the valley. Kennedy is reaching the point where he might just walk off. All Dudley can see is dollar signs, can't see all the effort it takes to solve these crimes, to protect the valley. I'm glad the crops are in. This will take some time and effort, but I'm going to get this process started first thing in the morning." *The best answer is to call for a public meeting, send notices to every address in the county and let the arguments take place.*

CHAPTER 8

L ittle Edna Pfaff was one of Jasper's more well-known madams, operating the Birdcage whore house and dancehall. Edna wasn't quite five feet tall, didn't weigh eighty-five pounds, and ruled her world as if she were an Amazon. There are some who believe she acquired the Birdcage by way underhanded activities.

It was late night, the Birdcage was alive with young men, some just boys, really, mostly loggers willing to spend big-time. Edna Pfaff had company but she wasn't entertaining him, she was working to save his life. Sam Bassett had arrived on her doorstep, bloody and drunk an hour before.

Jasper was a small logging village in Brookside County, a village made up of timber companies, saloons, and bawdy houses. The timber company workers were, for the most part, young single men making their first decent wage. The village grew up as a rowdy neighbor-hood and more small time outlaws maintained residence there than in Brookside about five miles south.

Edna Pfaff was able to purchase the Birdcage by way of a loan from the Brookside Bank, but in the name of

Ed Pfaff. The bank may or may not have known the little play on words. She found out, as so many have, that a man's name on a legal form will always be looked at. Edna became Ed when needed.

More than one business offered credit to Ed Pfaff but would never offer it to Edna. Not one of those creditors had ever seen Ed Pfaff in person. Edna was not one to back away from opportunity.

Edna had Bassett on the bed, the remains of his shirt cut away and was trying to get the infection cleared away as well. Gangrene had set in with a purpose, the smell was strong, and the sight was ugly. "You've made a mess of yourself, Sam. I ain't no kind of doctor and you need one bad. I can sew a shirt but I can't be sewin' on a man." Cringle's knife laid Bassett's arm wide open, shoulder to elbow. The wound was many inches long and many inches deep. Muscles were separated, tendons torn away, and blood loss was considerable.

"Doctors ask questions," Bassett said. "I ain't answering any questions." Bassett was smart enough to realize that the Cringle massacre was already known to Tobias Kennedy, and Kennedy might be aware that someone in the gang was wounded. "No doctors," he slurred.

Edna looked at him, shook her head and turned away. "You're gonna have a high fever shortly, Sam, and when you pass out I'm callin' the doctor. Ain't nothin' I can do for you, ceptin' either call the doctor or call the under-taker, cuz one of 'em is gonna get the call."

The widow Pfaff was a short woman, delightfully well put together, nearing thirty but still fine looking despite the rough life. She had come west as the wife of a man known as Winston G. Pfaff, geologist and surveyor, and he made enemies with the local Indians almost from the minute he drove a stake in what he called his homestead, what they called their land.

The Kalapuya tribe had lived and hunted on that land for thousands of years and was not going to allow this interloper to take it from them. Oregon Territorial land agents had not made the indigenous people's land available for homesteading, but Pfaff lived and died by his own rules. His body showed up near a saloon early one morning.

Edna took what personal property was left, the old man's geology tools and equipment, and sold it raising enough money to make a considerable down payment on the property on which her Birdcage brothel now operated. Brightly lit and painted on the outside, gaudy and cheap on the inside, the operation was successful beyond Edna's dreams. She had four girls working and the timber industry provided her with strong young men making good money in an area where single women simply didn't exist.

Sam Bassett showing up in this wretched condition was sure to put a damper on activities and she had to get rid of him any way possible. "Why did you come here, anyway? You're a fool, Bassett. Makes no difference right now what you say or think, as soon as you pass out I'm getting the doc in here."

Sam Bassett would be a kink in her operation if she let him stay and she figured he had a mind to stay until he was healed. Word around Jasper was that he was a wanted outlaw. He came to town often with sacked loot to sell, plunder from others, and that would surely bring questions from the county constable and others. He was right, she knew, that one who would have questions would be the doctor.

"Your choice, Sam. Doctor now or wait until the

infection gets so bad that you pass out and probably lose the arm. This isn't a hospital, it's a whore house, Sam. You can't stay here."

"I'll pay you, Edna. You know I will."

"Ain't the point, Sam. You're taking up a bed, a money making bed. How do you want it? Doc now or doc when it's time to cut the arm off?"

"Bitch," Sam spat out. "No feeling for a man what's hurt bad." He winced trying to move his arm to make it more comfortable. "Call the doctor," he snarled through drunken pain.

"And when he's through, you are, too. I want you out of here. I'll tell your man Porter to get the doc and then get you out of here."

———

"He was at the Birdcage, constable," Doctor Bruce Walling said. "Probably going to lose that arm. It was the worst cut I've seen in years. What's he done?"

"Still trying to find that out, Doctor. Were you able to talk to him?"

"What he said, that is, the words he used I don't use. I had to use my buggy and take him to his camp. He's with three other men and they have a camp set up down by the creek, about half a mile out of town."

Doctor Walling shook his head. "They are an ugly lot, constable. Mean looking. Certainly have some nice looking horses."

Kennedy hadn't been in Jasper half an hour and heard about men trying to sell some silver and some horses, and that one of them was seriously wounded. That led him to Doctor Walling and more information. "Thank you, Doctor. Keep all this close to your vest, eh? These men are involved in something serious, I'm afraid." *That verifies what I heard about these men having some nice horses. Ain't nothing wrong with a man having nice horses, but the description of these men don't jibe with men owning nice horses.*

He looked at the doctor and his rather spartan office. "If you had some fine silver dining ware such as bowls, gravy boats, serving dishes and spoons, where would you look to be selling them?"

"You believe that's what those men are looking to do? Let me think on that." Doctor Walling was a sparse man. looked to be in his fifties, had thinning white hair and wore an unruly Van Dyke beard. His clothes hung on him giving the impression that he might have carried a bit more weight in the near past.

"One couldn't just advertise such, could one?" He chuckled and his eyes wrinkled up in mirth. "Maybe casually spread the word in a tavern or two? Would these items be someone else's property, constable?"

Kennedy chuckled and stuck his hand out. "Thank you," he said, not answering the question. The doctor shook his hand, smiled at the reaction to his question, and ushered Kennedy out of the office. He enjoyed the sharing of a little humor.

"You might get an answer or two from Edna Pfaff, Mr. Kennedy. That's where he was when I was called. She owns the Birdcage. Or you might try the Knot Fir Nothing Saloon on First Street. It will be filled with young timber workers."

Kennedy nodded and made his way down the steps to his horse. The Birdcage was on Second Street almost directly behind the Knot Fir Nothing. *Good planning there*, he mused. *Young loggers get a snoot full and look for some loving. It's right out the back door.* The ride to First

Street was quick and the day was still early, leaning on two o'clock.

The Knot Fir Nothing was a tough, class-less saloon. The floor was roughhewn planks as were the walls. Lighting was by way of a few oil lamps hanging from the ceiling, and the bar top sat on barrels. The only tables in the long narrow building were set up for faro and poker, not drinking.

"Don't see your kindly and laughing face very often, Mr. Kennedy," the bar man and saloon owner, Sean McPherson said. "And you're not looking kindly at the moment."

"Ah, Sean, it's always good to see you. I'm afraid I'm not in a kindly mood at the moment. Do men try to sell items from time to time in here?"

"Items, constable? Such as?" McPherson gave himself away Kennedy saw, watching the elderly saloon keeper slowly drop his eyes. *He knows damn well what I mean.*

"Items, Sean. Maybe pieces of silver, maybe jewelry, maybe serving dishes." The constable could see McPherson not wanting to answer the question. *I think this fine barkeep just might be involved in some "items" himself.*

"You're following up on a thieving adventure, eh?" McPherson had been in the business a long time. He came west with the Canadian fur business many years ago as so many of the original residents of the territory had. There were serious political implications in creating the Oregon Territory, keeping it as a United States entity, not a British or Canadian one.

"I've been in these fine forests for twenty years, Mr. Kennedy, worked with traders in the fur business, dealt with Indians trading and stealing, dealt with American mountaineers, and all the time selling fine whiskey and beer. Traders are always working from saloons, sir."

"Of course," Kennedy said. "The fur trade couldn't have gotten along without friendly saloon keepers." Sean had a look on his face like he wanted to say considerably more but wasn't going to unless the right questions were asked. His eyes asked, 'did you have something special in mind'?

"Ah, Sean, a fine publican you are. There's been a man seriously wounded possibly trying to sell some silver items. Would you know something about that?"

"You're talking of that ugly mean Sam Bassett. Oh, yes, Constable I know the man." Sean turned to the back bar and grabbed an earthen jug. "Would you like a wee dram while I tell you about Sam Bassett?" Kennedy smiled and nodded.

"The man's not welcome in here, Mr. Kennedy, nor are those foul men who ride with him. Drunk, foul mouth, and a born troublemaker. That's what Sam Bassett is. This is a gentleman's drinking parlor. However, I've heard of some delightful silver items being displayed at the Columbia House Saloon another block west of here."

"Thank you, Sean. I won't forget this. It's a mean business I'm on."

"If it's taking Bassett out of the picture, then it's a good business, sir."

CHAPTER 9

"I'll be more than happy to place your notice, Jacob." Ben Thorndyke was looking at the broad sheet Hoagland offered. It proclaimed a public meeting to be held at the community park at noon on Thursday next to discuss public safety and criminal behavior in Brookside. "Give me two or three, please. We need to increase law and order and a public discussion of some of the problems will make many aware of them."

"Have you heard anything about your missing horse?"

"I had a long conversation with Constable Kennedy at breakfast this morning, Jacob, that's why I'm in compete agreement with your upcoming meeting. Seems as though our constable knows where my horse is, who has the steed, and is in a twit because he can't recover him."

"Can't recover him?" Hoagland asked. "That's a strange thing for Kennedy to say. Why?"

"My horse along with other stolen items are being held by a gang of four men, well-armed, and known for their mean and vicious attitude. The group is led by Sam Bassett."

"Bassett again," Hoagland said. "That name crops up too often. In the past Kennedy would put together a small group, a posse, and make his arrests. What's holding him back?"

"He'd be at Murphy's, Jacob. I think it's best if you talk to him direct. I know Murphy would want a poster or two from you, as well." Ben Thorndyke knew that Kennedy had been denied money to hire two or three men to help make the arrest but wanted Hoagland to hear it directly from the constable.

———

"You're absolutely positive that's what the county clerk said? No doubt at all?" Jacob Hoagland couldn't believe what Tobias Kennedy had just told him.

"I can still hear the words, Jacob. He said that commissioner Dudley told him there would be no more spending of any kind for anything including, or especially money for the constable's office." Kennedy's eyes were blazing, his fists knotted as hammers, and the muscles in his neck stood out like giant cables.

"I've got four men who I'm sure are those who attacked and killed the Cringle family and who stole Ben Thorndyke's horse less than five miles from where we're sitting and I am not allowed to form a posse and arrest them." Kennedy was ready to explode, face bright red, eyes narrowed to slits, and Hoagland was sure he was baring his teeth as well.

"I've always been able to hire a few men for special duties, usually at fifty cents a day and Murphy usually adds a dram of beverage to the pay voucher." Murphy gave him a smile and nod, and Kennedy continued. "It's bad enough that I can't have a full time man or two, commissioner, but now I'm hogtied by not being able to raise a posse to make an arrest? This, sir, is wrong."

"It is indeed." Jacob Hoagland could see what Dudley's plan might be. *If Kennedy is ham-strung by not being able to have men with him to make arrests, then Dudley will be able to say the man is incompetent. Why is Dudley doing this? What has Kennedy done, or what does Kennedy know, that Dudley wants him out of office?*

"Anyone at the family table, Murphy?" Jacob Hoagland asked.

"Shouldn't be. Not this time of day."

"Good. Constable, will you join me at the family table for a few minutes? Murphy, would you be kind enough to see to it that we aren't interrupted?" He led the way through the bar and into the restaurant area. "Have a seat."

Hoagland handed a broadsheet to Kennedy. "This won't help your current problem but I believe will give you your needed deputy when it's over. Now, let's talk about your current problem. How many men did you want and for how long?"

Kennedy hadn't had this kind of response from the county in a long time and sat back giving Jacob Hoagland a long look. *This man has come some way in a short amount of time. Working one of the nicest farms in the valley, raising a beautiful family, and taking on the duties of a commissioner? This is the kind of man we need leading the way into the future.*

"I like your style, Jacob but Dudley seems to think he has control over the county's purse strings. I need two men for two days to arrest the men responsible for the attack on the Cringle family and the theft of Ben

Thorndyke's horse. We're talking a grand total of two dollars, sir. I've always been able to simply notify the clerk that I would be hiring for day work. There's never been a question."

"Something has led to there being a question, constable," Hoagland said. "Dudley's comments to me tell me that he and you have some kind of personal problem. Would you like to discuss that?"

"I've never had any kind of personal relationship with the banker, Jacob. I can't imagine a personal problem with the man. I have my land, my home, all paid for. I've never done personal business with the man or his bank."

"Any kind of official business relationship? Coming from your official duties? Maybe helping someone who was having difficulties?"

Before Kennedy could answer, Ben Thorndyke stuck his head in. "I know I'm interrupting but I think this is important. It has to do with Dudley and Kennedy."

"Come in, Ben, and join us. We're talking about why it is that Dudley is so strongly opposed to our constable being able to do his job."

Thorndyke's large body filled the dining room seat to capacity and he leaned forward, elbows on the table. "As you know, Jacob, when Irene Creighton found herself in dire straits. I, along with others, came to her support."

"Yes, of course I remember. In fact, Ben, she's your book keeper now and is running her own business besides." Jacob Hoagland remembered that whole episode and looked at Constable Kennedy. "How does the constable or Dudley play into this?"

"You've been seeing the woman, have you?" Ben asked, looking into Kennedy's eyes.

"I've checked on her from time to time," Kennedy

said. "Uh, yes, I guess maybe a little more often than just time to time. She's had a hard time of it, her son in jail, bills dating back to when her husband was alive. She needed a friend, Ben, and I know you came to help her as well."

"I did but I haven't had supper alone with the lady, nor taken her and her daughter for walks along the levee, nor hired a coach for a drive in the forest to have a picnic." Thorndyke couldn't hold in the chuckles, his eyes bright with humor. "No, my help was to find her employment and legal help."

Hoagland chuckled and Kennedy's cheeks were even more red than normal. The constable took a drink of coffee, squirmed some in his chair, and took a long look at the floor. "She's a delightful lady and her daughter is lively and intelligent. And she needed some help."

"Let's discuss that help you offered, Tobias," Ben Thorndyke said. "I think that might be at the heart of the matter." Ben looked at Hoagland who was still smiling. "Mr. Dudley is single, Jacob, and was known, some weeks back to have a package delivered to Mrs. Creighton."

"How is it," Hoagland asked, "That you, Ben, know all of this? What was in the package."

"I know all this because my son Gerald has been seeing Mrs. Creighton's daughter, Carrie, who has told him about it all. The package was the threat of a foreclosure note on the Creighton residence."

"My god, no." Hoagland stood right up. "I'm sure Ed Creighton owned that property when she killed him. I'm sure of it. How could that be? Foreclosure? No, no."

"He did," Kennedy said. "That's what Irene, that is, Mrs. Creighton and I were discussing. Creighton took out a loan using the home and town lot as collateral and Dudley was threatening to call it in."

"After all this time?" Hoagland tried to remember but it seemed that Creighton had been killed just a year ago. "Seems a bit odd, eh?"

"Might be odd," Thorndyke said, "but for the fact that Dudley had also wanted the pleasure of Irene's company for supper more than once and the offers have been turned down."

"Your son should be in the detective business, Ben," Kennedy said. "She's never said a word about that. Most interesting."

"Dudley has had his eye on the lady for some time, constable, as have you. He's known in some circles as a lecher, I'm sure you've heard the stories. Her eyes, however have been on you, not him, and his jealousy has come to the surface by way of the collection note." Ben Thorndyke's grin told Kennedy he was enjoying all this.

"And by way of getting you out of the picture," Jacob Hoagland said. *Is this why the banker wants Kennedy out of office? Seems rather small to me. I thought better of the man but if that's going to be his game I'd best make sure I know a lot more than I know right now.*

Jacob Hoagland looked at Ben, looked at Kennedy, and looked a bit longer at the ceiling before saying anything. "You two might not be fully aware of this but Amos Dudley has told me that he will see to it that Tobias Kennedy is out of office before he will allow the county to hire more men in the office."

He took a minute for that to soak in before continuing. "It would be a small mind to take out his vengeance on both the woman who won't see him and the man who stands in his way of seeing her, but that's the picture I see at the moment."

"That's the reason for the public meeting, isn't it?" Ben Thorndyke said. "You're going to excite enough public pressure for more law and order and call Amos Dudley's game. Very clever, Jacob." Thorndyke turned to Kennedy. "You, my friend need to be at that meeting."

CHAPTER 10

"This won't be forgotten, Ben," Hoagland said as the two men walked from Murphy's Tavern and Inn. "Kennedy will have his two men, you'll be out two dollars, and you'll probably have your horse back in a day or two."

"I'm afraid you now have yourself a formidable political enemy, Jacob. Dudley's not the kind of man who takes a knocking. That's a shame, and it's Brookside that might be the loser."

"I'm not one to get knocked about without response either, Ben. If what's been discussed is what's behind Dudley's agenda, it has to be brought before the public. To use a personal grievance to deny public safety is simply wrong. We can't sift through the newcomers and only accept those we like so if we get some bad apples in the mix we have to have a means of staying safe."

It wasn't long after Thorndyke and Hoagland left that Kennedy departed Murphy's as well, feeling the weight of coins in his purse. *Just like that the man hands me money to form my posse. That's a bit of trust I appreciate. Now to find a man or two.* His thoughts wanted to stray away toward Irene Creighton and it was with brute force that he shoved them aside.

Work first, Tobias. Mr. Dudley doesn't want me in town because Mrs. Creighton appreciates my friendship? Well isn't that just too bad on Mr. Dudley. We'll have our discussion sir, but first, I'll see if I can stop a possible future murder. There was just the hint of smile, a squaring up of shoulders, and a thump or two to the dirt from Kennedy's cudgel.

IRENE CREIGHTON WAS STANDING AT THE STOVE, TRYING to concentrate on making dinner for her and her daughter, Carrie. "Are you crying, mama?" Carrie asked.

Irene quickly wiped away her tears and tried to smile with an answer. "I'm sorry, honey but I've received some upsetting news." She wasn't going to spend a lot of time trying to make her little girl understand how mean and nasty some men could be. She had enough trouble living down the fact she had married Ed Creighton, allowed herself to be beaten by the ugly man, and had killed him when he beat her one time too many.

"Your father made some wrong business decisions, honey, and I'm afraid we may have to live with them." How could she even try to explain how the banker held a foreclosure notice over her head, that could be done away with by just one evening's socializing?

Socializing? She thought. *That vile man wants me in his bed, and if I go, I keep my house? No! I've known too many men like this foul banker. He would come calling again and again. He would destroy my life, Carrie's life.*

"It's very difficult to explain, Carrie. In another couple of years you'll be old enough to understand. Let's just say there is a man who wants me to do something I will never do, and he says he holds papers that would make me do it. Well, sweetie, I won't."

She turned back to putting together bowls of soup for them. "Mid-day soup on a chilly fall day. That's what we get to enjoy."

KENNEDY TOOK A LEISURELY WALK ALONG THE LEVEE feeling the briskness in the early fall air. Waterfowl were moving south using the river for overnight accommodation, making enough noise to keep the predators away. He spotted Sidney "Hammerhead" Povolny out on a sand bar, shotgun in hand and waved him over.

He came in carrying two large birds, a white swan and a Canada goose. "Looks like you'll be eating high at the table, Hammerhead."

"They're flying fast, Toby, but I've got a good eye. What can I do for you?" Hammerhead Povolny was nearing forty, stood close to five feet eight inches and weighed in near two hundred pounds. His head was large, almost square, and his eyes were set close together. A massive chin jutted out, daring someone to take a swipe at it and his hands were those of a mechanic, large and strong.

If it was broken, Hammerhead could fix it. If you needed something built from scratch, Hammerhead could build it. But if Ben Thorndyke or any other business owner wanted to put Hammerhead on the payroll, the man would not move an inch. He was Mr. Fix-it in Brookside and worked on his schedule, no one else's. Hammerhead Povolny was his own man.

"I've got a bunch of nasty men I need to put collars on, Hammerhead. I believe they are killers, thieves, and worse. There are four of them and I'd like you and one other to join me in placing them under arrest."

"And just who is the other? You, I would trust with my life, Toby Kennedy, but there are some in this little town of ours that I wouldn't. Are we talking about the men who killed that couple and ransacked their wagon?"

Kennedy smiled and nodded. "We are. I don't have my third man. Have someone in mind to ride with us?"

"That knee bustin' gypsy king, Sonny Kniessel, is about as tough as us, and has strong feelings for the law. He's been nursing a sore rib or two, but that wouldn't slow him down in a fight. He's been meat hunting, as I, and has his squatter's camp up Third Creek. We could be there in an hour or so."

"Get your horse, Hammerhead and meet me at the courthouse."

———

SONNY KNIESSEL OPENED THE DOOR TO HIS LITTLE SHACK and invited the men in. "Only got whiskey. Ran out of coffee. Hope that's all right. Set your bums and tell me a story," he said. Kniessel was long and lanky, sad brown eyes protruded some from a long thin face, and what little hair he had, hung, dull and stringy, half-way down his back. From time to time he'd braid it and tie it off. Not this time. It waved about in the evening breeze.

"Got some fresh elk I could fry up if you're hungry. or some deer liver."

"Just here for some talk, Sonny. Got me a little problem," Kennedy said. "You heard about that couple got killed the other day?"

"Sad thing to happen to nice people. I helped get them across from Oregon City, Tobias. Was with them right up until the night before they was kilt. They had their parcel of land all picked out and plans made to build them a house and have a family. That little girl was the purdiest girl I ever did see. Why, Tobias, she just shone in being purdy."

Sonny Kniessel's sad eyes developed a leak that ran across a bony cheek bone and into his grayish beard. "What about them that kilt 'em?"

"Hammerhead and I are leaving first thing in the morning to arrest the men I believe are the killers, Sonny. I'd like you to ride with us. Need a strong man who knows right from wrong. You will be paid as usual."

"I would be honored to make that ride, Tobias. Honored. Ain't hunted a man since the last time I helped you out. My knife is sharp and my shotgun and rifle are ready."

Kennedy found it interesting that neither man had asked where they would be going or how long they might be gone. *Just good men willing to do good but dangerous work.* Kennedy looked at the two, sitting across from each other at a sturdy table, letting his mind go into free-fall.

Hammerhead and his wife came to our little valley three years ago and settled on a piece of property. He's working it alone today. Caught a terrible illness her first winter and died. His farm does well but the man's never been very social since. Sonny on the other hand has never been married, has no land, enjoys a free life hunting and guiding. These are good men, no shady past, no shadowed plans for the future. We could use a bunch more like 'em.

Kennedy chuckled to himself thinking that Sam Bassett and the mean, ugly, and dangerous men he rides with would be facing the terrible wrath of good men at some point come tomorrow.

CHAPTER 11

S andra Boyington had what was left of the canvas from their wagon stretched and hung between some trees, as a lean-to, and was tending a fire. Her daughter, Sonja, four-years-old and full of energy was stirring the fire after gathering several armloads of fallen twigs and branches. She stood up straight and tall and gave out a great whoosh, which brought a chuckle from Sandra.

"That's hard work, mama, but like you say, a woman's work is never done."

"You're a real clown this morning," Sandra said. The Boyington's son, almost one, named Harold, but who Ken insists on calling Spike was in his mama's arms. Sandra put the toddler down in some grass as her husband Ken rode in dragging a fine young buck deer. "We'll eat for another week," he called out.

Ken was an exuberant man, was able to see the good side of many problems and had a hard time with those who only saw trouble. "This guy had friends, too, Sandra. Big friends. I'm gonna like this country."

"Get him hung and I'll take care of him." She took the

lead rope he handed down and watched her strong man carrying a rifle and riding a big horse step to the ground. *Oh, the children we'll have. Big strong kids, not afraid of a day's work, not afraid to stand up for what they believe just as he.* "You like all this, don't you?" she said, waving her arms about. Sonja had her arms wrapped tightly around his knees.

He smiled and picked the girl up, giving her a peck on the cheek. "Just look at this land, Sandra. Just look. Great blankets of timber covering rolling mountains with streams down each seam or valley or canyon. Like it? No, little girl, I love it." He put Sonja down and stepped quickly to Sandra, swept her up in is arms and whirled about in the deep grass.

Sonja was giggling watching mommy and daddy do a little dance. Since arriving in Oregon Territory Ken Boyington hadn't slowed down. Sandra was sure he would hurt himself he was working so hard. He had leaned out considerably making the crossing and now was bulking up. She could see his shoulder and back muscles ripple even through his shirt.

He cut logs and moved them onto where he planned to build their initial cabin, worked from sun up to sun down. Boyington only took a break for a mid-day meal. "Grass grows so fast it moves you aside," he laughed. "We'll grow wheat and corn and beans and squash, we'll have fruit trees, and herds of cattle and sheep all over these hills next year. Between now and first snow I got to get us a house built."

Sandra looked at the lean-to, their bedrolls and clothing piled up, saw the roughly put together corral for the mules, horse, and oxen, saw rudimentary farm equipment scattered about and piles of cut timber. She was getting very good at skinning the logs, getting all the bark off and Ken was notching the ends so they fit the next log. With ropes, pulleys, and the mule, a cabin was taking shape.

"We'll settle for three rooms this winter," Ken told her, "but build this so it can easily be added on." She was at his side every minute of the day, helping to cut the trees down, helping to chain them up so as to be dragged to the home-site, skinning bark, sharpening axes, and cuddling under the blankets, watching the stars and sometimes scudding clouds roaming about.

It was fall and the threat of early winter hung over Ken but the threat simply made him work harder. Rains and snow would have a drastic effect on the building program but if he could get walls standing and a roof over the top, they would survive the winter. They had most of the tools necessary but there were things that would be needed inside.

"Sometimes I don't think I'm making any progress at all," he said. "Just look at this mess and I'm calling it our house. Just a bunch of logs spread around."

"Nonsense," Sandra said. "You've got walls up, you've got those pieces across the top."

"Stringers," he said.

"Yeah, those," she laughed. "And rocks, too."

Both wanted a big rock fireplace and knew that wasn't going to be, at least not this coming winter. They would settle for a large wood-fired cook stove in the kitchen and a Franklyn fireplace in the bedroom. "I'm just in a hurry," he said. He grabbed her again and held her tight. "We're gonna be fine. Just fine," and he kissed her long and hard. "Best to knock this off right now or I won't get another thing done today." She nuzzled him, kissed him again, and finally let go.

I am one lucky lady, she thought, watching him drag a

huge long around. *We're going to be just fine. He can actu-ally see this rough piece of ground as a producing farm and ranch. I can see children running everywhere, laughing and screaming.* She had to wipe her eyes as she picked Spike up and ducked into the lean-to for his feeding.

Ken was a fine carpenter and would build their tables, chairs, and beds but he knew he would have to purchase a cook stove. He was already gathering as many rocks as he could manage and was working on a fire-place and chimney. *So much to do and so little time to do it in. It took us more time to make the crossing than I antici-pated, than we were told. The extra days here and there, at the forts, rest stops for the stock. I'm paying for that now.*

Time. The clock ticks, the calendar pages turn, and nothing can slow it down. Heavy fall rains would slow the process to a stand-still and the snows of winter would simply end all building. Ken Boyington had to have the walls up and the roof on before those rains came.

The children learned quickly to stay out of the way when Ken and Sandra were moving big and heavy objects. Sonja and Spike were with them every minute of every day, sometimes getting in the way, sometimes being fussy and crabby, sometimes just sleeping in the deep grass.

Spike couldn't walk yet but could craw almost as fast as little Sonja could run. It was one of her jobs to keep him from getting in trouble. She was serious in that work, Spike thought it was a game.

"You know those beans and cows you talk about?" Sandra asked. He looked at her and nodded. "There's gonna be another baby screaming for milk, too."

Ken's knees almost buckled and he gathered her up, holding tight. "Oh, my," is all he could say and he said it over and over. He finally let go of her and walked to the fire. He knelt down and poured a cup of coffee. "Ain't that the most wonderful thing you've ever heard?" He was talking to Spike and Sonja. Sonja nodded but Spike was asleep under the lean-to canvas. "Oh, my," he said again.

"Going into town tomorrow to meet this Ben Thorndyke feller, Sandra. I'd like it if you and the kids came with me. There are things we need and that big store of his has 'em all. Stop at the grocer's, too. Get some potatoes, beans, and onions. Thorndyke is someone we need to make friends with."

"Should I make a list or have you already got one."

"I have but you need to go over it to make sure I haven't forgotten anything. We'll have to take the big wagon just to carry all the stuff back."

"I like the idea of a cook stove but you're already setting up the fireplace so I can cook there. It would be easier though having both available, particularly the way you go through biscuits and bread." She giggled some as he pretended to scowl.

"Well, getting the rocks for the fireplace is one thing, but the cement has to cure when you put it all together. Saw a man light his fireplace before all the cement was dry and it blew up like someone had put two pounds of black powder in there." More than one person had died from firing up a fireplace too soon.

"Think we should hire someone to work with you?" Sandra knew how worried Ken was about the weather, the possibility of winter arriving all at once, and knew, too, that he didn't want to spend what little money they had on things that might not be necessities.

"No, pretty girl. I'm so far along with the building that I'm not that worried about old man winter." It wasn't really a lie, he told himself. He really was close with walls standing straight and stringers in place for the roof. "It's next spring that I would really want someone to work with me in the fields."

Ken had spent so much time working for others, cutting irrigations ditches, plowing rocky fields, planting crops in those rocks, that he already had visions of his fields of corn and wheat, beans, potatoes, and orchards, and irrigation ponds, and ditches. "Yep, I'll want a little help come spring. We'll leave out for Thorndyke's first thing in the morning."

CHAPTER 12

S am Bassett's camp was in a deep stand of fir, pine, cedar, and other evergreens, and thick with ferns. The camp was well hidden from anyone on the little trail some thirty-five yards or so away. The trees were covered in moss, stood large and full grown, leaving the area dark on the brightest of days and cool on the hottest.

Kennedy and the other two slowly moved through the ferns and the constable wished it was a bright and sunny day. The day started at about five when the men rode at a trot out of the main part of the village and as it got lighter, they could see banks of clouds begin to roll in. They were heavy with moisture and breezes were cold.

"I imagine at some point you're gonna be tellin' us where it is we're a-goin, Mr. Kennedy," Hammerhead joshed. "Jist so we will know how to git back home, you see."

Hammerhead carried his rifle across the front of his saddle, a shotgun was nestled in a fine leather scabbard at the horse's side, and a big skinning knife was secured to a belt holding his heavy point blanket capote closed. Sonny Kniessel on the other hand had a flintlock pistol stuffed in his belt on the left side and an equally large knife on the other. His rifle was in a scabbard.

Kennedy carried his cudgel as he would a quirt, and had a knife at his belt. "We're going to Jasper boys and we're coming home with four outlaws, horses that belong to the Clinger's and Ben Thorndyke, and whatever other loot those pettish whelps might have with them."

It was a cold but beautiful morning for a ride through Oregon's gorgeous forests, crossing a few creeks on the way, kicking up deer and birds, hearing the sounds of building as they passed a homestead or two. three men in this majesty and knowing they might be killing other men before the day was out. Not giving a thought to the fact that they might be riding to their own death, not wanting to give it a thought.

Would it even be possible to have a negative thought in such splendor? None of the three were farmers, as such, but were fully aware of the value in the land offered by Oregon Territory. Rich ground begging to be planted, streams of fresh, clean, and abundant water splashed down every mountainside, and a warm sun created visions of being able to grow just about anything you might want.

Wildlife was abundant, some with four feet, some with wings, some moved with the seasons and some were available year round. There wasn't a family that hadn't learned the art of smoking elk and deer, of salting the meat, of corning it, too. Ducks, geese and swans flew through twice a year, great herds of elk and deer moved up and down the mountain sides, and black bears added to the menu.

Hammerhead was aware of the danger that was involved in this chase and simply accepted it. His life had been dangerous for as long as he could remember, what with the crossing and constant Indian aggressions, constant threats from others in the wagon train. His biggest mistake was not getting to meet others in the group before they left.

He would never have signed on. Four families made up of young couples, very young, inexperienced, and the women too young and pretty, almost open to assault by all the single men on the crossing. Thirty people on the train and almost half, single, hardened men.

Kniessel on the other hand may have been looking forward to the danger. After the loss of his wife he didn't give much of a damn whether he lived or died. "We will kill them if we have to, Mr. Kennedy. Just lead us on."

"They'll not roll over for us boys," Kennedy said. "We'll need to force them to their knees. Just remember what they did to the Cringle's. To that lovely Mrs. Cringle. To Mr. Cringle's throat. We'll make them roll over boys."

They rode out of town at a hard trot for about an hour and then slowed to a walk, letting the horses catch their breath. "Their camp is west of Jasper, slightly north of Jasper Creek, and in a dense stand of tall timber. We'll need to split up and come at them from three angles. I'd prefer not shooting any of them, but don't let that mean you can't," Kennedy said. Kniessel smiled and Hammerhead snarled his acceptance.

DESPITE THE LATE HOUR, SAM BASSETT WAS IN HIS bedroll, moaning, gasping for breath, mostly unconscious. Ames and Porter had finished their breakfast and were having coffee near the fire. Neither one had checked on Bassett. If he lived, fine, if he didn't, more of a share for each. Ambrose joined them after doing his business off in the ferns. "Time to make some decisions, my buckies. Old Sam's a goner, I'm sure of that, and we've got some goods to get rid of."

"You've got something on your mind, Ambrose. Spit it out," Ames said. "Sam's hurt bad but you might want to remember he's the man kept us alive coming across from Missouri. Saved your butt more than once."

"He did," Porter said. "Mine, too."

"Ain't sayin' he did or didn't," Ambrose said. "Only saying it's time to set him aside, sell all the goods and maybe split up. That big bastard Kennedy is sure to be looking for us."

"Ain't no way he could know it was us kilt them people. They be more comin' every day, too," Porter said. "Mighty easy pickin's if you ask me."

"I'm with Porter and with you," Ames said. "Need to just leave old Sam right where he is, sell all this in Jasper like we planned, and then find the next hit. Don't want to leave when we got us a golden goose in the nest."

Ambrose looked at the two men and smiled. "We'll leave Sam and ride into Jasper, sell all this, split the money, and then, I'll be ridin' south, into California. Going to Yerba Buena, get on a big boat, and go to South America or Mexico."

"Yer a fool, Ambrose," Porter said. "I'm staying right here."

———

KENNEDY MOTIONED FOR THE MEN TO STOP AND STEPPED down from his horse, tying the lead rope to a handy bush. Using his hands, he motioned that the Bassett campsite was just over the rise and deep in the woods. He led the men into the brush, being as quiet as possible. He sent Hammerhead around to his left and Sonny Kniessel off to his right.

The forest was thick and still wet from morning dew. Great fronds of fern got in the way. Huge fir trees were difficult to get around. And downed logs taller than a man they were so thick, had to be negotiated. The forest was not a friend to those walking through it.

"You'll hear me when I call those fools out so just follow my lead, boys," he whispered. There was no pathway and they could not walk through everything in a straight line. It took a long time for each to negotiate their way through heavy timber, downed timber, brush, and ferns. Staying as quiet as possible was made a bit easier because of the dampness in the ground and detritus.

Kennedy stopped suddenly, and took a quick sniff or two, picking up the aroma of smoke from the camp fire and eased his way through a stand of Oregon fir. Bent as low as he could get, he wormed through some wet ferns and saw three men standing around a camp fire. One man was thrashing around in a bedroll. *That's Bassett. Fever's got him and he's out of the fight, it looks like. What a shame. I have a great need to thump on men like him.* He waited a minute or so to make sure that Hammerhead and Sonny were in position.

"Stay where you are, gentlemen," Kennedy said in a strong voice as he stood up and walked quickly from the ferns, his cudgel at the ready. "I'm Constable Kennedy here to arrest you. Don't move as I have friends with me." He strode toward the three all the time he was talking.

Ambrose dropped his coffee and spun around, tried to wrench his single shot flintlock pistol from his belt. The cudgel smashed into his arm, breaking the bone and the second swing knocked him out cold. "I said, don't move, gentlemen. I meant that." Kennedy's face alone would frighten most men, with its square jaw, penetrating deep green eyes, and often-broke nose leading the way. His approach and that fine oak walking stick backed him up.

Porter and Ames didn't move as they each saw Hammerhead Povolny and Sonny Kniessel emerge from the surrounding forest. "We ain't done nothing. What do you mean busting into our camp?" Ames said but was slowly working to get a hand on his knife. "We just doing some meat huntin'."

"You might have been hunting but it wasn't for meat," Kennedy said. "You let that hand get one inch closer to that knife and you won't be able to ever use that hand again." He thumped the cudgel onto the forest floor, making the point, and took a step toward Ames who backed up quickly, right into the arms of Hammerhead Povolny.

"Be nice, sir," Hammerhead said, and smashed a massive fist into the back of the man's head, knocking him into Kennedy who quickly relieved him of his knife before shoving him back toward Hammerhead who dropped him with a terrific roundhouse to the man's kidneys.

Porter stood quiet, arms slightly out from his sides, looking down at the ground. He wasn't about to make any kind of move after what he just saw.

"That's a good boy," Kennedy said. "Now, drag your

two friends over to where Sam Bassett is moaning like a baby. We have a few things to talk about."

The five mile ride back to Brookside was far easier than the two hours it took to get the packs filled with stolen items on the horses. Then they had to get the bound prisoners on the horses, and wrap and tie off Sam Bassett's body. The man apparently died during the brief time it took to get his gang under control.

Kennedy was far more upset by what Commissioner Jacob Hoagland had told him about the banker than he led anyone to believe. *These people seem to think the job of constable is simply walking about, smiling at the ladies, and having a dram or two with Murphy. Well, now, I'm in a position to show them just how difficult this job can be.*

Kennedy led the parade through Brookside going out of his way to be seen by as many people as possible. The pack horses were led in by Sonny Kniessel and Hammerhead Povolny while Constable Kennedy lead the horses carrying the gang. One dead gang member laid out across a saddle and three members, two showing fresh injuries, tied to their mounts. It was a show and Kennedy nodded in grim pleasure to the many he passed.

It took less than ten minutes for the word to spread far and wide. Amos Dudley closed the brocade curtains of his office in the bank as the procession passed by. There's no record of what might have been said, whether it be a curse or not. There were some who saw Kennedy's brief smile.

"We'll need the undertaker and the doctor, Sonny. Could you round them up for me? And, Hammerhead, you can help me get these fine gentlemen into our rather comfortable accommodations. You gentlemen did a good job and I have some coin for you. Murphy of course will pour the first one on the house."

Oh, how I wish I had been in that bank's office when those curtains were pulled shut. I'll get these rascals behind bars, all doctored up, get Bassett cared for and pay a visit to Irene Creighton. I believe she said she was planning a large supper of lamb stew for me. I wonder how long it will take before word of Bassett's capture reaches Commissioner Hoagland? He'll be most pleased. I must remember to thank Ben Thorndyke for the money to pay those men.

The thoughts went back to Irene Creighton, not necessarily the lamb stew but the lady. *I've been a bit of a rounder in my past, not always been the kind and generous man I am now.* The chuckle rumbled through his chest, his eyes glistened with mirth, and he let his thoughts continue. *Would a refined lady like the widow Creighton even give a thought to a rough-out like me?* Tobias Kennedy's face was alive with anticipation as he made his way into the courthouse.

There are some in this little village of ours who would not consider trying to be friends with the lady. After all, she did kill her husband. And one must remember, she has a son who will remain in custody for many more years, and a daughter. We're not discussing unplowed ground here. Still... He let his thoughts trail off slowly. There was a softness to his eyes, and a gentle smile on his rugged face.

"Come now, gentlemen, get thee behind those iron bars." He got all three in the two cells and the doors locked. "A judge will be brought in and you'll likely be hanged, but in the meantime, any misconduct will bring pain and suffering. I'll not tolerate the least mischief."

CHAPTER 13

"Mr. Thorndyke, is it?" Ken Boyington asked, pulling the wagon to a stop at the loading dock in front of the large Thorndyke Emporium. "I'm Kenneth Boyington and this is my wife, Sandra with our children. Our homestead is up Third Creek a ways. They tell me you might have just about everything a man might need to survive in this country."

"I like to say Thorndyke's has everything except desire and responsibility. That is up to the individual."

"Well, then," Sandra said, "I can vouch for our desire and Ken's responsibility." She caught herself, realizing immediately that she might have been a bit out of line. Women were to be seen, not heard. That simply wasn't true in Sandra's mind.

"Wonderful," Thorndyke laughed. "And I'd vouch that you might just be a driving force, eh?"

Boyington laughed as Sandra blushed, and climbed down from the wagon to shake hands with the big man. "I've got a fair list here. Some we need immediately, for building the house and barn, and some we'll need before spring planting. Let's see how we do."

Ben Thorndyke shook the man's firm grip and gave him a quick look-over. *He's a fit young man, has an attractive wife and well-fed children, and is a gentleman as well.* "Let's step inside Mr. Boyington and, as you said, see how we do." He took the list and escorted the couple and their children into the large, crowded emporium.

It was a jungle of farm implements, forestry tools and equipment, and household goods for the kitchen and fireplace. Plows, harness, hammers, hoes, and saws were stacked everywhere. Double bladed axes, heavy wedges, and fence post diggers were scattered about, and bins of iron nails, spools of wire, and every hand tool imaginable was available. Sandra was amazed to even find material for curtains, spreads, and heavy work clothes.

"You've taken the word emporium to heart, sir," Ken said. "We've been in Virginia the last several years farming in rocks. I'm looking forward to this coming spring. I do want to turn the ground one time before winter, If I can beat the storms."

Thorndyke handed the list to one of the boys who was learning the trade and invited the couple to sit by the pot-belly stove while the order was filled. "Have some coffee and a biscuit, will you? It won't take Jerome long to put that list together and get it loaded for you. How will you be paying for this?"

Ah, there's the question Boyington was waiting to hear. Since arriving in the territory he'd heard rumblings of immigrants arriving and unable or not wanting to pay for their needs. He and Sandra had talked about the issue well before starting the adventure.

"We have cash, sir. Enough to keep us going for the first year or two. By then, I hope, the farm will be paying for itself. Where would I find some nice heifers and a bull or two?"

"Jacob Hoagland would be your best bet. He has a fine herd and is only about five miles out of town. Go south to the second road east and it will take you straight to his ranch. One of the nicest men in the valley and a county commissioner to boot."

Ken and Sandra were finishing their second cup of coffee when young Jerome told them the wagon was loaded. "Hope there's room for what we'll need from the grocer's," Sandra said.

Ben had the items and their costs listed and Ken produced the cash to pay the bill. "Itemized like that makes it nice," he said. "Will you be able to have those spring items in in plenty of time for planting?"

"Without question," Thorndyke said. "It's been a pleasure and welcome to Brookside. There's talk of a school being available soon. You might want to talk to Mrs. Hoagland about that."

Thorndyke stood on the loading dock of his store and watched Ken and Sandra drive off toward the grocer's. *Good people. Need more like them to move into the territory.* Thorndyke almost laughed right out remembering Constable Kennedy bringing in that load of criminals the day before. *Old banker Dudley is in a fit over that. And I paid for the men riding with Kennedy. That meeting day after tomorrow will be a sight, I think.*

THADDEUS YOUNGER WATCHED THE WAGON COME DOWN Main Street toward his grocery store. *Ah, yes. Just as I said to Murphy, here they come, hat in hand. First, a list of what they need and then the begging to be able to pay for it after their first crop comes in. Newcomers. Bah!*

Younger stepped back into his store and ducked

quickly behind the counter as Ken tied his team off and helped Sandra and the children down. "Late in the season," Ken said, "but the grocer seems to have some fresh vegetables. Plenty of dried as well. I wonder if he buys from local growers or if these come from his own farm?"

The Boyington family walked into the store and found bins of dried and fresh food, kitchen ware including cast iron pots and pans, and some tin ware. "Good morning," Sandra said when she spotted Younger. "What a nice selection you have. We've been on the trail from back east for so long I could eat a bite of everything you have displayed."

"Morning," is all Younger said. He had no intention of being friendly until he saw the color of their money.

"I have a short list here," Sandra said, handing it to him. "We'll be back for more after we have a place to keep it." Her smile almost lit up the store as she looked at a bin full of beautiful apples. There were peaches, too, and even plums. "Let's get some apples, Ken. I'll make pies to go with supper."

Little Sonja yipped at that. "Yes, Mommy, yes," she cried out.

"How are we paying for this?" Younger asked. There was no smile on his face despite the fact the family was filled with joy at what he offered.

"Oh, we have cash, sir," Ken Boyington said. He looked at the man's rather glum face. "I have the feeling you don't much care for those of us moving into the territory. Mr. Thorndyke on the other hand welcomed us with open arms. We'll not be beholden to anyone, sir. Please fill the order and we'll be on our way."

The brusqueness had no effect on the storekeeper. It seemed to go right over his head, but Sandra turned quickly at Ken's comment. *The storekeeper is a cold one, for certain but I don't think I've ever seen Ken react this way.*

The man standing off behind bushel baskets of apples wasn't noticed by anyone and was out of the store in moments. Sandra was much interested in the apples and picked up several for her pies.

Thaddeus Younger stood behind the counter with a small list of necessities they wanted and was not pleased by Boyington's attitude. On the other hand, the man would be paying for what they wanted. *This young man is a little more uppity than I like. He'll not get any favors from me.*

Ken Boyington had a sad look on his face standing in front of Younger. *All my life I've worked hard for other people. Even to the point of having to work off my father's debt. Always looked down on by those who felt superior because they had and I had not. Well, today I have. I have land, I have family, and I have money to pay for what we need. Don't turn your nose up at me, Mr. Storekeeper or I'll not sell you any of my fine produce next fall.*

Ken Boyington and family were back in the wagon and on their way home in just minutes. "Man never even said thank you. He had that sour face the entire time we were in the store, Sandra. I'm afraid we're not welcome everywhere in Oregon Territory."

"Maybe it was something he ate," she giggled, reaching over and pinching Ken. "We were told at the land office that not everyone looked with favor on those of us moving in. It's a big country we're moving into, so they'll just have to accept us and if they don't, it's their loss."

Boyington chuckled at the comment and tried to get the mules to move a little faster. "Gonna take some effort to unload this mess we bought." He looked at Sandra.

"Knowing I've got apple pie in my future will make the job a little easier."

"I think you should plan on visiting that Jacob Hoagland that Mr. Thorndyke told you about. Maybe tomorrow, eh?"

"He's got a public meeting scheduled at the civic center tomorrow, Sandra. Mr. Thorndyke showed me the poster about it. I'll be at that meeting and I'll introduce myself. Something about public safety." He looked back over his shoulder and enjoyed the view of so much material to use on their new home. "I really thought it would cost a lot more than it did. We will have to watch our spending though over the next year. We'll need that first crop to be a good one, too."

Sandra looked at him a long time. "You're not getting second thoughts or something are you?"

"Not a chance," he laughed. "With that ground? With you standing at my side? No, my sweet little girl, there aren't any second thoughts."

The ride back home gave both a chance to think about what they've done, what might be in their immediate future. Would the ground really produce the way Ken thinks it will? Will he be able to get the roof on their little cabin before the rains and snow arrive? Will she be able to help as much as she thinks, being pregnant and having one child not walking yet?

"My head hurts from all my questions," Sandra laughed. "We'll be all right, won't we?"

Ken smiled, reached across and patted her knee. "More than all right. We'll be fine."

CHAPTER 14

Amos Dudley was pacing the floor in his ornate bank manager's office, angry and for one of the few times in his life unsure of exactly what to do. Go to the damned public meeting and face off with Jacob Hoagland? Ignore the meeting completely? Have it out with Hoagland at the next commissioner's meeting? He paced around the office and stopped in front of the large windows on every circuit, looking out to see how many people might be gathering at the civic park across the way.

Interestingly, the Brookside Civic Park was Amos Dudley's idea, a place of pristine beauty, a place where public men could make public speeches, where ideas could bloom. It was the irony of all that that was at the heart of Dudley's contempt for Kennedy's successes. Success at being able to spend time with the lovely, warm Irene Creighton, success at parading dead and wounded prisoners through his park. Kennedy did not parade those men through the park, but the street alongside the park.

It was bad enough having to stand in front of that

window and see constable Kennedy parade his prisoners around. Where did he get the money to hire those two yahoos, anyway?

A wise man might see the folly in standing in front of a window being angry at those who in reality have nothing to do with the problem. The problem in Irene Creighton not wanting to have anything to do with Amos Dudley wasn't Tobias Kennedy, nor was it Jacob Hoagland. Very simply, it was Amos Dudley and his lecherous behavior.

Gentlemen of his social standing do not treat women as whores, but Dudley had never had social intercourse with women of social standing, in fact, with women of any standing. He was coarse, his intercourse with those he does business with was coarse, even his treatment of those who worked for him was coarse.

Some of his anger was aimed at Jacob Hoagland, and some at the way Hoagland out-foxed him setting up this public meeting, but the furious part of his anger was aimed straight at Tobias Kennedy, Constable, Brookside, Oregon Territory. Dudley passed by Irene Creighton's home on his evening walk the night before and, just by accident, of course, noticed Kennedy and Mrs. Creighton having supper.

After all, if you leave a curtain open, one can be seen from outside. It wasn't as if he was purposefully searching the shadows. The rest of the evening's walk involved kicking every stone in his path and snarling invectives at children out playing. He so desperately wanted to be at that table, to gaze into those beautiful eyes, to slam Irene Creighton into bed.

He stood in front of the large window in his office, saw fifty or more people gathering in the civic center and decided that today was not the proper time to have a face-off with Hoagland. "Charles," he called out. "Come now."

His bank clerk rushed into the office, fear writ large on an open and youthful face. "Go to that meeting in the park and note what's being said. I will expect a full and written report before tomorrow morning." Charles bowed slightly and left in a hurry, grabbing paper, pen, and ink bottle.

Jacob Hoagland and his wife Martha, she holding their baby daughter, and son Lucas drove the family buggy up to the hitching post and Luke jumped down to take care of the horses. "My goodness, Jacob," Martha said. "This is quite a turn-out. Did you expect this kind of reaction?"

Families had gathered as if to have a picnic, sitting on spread blankets, groups of men passed flasks back and forth, engaged in vigorous debate, and women attempted to corral running and screaming children. It was only slightly organized chaos on a delightful Autumn day.

Jacob had a satisfied smile as he looked the crowd over. "No, dear lady I did not. I knew our friends and neighbors had concerns about our growth and lack of law and order, but I did not anticipate this large a crowd." He kept looking out over the crowd and Martha gave him a questioning look.

"Just looking to see if Amos Dudley was here. He really should be. I sent him and Clyde Peabody invitations. There's Peabody, over by the oak tree. Looks like he brought his family along, too. Dudley really should be here." Hoagland wasn't thinking of Dudley as the bank manager but rather, Dudley the county commissioner. All three commissioners should be at this gathering.

Hoagland moved his family over to where Commissioner Peabody was standing. "Nice turn out, eh? You look fit," Jacob said.

"Hello, Jacob. Yes, I like the way you put this little gathering together. How do you plan on handling this? Oh, and where's Amos?"

"I have a feeling he might not show up, Clyde. I'm going to open it up with a very brief speech about growth, lack of people in the constable's office, and the necessity of growth in that department. I received a note from Ben Thorndyke about the need for at least one more volunteer hose wagon for the fire department. Then I'm going to ask if anyone would like to add anything."

"That could get lively," Clyde Peabody chuckled. "I'd like to say something, if you could fit me in."

"More than glad to. Absolutely. Ah, here's Kennedy now. Hello, Tobias. Glad you could make it."

"Wouldn't miss this for anything, Jacob. Not for anything. Ben Thorndyke will be here shortly. He asked that I ask you if he could open the meeting and have the pleasure of introducing you."

"Good old speechifying Ben Thorndyke," Clyde Peabody chuckled.

"Of course he can," Jacob chuckled. "Of course he can."

———

"I THINK THE HIGHLIGHT OF THE MEETING WAS WHEN Kennedy publicly thanked Ben Thorndyke for the two dollars he used to hire two men to bring in the killers of the Cringle family." Clyde Peabody and his family were at the big table at Murphy's along with the Hoagland family, the Thorndyke family, and Constable Kennedy. Kennedy fought with himself for an hour, wanting desperately to invite Irene Creighton to be with him at this supper.

She was right in saying no. This wouldn't be the right place, the right time, for us to have supper in public. Soon, he thought. "I do want to thank you, Commissioner Hoagland for putting on this public hearing. Many people had a lot to say and most of it was positive," Kennedy said.

"All except for what that fool grocer, Younger, railed on about." Murphy said. "That man has a serious dislike for a lot of people he's never met or laid eyes on. Some of the young hot-heads are liable to follow his ideas of running people off. He's enflaming a lot of anger."

"He won't listen to anyone, either." Kennedy shook his head. "Claude Atkins has spoken to him, Jacob, you've spoken to him, I've told him he's wrong more than once, and he simply won't listen. He is going to cause trouble, sure as I'm sitting here."

Discussion on the plusses of those moving into the territory continued as Mrs. O'Reilly and a young girl brought on the food. Murphy and his wife laid out a spread fit for kings and queens not to mention county commissioners and their wives.

"The highlight for me, Ben Thorndyke said, "was when somebody told Younger to shut up and sit down."

"I was most interested in watching the young man near the oak tree, writing furiously all afternoon," Martha Hoagland said. "I don't think I recognized him. Is he a newcomer?"

"No," Murphy yelped. "It was when that gentleman standing near an oak tree wanted to know why commissioner Dudley wasn't present."

"That gentleman," Kennedy said, "was Amon Dudley's bank clerk. Rather sly of the young man."

"No," Ben Thorndyke said, "It was when Thaddeus Younger proclaimed that there should be a law prohibiting any newcomers at all. The boos and cat-calls drowned out anything Hoagland could have said in retort. It was wonderful."

"I met one of the newcomers," Jacob Hoagland said. "A most interesting man named Boyington. Ken Boyington, from Virginia. He and his wife have 320 acres up Third Creek. A real gentleman. He met Mr. Younger the day before and wasn't surprised by what Younger said at the park."

"You're being rather quiet, constable," Thorndyke said. "From where I sit it looks like you might have a deputy or two in your office."

"Possibly, Ben. Possibly. But," and he looked around the crowded table, "what bothers me is Amos Dudley not being there. He has said to you, Ben, and to you, Jacob, that I should be relieved of my position if I can't keep order in the county. He wasn't there, but what will he do at the next commissioners' meeting? Is he in a position to either let me go or ham-string the office to the point where order in the county can't be kept?"

Clyde Peabody shook his nearly bald head slowly back and forth all the time saying, "No, no, no." He looked at Jacob Hoagland and smiled. "There are three commissioners, constable, and two of them are at this table right now. No, Mr. Dudley is in no position to have you ousted from office. Whatever is driving Amos is personal and I don't think we'll know the answer until he lets it out of the bag."

Hoagland noted that neither Thorndyke nor Kennedy said anything. *Is Kennedy aware of what Dudley's problem is? Has anything been said to him. Ben isn't going to say anything and neither am I. It's up to Amos Dudley now. Will he bring his personal problem to the commissioner's meeting next week?*

Murphy and his wife ended the discussion bringing great platters of roasted lamb, roasted goose, and roasted venison to the table. The Hoagland and Peabody children were sitting with the Thorndyke children at a table of their own, overseen by Gerald Thorndyke and Luke Hoagland.

The conversation turned to the upcoming winter months, the just completed harvest, and what plans were already in place for next year's planting. It was a lively supper and a long ride home for the Hoagland family, well after dark.

"You should be more than proud of yourself, Jacob," Martha said. "I thought the whole thing was just wonderful. So many people had so much to say, and for the most part said it well."

"I am pleased," Jacob said. "I am and sad that Amos wasn't there. Didn't hear how some families have been hurt by the lawlessness of a few, how fear has been part of some lives because of these few thugs running amongst us. He needed to hear that."

"Don't you think it will get back to him?" Martha asked.

"Oh, yes," Jacob laughed. "His man was there taking notes, but that won't be the same. He's got it in for Tobias Kennedy and it's very personal. He can't separate his feelings from the needs of the community. The passion shown by our community at the gathering might have done that."

CHAPTER 15

"Charles," Dudley bawled. The young man was sitting at his clerk's desk and jumped to his feet. He grabbed a hand full of papers and rushed to Dudley's office. He was thrilled to sit under an old oak tree for a wonderful afternoon of debate and wrote extensively on what was said along with the general attitude of the people speaking. Now he had to face the wrath of the man who told him to sit under that old oak and write what took place.

Charles had his position at the bank at the insistence of his father, not at his own pleasure. The Lawrence Nixon family had been in the west, not by way of a wagon train or led by a mountain man, but on a schooner brought north from Panama. Nixon ran a trading post on the British side of the Columbia River during the height of the fur trade but wanted his son to learn the banking business.

Charles was a bright young man, detested the work, and wanted more than anything to be a writer and own a newspaper. The people of Brookside read a broadsheet that was distributed once a month and never signed. No one ever took responsibility for what was written and only Charles Nixon knew who the writer was, not Anon, but Charles Nixon. Each sheet was hand written or lettered, a pain's taking enterprise but one loved by the young man.

Hours spent at his writing table hand writing in beautiful script, the month's activities in Brookside. Some rather humorous happenings, some sad, and always accurate. One name kept cropping up, Travis T, commenting on various activities in the community. Travis T. had a wit along with a sharp tongue. People were beginning to ask, just who is this Travis T? What's more, they kept asking, who is it that's producing this little piece of literature?

Charles Nixon has endured the ravings of Amos Dudley for two years, stuffing every loose farthing he could find into a drawer in his one room shack, hoping to buy his very own printing press. Until then, he would hand write twenty-five or so copies of his newsletter.

"Right here, sir." Charles's position at the bank was always vulnerable, Amos Dudley saw to that. Dudley was of the belief that a good manager terrorized his employees. Management by intimidation had been taught to him by his father and his grandfather. Young Amos Dudley had been terrorized from his day of birth and was now in a position to do his own plundering of souls.

"Where's that report. I said I wanted it this morning."

"Right here, sir," Charles said. A close look would see bright eyes shining with anticipation. Would this pompous banker understand that the citizens of Brookside were worried about the lack of protection? Would the words of the commissioners and the constable have an impact on the banker's feelings about increasing the size of the constable's department? Or would Charles

Nixon's way of outlining what happened at the civic park lead to his being ushered from the slate and marble halls of Brookside's bank?

Dudley took the offered papers and flicked his hand as if saying, "That's all. Leave." Charles turned and walked back to his desk and methodically sorted what belonged to the bank from what was his. Just in case he had to make a hasty retreat.

Amos Dudley paged through the notes and made some marks, jotted some notes, and grew more and more angry. Within ten minutes Dudley had the bottom right drawer of his impressive desk opened and the porcelain flask open. A small silver tea-cup was filled three times before Dudley put the flask back in the drawer.

So, our grocer doesn't want more people moving into our little valley, eh? Doesn't he understand that they must eat, must purchase farming equipment? They are an asset. He stopped the thought process immediately and turned his mind back on getting Tobias Kennedy out of the county. Irene Creighton was not even aware that she was at the heart of the problem. She had been made aware of just what part she would be playing, however. *She'll be mine, one way or the other.*

THE MAN HAD SURVIVED THE CROSSING, WHICH IN ITSELF says a lot about him, but surviving at life seemed to be different somehow. Dudley was nearing forty years of age, and had never been close to a woman more or less in a romantic way. His mannerisms were of the Boston variety, Boston elite, that is. Some simply call it arrogance.

His family had been successful bankers for several generations despite being at odds with the king before leaving England, and somewhat shady from time to time with proper behavior in the new land. It was expected that Amos would act in the best traditions of the Dudley family also. It was expected of him. Yes, he was to marry into a family of influence and money. It was expected of him. But several generations of arrogance peaked with Amos Dudley and he found it, not just impossible, but repulsive to have a close friendship or relationship with another human being, more or less with a woman.

What developed was a great need for female companionship without the least idea of how to accomplish such a task. Desire and demand, and soon, Amos Dudley had a reputation of being more a lecher than a gentleman. After several threats of lawsuits, the family found it convenient to open a banking enterprise in the up and coming Territory of Oregon, naming Amos as manager of the operation. The women of Brookside were not appreciative.

Amos Dudley, after all these years only wanted the facade of a relationship. He wanted carnal knowledge without benefit of wooing and romance. That is, until he met Irene Creighton. What was so different? Why did he have this desire to be close to this woman? Irene Creighton, you must remember, killed her husband, the father of her children. Yes, she was fully justified in the eyes of the law, but the deed itself, one would think, might keep another man at arm's length.

She has a vitality I've never seen in another person, more or less a woman. And she knows her numbers. A book keeping business run by a woman? Some pluck there. Amos Dudley was enamored, needed to know more about this woman who Ben Thorndyke lets maintain his financial empire.

This woman who seems to have eyes for constable Kennedy, not for Amos Dudley.

Was it the thought there might be danger in a relationship with a woman who killed one husband? Or was it the fact that she was the owner of a successful book keeping business? A woman who understood numbers, profits and losses, managing enormous amounts of money, as she did for Ben Thorndyke?

Irene Creighton was a lovely and generous woman, well-liked by the community, who had faced bad times. Her husband was physically abusive and she ended that problem but he taught their son that it was a man's right to be abusive and to take advantage of women. The boy is in custody because he followed his father's training.

There was a daughter, too. Carrie was almost ten-years-old, and just as attractive as her mother. She was a reader, loved learning, and had many friends. Amos Dudley found her playfulness obnoxious, found her ability to laugh irritating, and wanted nothing to do with her or any child. But he wanted to be close to her mother and had no real idea of how to make that happen. He knew, though, that he had to get rid of Tobias Kennedy.

Kennedy's outgoing personality, his ability to enjoy life, tell a ribald story or two, quaff a brandy or rum, was disgusting to the banker. The fact that so many liked the man, so many felt safe because he was on the job, and that Irene Creighton enjoyed his company festered to the point that Dudley's thoughts concentrated on ways to get Kennedy out of their lives.

Dudley was a bully, had been since early childhood, and was putting together a plan that would end any possibility of the widow Creighton wanting to be near anyone but Dudley. *She'll come to me on bended knee, demand that I take care of her. She'll beg for help and I'll be the only one who can help.*

———

THE WIDOW CREIGHTON WAS SITTING AT A SMALL DESK IN an equally small alcove just off the living room of her home, trying to work on the profit/loss statement for her own book keeping business. It had been a long and difficult, but fruitful, year for the family. Her son still in the boy's home after being found guilty of actions dealing with young girls. Her daughter was growing up fast, and her business had blossomed.

One year. It's been one year since the death of Ed Creighton. She always referred to it as 'the death' of her husband. The constable said it was justified, the court said it was justified, but Irene had a hard time saying something like, 'it's been one year since I killed my husband.' *I'm keeping the books for Ben Thorndyke's many businesses and three others in the community, and I and Carrie are healthy. Why do I feel like there's something missing?*

She knew why but was unwilling to accept that she wanted, needed a man in her life. She was pleased at the attention paid her by the constable, but he scared her. He was big, so strong, and his work, having to be with nasty and dirty people all the time. On the other hand, Amos Dudley was, to put it in simple terms, a boor. *He's a little bit more refined than Ed Creighton was but still makes uncalled for remarks about my having a business. As if women were to be placed in either the kitchen or the bed, never anywhere else.*

Most of the other single men in the community were scared off by her independence on the one hand and her having children on the other. She got up from the table and walked into the kitchen for a cup of coffee. Carrie was sitting at the table reading what Charles Nixon was calling *FYI*. *For Your Information* was penned on just one side of a single sheet of paper, black ink and no etchings or wood cuts.

"Where did this come from?"

"Gerald Thorndyke had it," Carrie said. "He says big cities have real newspapers, but this is all Brookside has. He said it's delivered to the store early in the morning, once a month, and nobody knows who writes it. It's easy to read."

Irene poured a cup of coffee, put a sweet roll left over from breakfast on a plate and sat down. "Let me see." It only took a few minutes to read three little stories. "My, my," she said. "Whoever wrote this was right there with us, Carrie. He has some nice things to say about Mr. Kennedy."

"I like the constable," Carrie said. "He's funny when he's pretending to arrest me, or when he sits at the head of the table and recites those funny little sayings of his."

Irene looked at her daughter and realized that she was saying almost exactly what she, herself was thinking. "Yes, he is a charming man, but so big, so strong." She realized she was about to say, 'and so good looking.' A quick look at Carrie and she sipped some coffee to hide the smile.

"Think we could visit the seamstress this afternoon, honey? I wonder if that new dress of yours is finished?"

"Oh, yes, mommy. Yes."

"Good. It's cold outside so dress warmly. I'm sure we have our first snow of the season coming our way." She looked around the kitchen and once again realized just how lucky she was. Not only was the wood bin and kindling box inside filled, but there were several cords of wood stacked in the wood shack as well.

The men from the timber mill along with Ben Thorndyke saw to it that she and Carrie would have a warm winter. She insisted on paying the men for delivering the wood, and they insisted that they only delivered the two cords that Ben ordered. Anyone could see there were at least four cords of wood stacked under the shed roof.

Ed Creighton was such a fool, not responding to those wishing to be friends, never being a part of the community. We never had friends over, were never invited out because of his personality, and now? Amazing just how many friends I have.

CHAPTER 16

T he Creighton residence was at the intersection of First Street and Eagle Avenue and it was a nice two block walk to Second Street and Apple where Mrs. Bendix had her dress shop. It was just a block south of the courthouse at Second and Main. Irene and Carrie were dressed warm for the walk. November was starting to feel more like winter than fall.

Irene waved to one of the men who had delivered split cord wood to her home during the past week as he drove a four-up team and wagon load of wood for another customer. There were several men in town who made part of their living cutting, splitting, and delivering wood for the hungry stoves and fireplaces in the community.

"That wind has a nip to it," Irene said. "Just look at your rosy cheeks. Maybe we can stop by the café on the way home for hot chocolate."

"I'd like that," Carrie said. She was walking with her mother, prim and proper for a few steps, then skipping and laughing for a few steps. She was ten-years-old and full of life. Irene couldn't keep the smile off her face, and remembered what it was like for her.

If I'd listened to my father I would still be living on the east coast, would never have married Ed Creighton and would never have had Carrie. Life is complex, Irene, complex and scary. It's just been one year since the death of Ed Creighton and what a year it's been. Look at her, dancing and skipping, loving life. She was more contemplative than she had been in months.

I'm loving our life, too, and it's been a long time since I've even been able to think something like that. How different it had been living back east compared to out here. These men and women turning a wild and fearsome territory into an agricultural paradise. My god, the fresh food we have literally at our fingertips.

Clouds had been building to the northwest, the wind had picked up, and the temperature was falling fast. Late November and if it was rain it would be a cold, almost icy rain, but if it was snow, it would be slushy. No matter which, it would mean mud. Muddy streets, muddy pathways, muddy boots and shoes. Irene held in her laugh, thinking that mud was one of the most prevalent crops, as rocks were in the east.

The dress that Carrie wanted was fitted and she looked lovely in it. There were yellows and greens, some muted pinks and even some of the designs were in white. "It's spring, momma, look, it's spring in my dress. Frilly spring," she giggled. She changed back into her more acceptable winter wear, Irene paid for the dress and let her daughter carry the package.

I paid for that. I reached in my purse for money and paid for the dress. It took a long time for Irene to realize just what a change had taken place. *When Ed Creighton was alive he would never let me have any money. None at all.* She looked at Carrie with her package and smiled.

"Hot chocolate, coming up," Irene said, leading the way across the street to Newman's Café. "And maybe a piece of pie?"

"Apple pie," Carrie said. "Luke Hoagland brought us a whole sack of apples, momma. I forgot to tell you. He and his father left them on the steps and I put them on the back porch, in the cool air."

"Thank you," Irene said. Her daughter was growing up so fast. *Young boys bringing gifts? Well, it's time for us to have a little talk, I think.* There were also the horrid memories of her son attempting to take advantage of Carrie, and a friend, and at the suggestion of his father. They were just getting settled in chairs at a table by the front window when Constable Kennedy walked in.

"Ah," he said, doffing his wool hat and giving a sweeping bow to the ladies. "Two charming young ladies in distress. I must fend off the evil dragon and save them. I must," he said, bending down and saying it right into Carries laughing face.

"You're funny," she giggled. "Want to see my new dress?"

"Please, Constable, will you join us?" Irene said.

"Yes to both questions," Kennedy said. "We have a storm coming our way, ladies so don't stay out too long. I saw you at the civic park yesterday but couldn't get away from everyone. Did you enjoy the debates?"

"I did," Irene said. "Mr. Thorndyke seems to be under the impression that Mr. Dudley won't let you hire extra help because he wants you to fail in your job. Is that right? Why would he want that?"

Kennedy looked at the woman for several seconds before trying to come up with an answer. "He's a strange man to try to get to know, Irene. He is demanding that a certain level of protection be offered to the county but isn't willing to pay for it. I think it's simply that he doesn't like me. Hard to believe, eh, Carrie? That somebody doesn't like me?"

Carrie giggled and Irene laughed right out. "Hard to believe," Irene barely mumbled but Kennedy heard it. He winked at Carrie but tried to keep a somber look on his face. "May I have the honor of escorting you charming ladies home?"

"Yes," Irene said. She realized how quickly she said that, blushed and kept her eyes from both Carrie and the constable. *Oh, dear. That certainly wasn't proper.* She let him hold her chair and helped her with her coat, and found she simply couldn't keep the smile off her face.

As they approached the walkway to the house, Amos Dudley came around the corner holding a sheaf of papers close to his chest. The wind was blowing hard and Dudley was sure the papers would blow away.

"Need some help there, Dudley?" Kennedy called out. "Wind's got a bite to it, eh?"

"I'll manage," Dudley growled out, but he didn't. A strong gust ripped half the papers from his hand and he watched in alarm as they tumbled through the air, blowing and twisting, some falling and then rising again. He fumbled with the few left in his grasp, tried to catch those flying about, only to lose some he held.

Rain and globs of snow started falling, blowing hard, wetting everything. The wind made catching flying sheets of paper impossible. When they fell to the ground they were soaked instantly. "Must be important to be delivering these papers without putting them in a sleeve," Kennedy said.

"Damn it," Dudley said, and caught himself. "Oh, dear.

I'm terribly sorry, Mrs. Creighton. Please, I apologize." He made a complete fool of himself, trying to hold a few sheets of paper, wanting to hold Irene's hand, and trying to catch a flurry of papers dancing in the wind.

Never seen a more awkward man in my life, Kennedy thought. He started gathering some of the papers, knew many were lost, and handed the gob he had to the banker. "Might want to bind these next time, Dudley."

"Yes, of course," Dudley said. He didn't really have a good hand on them, harrumphed a hurried, "Good day." He turned, hands full of crumpled papers, and stalked off down the street, not looking back.

"A most unusual man," Irene said. "Would you join us for coffee, Mr. Kennedy?"

"Indeed," the constable said. Maybe it was seeing the flying papers, maybe it was a tick of memory, but Kennedy remembered what Hoagland had said about the bank foreclosing on Mrs. Creighton's property. "And, yes, coffee would be fine, Irene."

Inside and in the warm kitchen, Kennedy said, "There's something we need to talk about. Has Dudley said anything to you about ownership of this property?"

"No," she almost gasped. "What do you mean?" She was standing at the wood fired stove, coffee pot in hand. She felt her knees weaken, eased the pot down and moved quickly to her chair. "What?"

Her face was chalky white, her breathing quickened, and she remembered, a year ago, both Constable Kennedy and Ben Thorndyke saying that there might be moves by men to take what was rightfully hers only because she was a woman.

"I've heard that Ed Creighton made loans from the bank, Irene, and used this property as collateral. Dudley may be getting ready to call in those loans. Has anything been said?"

It was as if time took that moment to stand still. Her breathing quit, her eyes clouded over, and she couldn't feel her hands on the table. How could this be? It's been a year. Thoughts were jumbled, fear ran rampant, and she wanted to grab Carrie and hold her tight. It took just moments and she tried to put her thoughts in order, stifle this mad fear, and think.

"There was nothing in any of his papers to suggest anything like that." Irene sat, stiff, staring at her coffee cup, trying to think if she had ever heard of any kind of loan through Amos Dudley. "I've never heard of any kind of loan. Mr. Creighton was loose with our funds, as you well know, Tobias, but a loan? Using this property to fund it? No, I know nothing of this."

It was quiet at the table for many minutes as the two simply let their minds flush out what had been said. "Can he do such a thing?" Irene finally asked. "Can he call in a loan made by a man who is now dead? What should I do?"

"A nice long talk with the county attorney might be the best thing to do," Kennedy said. "Claude Atkins is one of the smartest men I know. If you want, I'll be happy to escort you to the appointment."

"Thank you, Tobias. You're so kind. I'll make the appointment first thing in the morning. This is frightening. First I learn Ed Creighton is a criminal, now I find out he was more than just loose with our money, he was foolishly so."

CHAPTER 17

"**A**re you sure of what you heard from Kennedy?" Ben Thorndyke was sitting in his oversize leather chair, looking out the window to the pasture across the creek. It was the kind of office that men with a vision dream of. Built in the style of a log cabin, simply because that's exactly what it was, with a rock fireplace dominating one wall, a desk looking out the large window, and elk antlers, buckskins decorated with Indian beadwork hanging from walls, and a double-barrel flintlock shotgun standing near the fireplace. The little building stood off, well away from the main Thorndyke complex. It was Ben Thorndyke's castle.

Thorndyke turned in his chair to look directly into Irene Creighton's eyes. "Creighton was a fool, did some stupid things in his life, but taking out a loan against his property without your knowing it?" He wagged his head a bit. "Even for Ed Creighton, that's simply not logical."

"I've not seen a shred of paper on such a loan," Irene said. "Nothing, and you know I went through his office and papers. There is not a single indication he ever made such a loan."

"And Dudley hasn't said anything to you?" Thorndyke's brows were knit, his eyes blazing as he asked. "Our fine and upstanding banker can be mean in his dealings with people." He coughed out a chuckle. "He's always been a bully, sadistic, and uncaring. He would have to have papers even if Creighton didn't keep his."

"He's a strange man, Ben. He's asked me to have supper with him twice. My goodness, I would never do that. He even invited me for a carriage ride up Third Creek. My heavens, Ben. What does he think I am? No, nothing about a loan has ever been mentioned."

"I think the constable was right, then. You need to see Claude Atkins as soon as possible. I'll make the arrangements for you."

"Thank you, Ben. Would Dudley really be able to take my house?"

"That's the question, isn't it?" He looked out the window, across grasses and brush to the creek flowing through the meadow and wondered just what Dudley was up to.

Irene Creighton went back to her desk in the main building of the Thorndyke complex and Ben sat at his desk looking out the window. *It's been a year since Ed Creighton's death. If Dudley does have loan papers why has he waited a year to do anything with them? Is any of this related to Kennedy?* It hadn't reached the point of being the talk of the village but the visits between the constable and the widow were discussed over more than one fence, across more than one pot of coffee.

Thorndyke's dealings with the banker had always been strictly at the business level. He and others had invested in the bank, was a member of the board of directors. Dudley was the majority stock holder at fifty-one percent, and served as bank manager.

Unlike Dudley, Thorndyke was open and friendly, ready to help anyone willing to help themselves while Amos Dudley was willing to take advantage of anyone not protecting himself. There was no friendship between the two men. More than once Thorndyke had suggested that Brookside would do well to have a second bank in the community. The man even offered to finance one if Dudley wouldn't sell out his interest.

Thorndyke jotted down some notes and made the short walk to the county courthouse for a visit with Claude Atkins, County Attorney. He couldn't help trying to tie Dudley's asking Irene out for supper or a carriage ride to pledging to have Tobias Kennedy relieved of his office.

Kennedy has been seeing Irene and Dudley wants to. Would that sadistic bastard stoop so low as to intimidate Irene into seeing him or losing her property? That's mighty low, even for Dudley.

Thorndyke had to pass by the constable's office to get to the stairway leading to Atkins' office in the court-house. Kennedy was looking at a rather nice looking shotgun. "New shotgun, constable?"

"No, Ben. Sure is good looking, eh? I think this is the one reported stolen by old Mr. Parker recently. It was delivered to my office while I was out, but of course, I don't know who might have delivered it." Kennedy didn't mention the note that had been attached. "I'm about to take it up to Parker and see if it is his."

Thorndyke nodded and headed for the stairs and Claude Atkins office. *There's just too much crime going on. Brookside is too small a village for this much crime taking place. We've got to get Kennedy some help. My horse stolen,*

112

Parker's shotgun stolen, families murdered, and stores plundered, and we have just one lawman.

"Hello, Claude. How are you feeling?"

"Ah, good morning, Ben. I'm getting along. These old lungs still giving me hell but I ain't leaving my trees. By God, I'm not. What brings you this way?"

"Don't really know how to explain it," Ben Thorndyke said. He sat down and shook his head. "It's possible that Ed Creighton took out a loan on his property. That would be more than a year ago, and there are rumors that Amos Dudley is going to call in the loan. Mrs. Creighton needs some hard and fast legal help."

"The constable was just up here saying the same thing, Ben. Interesting. Creighton was so cold hearted, rough as a cob, and it looks like his problems are still around for his widow. If Dudley has papers, legal papers, there isn't much she can do about it. Have her come in any time. I'll have a talk with her."

He shook hands with Thorndyke and wondered why the banker would wait a year to want to close the loan. *Between the constable and old Ben Thorndyke, that woman has some strong allies. Wouldn't want to get between those two.* Atkins chuckled. Together Thorndyke and Kennedy would weigh in over four hundred pounds while Dudley's pompous frame might weigh one-eighty-five. *It would be fun to watch.*

———

"GOOD MORNING, MR. PARKER," KENNEDY SAID WHEN THE old man answered his knock. Parker lived along the edge of Brookside's eastern limit, at the very end of Third Creek Road, in a small cabin he built several years before. The road becomes just a trail leading deeper into the canyon that supports the creek. Parker came to Oregon Territory, working in the fur trade and then settled and made his living as a hunter.

When he arrived he had a lovely Shoshone wife but they weren't able to have children. She caught the flu that swept through the tiny village and died from fever. He told stories of riding with Jim Bridger and Broken Hand, stories of Indian fights, and wild nights during rendezvous. He favored buckskins over cotton or wool, and ate what nature provided. Despite his age his eyes sparkled with life and he was always ready to tell or hear a good story.

It had been a nice ride up and into the mountains and Kennedy enjoyed the sights and smells. The leafy trees were ablaze in their fall finery, rabbit brush was a brilliant yellow, and he could hear bull elk way off in the higher country calling for their does. From the courthouse it was almost eight miles to Parker's cabin. Third Creek road crossed the creek several times and it seemed he had seen fish at each of the crossings. *I got to come up here more often, and with my bamboo pole.* He chuckled at the thought.

"Tobias, well my goodness, come in, come in." Parker held the door open and Kennedy walked into a warm and friendly two room cabin. Parker had a rock fireplace burning well with a cast-iron pot of stew on a hanger spewing a delightful aroma. There was a table with two chairs not far away from the fire. The other room would have been for sleeping. Kennedy opened his heavy bearskin coat and pulled the shotgun out.

"Recognize this, sir?"

"You found her," Parker said. His eyes lit up and he grabbed it away from the constable. "Oh, little girl, you've come home." He raised it to his shoulder and smiled. "That was fast work, Toby. Where did you find her?"

Kennedy enjoyed the little show Parker put on with the gun and sat down with a cup of coffee. "Somebody dropped it off at the office," he said. "I think whoever took it was afraid of trying to sell it. Too many people would know it was yours. Do you have any ideas about the theft?"

"For a day or two before it disappeared, those two ruffians, Evan and Travis Kinsey were hanging around. They were pestering me about cutting wood for me, or some such nonsense. I cut my own wood. Don't need them troublemakers around."

He looked at Kennedy. "Think they did it?"

"Might have been looking around to see what you had worth taking. They've been known for that." He stood up to leave. "Keep your eyes open, Mr. Parker. Times are changing, new people aren't all good people, sir."

"Thank you, Toby. I think I'll go shoot me a goose or a turkey. Best shotgun I've ever had. Back in the day," he said, "When the likes of Old Gabe and me wandered those far mountains, a shotgun like this would be worth a hundred beavers."

Kennedy was smiling walking his horse down the path that led to Third Creek Road. *Gonna have to have a word with them Kinsey twins. Too young to be getting in as much trouble as they get in.* He reached in his jacket and pulled the note out that had accompanied the shotgun when it was returned. *Strange,* he thought. *All it says is, 'found this. thought you might know the owner.' Nobody signed it, doesn't say where it was found.* The ride back to town was filled with more questions than answers.

CHAPTER 18

Ken Boyington rode the mule into their little home place, a couple of walls up so far, and found two men with rifles, one holding Sandra who was holding Spike. Little Sonja was holding onto Sandra's skirts crying.

"What is this?" Ken cried out, jumping from the mule and rushing toward Sandra. The man holding Sandra swung his rifle, knocking Boyington to the ground. He got up quickly, wiping blood from his forehead, and rushed the man who hit him.

It was the other man who knocked him to the ground this time. "All we want is your money, mister. Give us your money or else."

"Or else what?" Boyington said, getting slowly to his feet.

"Or else this," the man said. He grabbed Spike right out of Sandra's arms and had a large knife at Spike's throat. "Money, mister or this boy's gone."

Ken stood stock still, not daring to move. Nothing like this had ever even been considered in his wildest dreams. "No," Ken said, as quietly as he could, fearing something loud and aggressive would startle the man.

"We ain't got no money," Sandra cried out. "Tell them, Ken." The man holding Sandra had his hands all over the lovely lady and Ken's blood was boiling.

"Let them go and I'll get you your money," he said. His voice was quiet, almost soft, and Sandra knew he was going to try something, anything, to get them free.

"No, mister. Put the money down in front of me and we'll see if this fine woman stays or goes with us. She's a fine one, ain't she, Torch? My kind of woman."

Boyington rushed him, knocking the man, Sandra, and himself to the ground. Sandra wrenched free but the man swung the rifle, even while on his back, and knocked Boyington back into the dirt. The man jumped to his feet, grabbed Sandra, and kicked Boyington before he could get to his feet.

"Enough of this," the man holding Spike shouted. "Get up, mister, get that money in my hands before I count to ten, and I'm counting now."

Boyington got to his feet and made one more quick move at the man holding Sandra. As he fell to the ground he saw the knife swiped across Spike's throat and the boy's body fall to the dirt.

Sandra screamed, Sonja screamed, and Ken howled in pain when the man with the rifle pounded it into his head. "You get the money, then," he said to Sandra. "Get it or that little girl over there joins her brother."

Sandra fainted and the man simply let her fall to the ground. They tore what was starting out to be the Boyingtons' first cabin on their homestead to pieces, finding a leather pouch with more than a hundred dollars in it. "That old man was right. Here's their poke, Torch. Let's get out of here."

"Bring that woman, kill that screaming kid," Torch said, walking to his horse.

"She'd be fun for a day or two and then not. Let's just ride." The dust settled on little Sonja holding dearly to her unconscious mother, blood still easing its way to the dirt from Spike's ripped open neck, and Ken Boyington slowly coming to.

———

THERE WERE SEVERAL PEOPLE STANDING AROUND OUTSIDE the courthouse when Kennedy rode up. He tied his horse off and walked toward the stone steps. Claude Atkins was the first to say anything. "There's been another killing, Tobias. The Boyington's are in your office. He's a wreck, Toby."

Kennedy found Ken Boyington, bloody and filthy. standing next to a chair at his desk. Sandra, bleeding, and holding Sonja, were in the chair.

"Boyington," he said. "Tell me all about it." There were no preliminaries, just get right into it.

"Two men, tried to grab Sandra," Ken said, shaking in anger and frustration. "I was coming in for mid-day and found them. Oh, God, Constable, it was horrible."

"Take it nice and slow, Boyington. Tell me what happened." Sandra's soft crying was constant and Kennedy saw that Sonja's eyes were open but she was just staring off into the air. *That dear little girl saw it all. She'll have that picture forever, I'm afraid. So young and vulnerable.*

"I rushed them and one of them slashed at me with his rifle, knocking me down. I got up and rushed again, and the bastard hit me hard. He grabbed Spike and put a knife to my boy's throat. My God, Constable, he put a knife to Spike's throat."

Boyington's anger flashed to the surface. "I wanted to kill that man, Constable. Kill him over and over."

"What happened?" Kennedy asked.

"The other man had Sandra, had his hands all over her and said they wanted all my money. They knew we had some money, Constable. I said we didn't have any. The man holding Spike said give it or else. He swiped that knife right across Spike's throat. Oh, God," Boyington cried out and fell to the floor.

He was slumped on his knees by the chair, crying, blubbering words that couldn't be understood. Sandra, holding Sonja so tight, reached down and ran her fingers through Ken's hair, still sobbing.

"Please, Boyington, go on." It was a horrible, terrifying moment in the constable's office and Kennedy, as big and hard muscled as he was, had a huge and tender heart. "Come now, Mr. Boyington, come now. Let's get you up in the chair." He helped Ken up, got him comfortably seated, and again asked him to continue. "I've got to know everything, sir. Please."

"The man holding Sandra kicked me in the head. When I came to, they were gone. They found my little pouch where I kept our money. My boy, Constable, they killed Spike."

Yes, Kennedy thought, *they killed Spike but have they now killed the spark that brought you to Oregon Territory? You don't look like the type to roll over and quit, Ken Boyington. Don't let this destroy what you and Sandra are building.* The big constable helped Ken to his feet and walked him around the desk to sit in his own chair.

It was Irene Creighton who took control of the situation. She had been visiting the attorney when the Boyingtons arrived. "Let's get all these other people out of here, Toby, and let's get some medical help for these folks."

Kennedy ushered those who had come right on into his office out and sent a youngster off for the doctor. "This is horrible, Toby. these people just arrived a few days ago. I saw them at Younger's Market."

"You take as good of care of them as you can, Irene, but I have to keep asking questions." Kennedy looked at Ken Boyington, trying to get back on his feet, wiping blood from his head, reaching for Sandra's hand. Sandra was weeping silently, holding desperately to little Sonja.

"You said there were two? Did you recognize either of them?"

"No," Ken said. "One was called Torch. Never heard the other's name. Torch killed Spike. They arrived on horses. Torch was heavy, not tall, but very heavy, strong from hard work. The other wasn't very big, but he was also strong. Swung that rifle hard."

Kennedy knew it wasn't the Kinsey twins. Their long red hair and freckles would have been first to be described. He was trying to come up with names of two men known to work together. "One called Torch? I wonder if that's his last name or a nick name? Can't place anyone named Torch."

Doctor Ralph Winslow knocked and came into the office. "You'll want to be at the Boyington place, Constable. I'll take over here. I alerted Shorty Salinski, so the undertaker will probably meet you out there. When are you going to do something about all this crime, Kennedy?"

Kennedy bristled at the comment but held his tongue. Doctor Winslow had a sharp tongue, never held back when he voiced an opinion, never gave a damn if his opinion hurt someone's feelings. Acidic is how some people referred to his personality. Kennedy scowled at Winslow and turned to Ken Boyington.

"We'll talk when I get back," he said. "Let the doctor get you two fixed up."

It was a lonely ride out to the Boyington homestead and it gave Tobias Kennedy plenty of time to think. As so often happens when a man is riding alone, his conversation was right out loud. "Two men who seemed to know that Ken Boyington would have some money. How would they know? Killing that boy was insane, stupid, and just guaranteed that I will catch him and break a lot of bones before we hang him. Torch. Somebody named Torch. Can't have been here long or I would have heard that name."

He rode onto the Boyington property and found Shorty Salinski bent over Spike's mutilated body. "So young, Toby. This just isn't right."

CHAPTER 19

K ennedy left Salinski to his work and began his search around the area. It didn't take long for him to find where the men had ridden off. "Heading out toward the northeast, eh boys?" He looked off that way and wondered why they would choose that direction. The rolling hills where the Boyington property was became steep and rocky mountains in short order, going east with thick stands of big trees to hinder travel.

"Wouldn't be my first choice," he muttered as he mounted and followed, noting that one of the horses was missing a shoe. "Sloppy with your horses, and ugly in your behavior, are you? You'll find the noose an unpleasant experience."

Kennedy was angry at the men for committing such a brutal crime, angry that he had allowed himself to be put in such a terrible position. "I should have been at every meeting of the commissioners, demanding that this little office be fully manned." It was more than murmuring but not quite outright talking. "Who are these men I'm following? Why are they in Oregon Territory? What brought them to Brookside?"

He chuckled softly. "That is the question, isn't it? What brought me to Brookside? Or Jacob Hoagland? But neither I nor Jacob have committed heinous crimes, have we?" He was on a run, could feel it, needed to get it all out even if he was the only one listening. "Is it possible to see to it that only the good souls come to the territory? No, of course not. Then how do we weed out the bad?"

He looked around as if expecting someone to answer. "The answer to that question is to have a fine means of law enforcement, which means in anyone's mind, more than one person doing the enforcing. These are the things I should have been screaming at the commissioners all along. Now, our fine banker has decided that I may not be qualified to keep order in Brookside. Well, Amos Dudley, I'm afraid I'm going to prove you very wrong."

The trail led Kennedy more north than east, winding through deep forest country. "Such beauty and I'm searching for the most ugly. That little boy, denied a lifetime of this beauty. Senseless, stupid, and so brutal. I'll find who did this, Spike. I promise you, lad, I'll make who did this pay and pay and pay."

While the hunt was for the ugly ones the trip was filled with the natural beauty of high, forested mountains. The once green leaves were brilliant in the sunshine, reds, yellows, and gold, while the evergreens were dressed in their deep green with a sheen to them that sometimes seemed a bright silver. The clouds, scudding across a deep blue sky carried their own colors which of course was mostly white.

"It's wrong to have to have murder on my mind in this splendor of beauty." Kennedy let his anger over the boy's death continue to build.

The trail dropped down quickly to near the valley

floor and connected with Third Creek Canyon and the road back to Brookside. The two horse's prints vanished into other prints when they got close to town. From time to time Kennedy would spot the one shoeless print, but then traffic got so that even that didn't show up.

It was nearing dusk when he walked back into his office finding Irene Creighton and her daughter Carrie sitting by the desk. "You've been gone some time, Toby. You must be starved."

He was surprised to the point that he forgot his manners and simply blurted out what was first and foremost on his mind. Getting answers. "Where is the Boyington family? I still have many questions." Being abrupt wasn't his intention and he tried to cover it up with a quick smile to the lovely lady. "Sorry, Irene. I know better than that. I've just come from the Boyingtons and I don't think I'll eat or be friendly for a week or more."

He slumped into his chair, wiped a hand across his ruddy face, and stared at the charming lady who stood in front of him. What was she doing there? Why had she come to his office? To clean? That's not even logical, he thought. *I would really like to get to know this woman. Really know her. Such vitality.*

"You're a good man, Toby and you've a giant heart beating in that broad chest. Doctor Winslow took them to his place for the night. Mr. Boyington's head injuries were more than just lacerations. Come home with us and have a decent meal, please. You can finish this up in the morning. It won't be going anywhere."

No it won't, he thought. *Having supper with you would be most wonderful, Irene, but I'm afraid I can't just shunt something like this horrible killing aside. Oh, how I'd like to. How I'd like to sit at table with you and Carrie, sit before the fire and read, maybe even hold your hand.* He sat bolt upright and had a sheepish look on his face. *Forget it, Tobias Kennedy. Forget it now.* He tried to put those warm thoughts aside, knew he had to stay on the hunt.

"There are two men somewhere nearby, Irene. They have Ken Boyington's money, maybe even his dreams, and they must be caught. I have three stops that must be made and I will have something to eat at the first one."

"You're going to Murphy's aren't you? Well, at least I know you'll be fed well. Be safe, Toby," she said, looking deep into his brilliant eyes. *I wish I'd met you before I met Mr. Creighton. You're the man my father would have approved of, and the man who should have been father to my children.* "Be safe, Toby. There are things we need to discuss, need to understand."

She turned suddenly. Had she said too much? Would he be offended? She took Carrie by the hand, and almost rushed from the office. "What did she mean by that? Need to discuss? Understand?" He looked around the office and realized that she had done more than just clean it while he was gone. Blood stains gone, floor swept, even a nice fire in the stove. "Her home is like this, too. Clean, tidy, and warm. My little cabin isn't as tidy, but I do keep it warm when I'm there."

He didn't let his mind go any further on that track and slipped into his heavy coat for the short walk to Murphy's. A stop at the stables to put his horse up, wipe it down, and feed it, and he realized just how tired he was. "Lamb stew, a brandy or two, and I'll find my bed," he chuckled, walking out into a light drizzle. "Well, there go any sign of horse prints I might have found." The drizzle was full blown cold rain by the time he reached Murphy's Inn.

———

THE ROAD BETWEEN BROOKSIDE AND JASPER WAS SHARED by several homestead pathways off on either side. Farmland occupied most of the ground on the west side of the five-mile roadway. There were three large homesteads and the rolling hills were filled with crops and orchards, while timber tracts of two logging companies took up the mountainsides to the east. Each of those concerns had operating mills and hired a number of men.

Creeks from springs and from runoff helped drive the mills and crossed the roadway in several places. One of the crossings featured a trail that followed the creek back up into a steep sided canyon filled with rock that had tumbled, broken tree trunks, and dense stands of willow. The canyon broadened into what might have been meadows if not for all the fallen rock and weather whipped trees.

It was a no-man's land on the one hand and home to several groups of deer. In a small side canyon, a fire was burning in front of a quickly built, thrown together log structure where two men were hunched down out of the rain. Two horses were standing in the rain inside a rope and brush corral.

"That's a lot of money, Torch. That old man didn't know just how right he was, talking the way he did."

"He's gonna tell that Kennedy brute all about us. Hawk. You can bet on that. We got to kill him before he does. Should have brought that gal. Could sure use some of what she had right now. Have to satisfy myself counting this gold again," he laughed. He grabbed the earthen jug and poured a tin cup full.

Torch was known to the New York police as Albert

McGhan and Hawk was Wendell Spivey, both small time thieves. Torch was known for burning down or killing off what evidence might be around and Hawk got his name from a large and protruding nose. Both had made the crossing by doing odd work for the train they were with, but were ostracized after they were found pilfering from wagons.

They made the last eight hundred miles or so by pure luck and settled in this canyon a month ago. Their backgrounds were safe, them being far out on the frontier but their work ethic, that is, zero at the thought of hard labor meant they could not be hired by any of the concerns in the territory. Neither man could hold a job for more than a couple of hours, being let go for bad attitude, unwillingness to work, or unable to get along with others on the job. Drinking had a lot to do with it as well.

Pilfering from homesteads, robbing from those traveling between Jasper and Brookside, and theft from businesses in Brookside had kept the two in food and whiskey. The attack on the Boyington family brought them their first real money.

"I need to spend some time in one of them whore houses in Jasper," Torch said. "Five dollars will make me a happy man."

"Ain't going nowhere in this rain," Hawk said. "That creek's liable to go over the banks too, before morning. Just gonna drink myself into a good long sleep. If you go to Jasper, don't be gettin' drunk and talking."

Hawk was a short man but stocky, heavy in the shoulders. His arms were short and meaty, stubby fingers that once they had a hold on a neck, couldn't be torn loose. Torch was taller, leaner, and by most accounts the uglier of the two. His face was crisscrossed by knife wounds, he had part of an ear missing, and his thinning hair was a dull brown that simply hung from his head.

———

MURPHY WAS BEHIND THE BAR WHEN KENNEDY CAME IN. "Looks like the rain's started up," he said. "Mud ain't far behind." He watched Kennedy struggle out of his heavy and wet coat. "That true what we heard? That two men attacked one of our new families and killed 'em all?"

"Ain't true, Murph." Kennedy almost growled it out. "Don't take long for the rumor mongers to get hold of something, does it? People need to mind their own business." Kennedy found a seat by the fire and tried to let his system ease off. Other men standing at the bar knew immediately that he was angry. They would give the big constable as much room as he wanted.

"People dyin', Murph and I'm angry because I got no help, because I can't be everywhere at every minute. I'm not willing to take the blame for all this, either, damn it. Banker told somebody that if I was a good constable I wouldn't need help. Damn fool is what he is." He took the full glass o of brandy from the inn-keeper and downed it, wiped a hand across his face and tried to get a smile started.

"I'm sorry, Murphy. I'm not angry at you. It's been one long damn day. Two men attacked the Boyington family and killed their little boy and I'm gonna find 'em. You can write that down in big letters. I'm gonna sit right here and have you serve me a bowl of lamb stew and set up a bottle of good brandy next to it. And I'm going to find those two fiends and they are going to die a very harsh and painful death."

"You remember when Joe Clausen was in the other day?" Kennedy nodded, pouring a cup of brandy. "He just left, said he was talking with Sam Petersen about the Boyingtons."

"Petersen? That old windbag talks too much. Tells stories that shouldn't be told. Worse than an old woman talking across a fence."

"Well, he told Clausen that he saw Ken Boyington reach into a leather pouch when he was at Younger's store, and pull out a hand full of gold coins." Murphy said.

Kennedy's brow knitted visibly at the comment and he looked around to see if others picked up on what was said. "I wonder how many other people he told that to. Those two men who killed little Spike Boyington knew the family had money. That's what they were there for. They kicked the hell out of Ken Boyington, beat up on the missus, and killed the little boy. Did Petersen tell them about the money?"

Tobias Kennedy was getting louder than he liked to do, but the anger flowed through his system like a river at spring thaw. Murphy had seen this before and quickly stepped back. Kennedy looked around to see if he'd talked too loud, and looked at Murphy. "So help me, Murph, those two men are going to hurt when I find 'em. And If I find out Petersen told them about the money I'm gonna knock him about as well. We're supposed to be welcoming these newcomers, not killing 'em off."

Two men, one named Torch, come west and settle in or near Brookside. Why? Did they fight their way across the plains, through the majestic Rocky Mountains just to rob a family and kill their son? What kind of people am I dealing with? From his thoughts of Torch and his partner, Kennedy's thoughts turned to Sam Bassett.

All those same questions can be asked about Sam Bassett and those men who rode with him. for Sam, he was running away from the law back east. Is that why Torch is here? How many like Torch are there, already here or on their way? He sat back, looked deep into the fire, took a drink of brandy, sighed some, and looked into his empty bowl of lamb stew. There were no answers. At some point, maybe, there might be.

The bowl of lamb stew was followed by a second bowl, the cups of brandy had a total well up in the numbers, and Tobias Kennedy fought his way into his heavy coat. "Maybe a long walk in the rain will ease the pain, Murphy. The scene with that little boy in the middle won't go away. The cruelty was immense, Murphy." Anger, sorrow, and irony, were writ deep on the man's brow, Murphy saw, watching him leave.

Kennedy walked to the door, pounding that walking stick of his with every step and Murphy knew not to even try to say anything to him. Kennedy was a loner, as big as a grizzly bear, he could be as warm hearted as the cutest puppy ever seen, or as raucous and mean as any Bowery criminal.

"God help those two buggers," Murphy all but whispered. He remembered when Tobias Kennedy first arrived in Brookside, more than five years now, brought to town in the back of a two-wheel cart driven by one of the men in the fur trade who had found him battered and bleeding alongside a creek high in the mountains.

The story emerged that Kennedy found three men ransacking his lean-to where he had been hunting. Two were discovered, dead, not far downstream, their heads mashed by a heavy oak walking stick. The third turned up near Jasper with broken bones and died not long after. Murphy and his wife took the battered Irishman in and nursed him back to robust health. "He'll find those two, sure as I'm standing here," he said, "and they'll die."

CHAPTER 20

Word of the attack on the Boyington family spread through the little community quickly and by the next morning it was the talk of the neighborhoods. The gossip of course increased the level of the crimes committed to the point that the entire family was dead, skinned, and hung to dry.

Small communities such as Brookside existed on the east coast as well and the residents of these communities were often separated by where and how they lived. Those inside the confines of the village and those surviving as farmers and ranchers. What few conflicts that took place usually were started by those simple differences.

However, an attack such as suffered by the Boyington family drew the two sides together. The attack was more fearsome because it came on the heels of the attack on the Cringle wagon and men talked about having firearms close to hand as they worked their fields, women asked that loaded shotguns be made available in their homes. It wasn't panic, yet, but Tobias Kennedy saw signs that made him cringe.

One of the things he feared was vigilante justice. Rabble rousers getting a bunch of people overly excited to the point of taking the law into their own hands. Always the possibility of an innocent person getting hung. Those who had ugly feelings toward the newcomers were already stirring up the dust and it might not take a whole lot to turn that whirly dust into a tornado of death and injury.

The storekeeper Younger was behind most of the angry talk of the immigrants moving into the valley. He had followers, Kennedy knew, and feared the carnage that was possible.

I need to have a little talk with Thaddeus Younger. He's spending too much time telling ugly stories about the immigrants and he needs to stop. Men like Joe Clausen are spreading his filth and believing it. There was so much to do, so many people to talk to, and so much criminal activity facing the one man. He shook his shaggy head and remembered a few nasty words in the old language.

Rain fell all night and come morning the streets were rivers of mud but life must go on, the economy of the town must be kept alive. Stores opened, but maybe just a bit late, storekeepers were seen carrying loaded weapons, horses and buggies were used to get from one point to another because walking wasn't in the cards, and normal early morning greetings were short, sometimes gruff.

Jacob Hoagland and his son Lucas brought in a wagon load of late season apples for Thaddeus Younger's grocery and the county commissioner was stopped twice by people wanting to tell him the story. Most demanding that he get Constable Kennedy help. Crime in the little frontier village was "getting out of hand," some said.

"Is it true, papa?" Lucas asked. "Are most of the

people moving here criminals? Why would they want to come here?"

"No, son, it isn't true. Most of these newcomers are just like you and me and your mama. They are coming here for the same reasons we came, good land, opportunity to make a good life. No, very few of them are criminals, Luke. Some people like to spread rumors, and some people are just afraid of what they don't know about. There's nothing to be afraid of."

"As long as they buy our produce, right, papa?" Luca was laughing as they got close to the store. Jacob smiled and poked his son in the ribs making him laugh even more.

Jacob was in a shaggy buffalo robe pulled up and over his floppy hat while young Luke, nearing eleven-years-old braved the elements wrapped in a wool blanket, his head covered in a wool cap pulled over his ears. "I'm cold," Jacob said. "How are you doing?"

"Think Mr. Younger might have some hot chocolate when we get there?"

Hoagland chuckled, thought he would like hot coffee with a touch of good Virginia rum, but either one would be just right. "Sounds good," he said, "but Mr. Younger isn't the type to think of offering something to someone."

Some in Brookside took banker Dudley's position and wondered if Constable Kennedy was really up to the job. "People are dying and he's not doing his job." The commissioner's regular meeting was to be the next day and Hoagland wished it was this day. "We'll stop at the courthouse after and you can find some hot chocolate, I think." He drew the loaded wagon up to what Younger called his loading dock. It was just an extension of the board walk across the front of the store and one needed a set of steps to climb into a wagon.

"Morning, Mr. Younger. I have those apples you ordered. Perfect weather for apple pie, eh?" Jacob called out, climbing down from the high seat.

"Perfect weather for murder," Younger said. His wizened old face hadn't carried a smile in years and surely wouldn't this morning. "That whole family dead because of these newcomers. Stores being robbed nightly, men, women, and children killed almost daily, and still more people flooding in, ruining our way of life. Don't tell me good morning."

"The commission will be meeting in the morning and I'm hoping we'll get the constable the help he needs," Hoagland said. He hadn't seen the constable, wasn't aware that the entire Boyington family wasn't slain. Hoagland was aware, though, that Younger was one of those who was not only against the influx of immigrants but was instigating trouble maybe even by way of taking the law into their own hands.

"What we need is a law banning all these immigrants, Hoagland. Stop these criminals before they get here. Don't let any more people into the territory. That's what we need."

"I guess we're both glad there wasn't such a law when we arrived," Hoagland said. He looked into the angry eyes of the storekeeper and saw that his comment wasn't even heard. "I'm sure as much of the crime taking place comes from a few who have been here for some time and from a few who are newcomers, Mr. Younger."

He motioned for Lucas to start bringing in the baskets of apples. "Newcomer or old-timer, they have to eat, eh Mr. Younger? I have dried beans as well, today if you'd like a large basket. Twenty-five pound baskets."

"I'll take two, Hoagland. You're right, people do need food, but too many of the newcomers want their food on the cuff, and too many of them are criminals. Do something about that, Hoagland. that's your job."

Jacob Hoagland had heard that story from others as well but also upbeat stories about some of the newcomers and knew that the crime problem wasn't so much the new people moving into the valley and territory as it was a lack of people in the constable's office. Criminals take advantage of situations like that. *Opportunity,* Jacob thought. *Many of these are crimes of opportunity. Given decent enforcement, the opportunity diminishes.*

Father and son finished their business with Younger and, still sopping wet, settled into their seats on the wagon. "Mr. Younger doesn't like very many people, does he," Luke said. "Are we a newcomer or are we an old-timer?"

Hoagland laughed right out, snapped the reins to move the horses out, and looked over at Lucas. "We've been here for quite a while, son, but everyone's a newcomer at some point. We came for the opportunity to build a good life. That's why most of the people come to Oregon Territory. We're free to move about as we choose. Some who move here weren't welcome where they came from either, and aren't welcome here, but it isn't up to us to determine who is and who isn't welcome. Each person has to make himself welcome."

"I'm not sure I understand," Luke said, "but I'm just glad that we're welcome."

Jacob had to laugh again and gave his son a little poke on the shoulder. "I want to have a chat with Claude Atkins, Luke. Think you can find some hot chocolate to keep you busy for half an hour?" Luke smiled and nodded. He had a few pennies and the bakery was just down the block. "Meet me back here at the wagon in half an hour."

Hoagland shook as much rain off as he could before he walked into the courthouse and straight to the county attorney's office. "Morning Claude. Got a minute?"

"For you, Jacob, even two," Atkins laughed. "Took a ride out your way yesterday. You've done a lot with that new land of yours. Saw Luke driving a mule, raking where the beans had been. How was the wheat this year?"

"Good wheat crop, Claude. Understand you've brought another steam engine in for your mill. Timber business is holding up, eh?"

"It is," Atkins said. "Hard sometimes to keep the men working, what with the rain and all. Sit down, Jacob. What's on your mind?"

"A little legal talk. You've heard Amos Dudley say right out that he will never allow any more money to be spent on the constable's office. I am under the impression that the budget is controlled by the county commission as a whole. That he, I, and Commissioner Peabody have control of how the money is spent. Not Amos Dudley alone. Am I right?"

"That's how it's spelled out, Jacob. I've heard him say that several times, even tried to correct him once. That's also why there are three commissioners. No chance for a tie unless one commissioner decides not to vote. That's happened in the past, too." He gave Hoagland a long look before continuing.

"You're meeting tomorrow, right?" Jacob nodded. "If I were you I'd make sure that Peabody is in agreement with you. Something must be done about the increase in crime and I'm sure Kennedy is up to the job if he had people working for him. He's a good man. Brookside is lucky to have someone like him."

"Dudley's been working to ease Kennedy out of the job. He's wrong about that. I'm glad I got through the harvest before all this kicked up. Thanks for your time. I'll go find Peabody. He should be in his saddle shop, I'd think."

Peabody's saddles, harness, and other leather work were known around Oregon Territory and the man had his own tannery besides. Luke was sitting in the rain eating a doughnut when Jacob got back. "Got two, papa. One for each of us."

"Gonna keep you around, boy," Jacob said, giving the horses their head. "Going to Peabody's leather shop so finish that doughnut before we get there. Don't want to get sugar all over those saddles."

Lucas laughed. "I sure would like a new saddle. Buddy would appreciate it, too." Buddy was an old black farm mule that Lucas got for Christmas a year ago. In the boy's mind that mule could outrun, outwork, out pleasure any animal in the territory.

"Ain't gonna happen, son," Jacob chuckled. He remembered last year and the economic change that's happened to the Hoagland family. *Wasn't sure we'd even have a Christmas last year. Now, another hundred and sixty acres of good land, good crops, a new baby on the way. Life can change so fast, good or bad.* "This will be business talk, so just enjoy looking at all the fine work the man does."

Clyde Peabody was standing under a wooden over-hang in front of the building shaking his head when Jacob pulled the team up. "Morning, Jacob. Wet enough for you? More rain coming, too, I'm afraid. What are you selling today?"

"What I grow you don't sell, Clyde," Jacob said. "Need to talk about what's been going on around Brookside and the county."

"Can't it wait until tomorrow's meeting?"

"That's part of it," Hoagland said. He and Luke climbed down from the wagon, shook off as much as possible, and followed Peabody into his shop. The aroma of tooled leather was warm and sweet and Luke's eyes tried to see every saddle, every bridle all at the same time. In his mind he was saying, *I want that one and that one and that one.*

"Buddy the mule would sure be proud wearing one of these, Mr. Peabody. They're beautiful."

"Thank you, son. Well, Jacob, let's see if I can find us some coffee, eh?" Peabody had come west during the fur trade years and made enough money with the American Fur Company to settle down on good land in what is now Brookside. He raised cattle for their hides, not necessarily for just the meat, built his tannery, and made magnificent leather goods. His saddles and bridles were known in California as well.

As today, Clyde Peabody often still dressed as a mountain man, buckskin trousers, high moccasins laced tightly, and a wool sweater over a soft, doe-skin shirt. He led them across the store toward a pot-belly stove showing some deep red in the iron. Peabody's full reddish beard seemed to glow as he neared the stove. "You must have the biggest pot-belly stove that's made, Clyde."

"One of the crews from Canada had it shipped in. Not sure how I ended up with it. Got to feed it regular like, but it heats this old barn." He gathered a couple of tin cups and poured the coffee. "You just missed Constable Kennedy. That's one angry Irisher, let me tell you. At least I got the real story on the attack on the Boyington family. Two men heard that Boyington had money and they meant to steal it. When Boyington wouldn't give it up, they killed his boy and beat the tar out of he and his wife. Ugly times, Jacob."

"Is that, Clyde. Is that. Thank you for passing that on. All we've heard this morning is wild rumors." Hoagland frowned. "People are strange, Clyde. Just make up stories when the truth is about as ugly as one can stand." He walked toward the stove, shaking his head.

"I just left Claude Atkins office and got the real word on how we spend county money. Amos Dudley is wrong when he says that he won't allow another dollar to be spent on the constable's office. The commission has to decide that, not Dudley."

"I know. I've told Dudley that twice this week. Let me show you something." Peabody walked around behind the little counter and pulled out a ragged newspaper. "My sister in New York sent this to me. It didn't fare the trip around the horn very well," he chuckled. Most of the mail and commerce made its way to Oregon Territory by sailing ship coming from the east coast, around the southern tip of South American, and north to the ports along the west coast.

Peabody folded the torn pages so Hoagland could read the story. The headline proclaimed "The Finest Agricultural Land Free" and the story extolled the virtues of Oregon Territory and its land acquisition policies. Hoagland didn't have to read past the second or third paragraph before Peabody started talking.

"These few people we've had coming in over this last year or so are tiny droplets in a mighty big bucket, Jacob. We're about to see massive waves of immigrants. Stories like this are being printed daily in the newspapers along the east coast according to my sister."

"It started when Lewis and Clarke got back east," Jacob said. "First the fur trade and so many talking about this little paradise of ours. Oregon Territory will have a strong economic impact of the western edge of this country, Clyde. You can make book on that."

Jacob Hoagland finished the story and handed the paper back to the storekeeper. "Makes me want to move here," he smiled. "Did you show that to Kennedy?"

"He just stood there and stared at me, unable to say anything. Think of this," Peabody continued. "Thousands of people moving across that vast area of the plains out there looking to be here. Some will be good citizens, do what's right, make for good neighbors, but others won't. Kennedy will have to deal with those who won't be good neighbors."

"We can't let that happen, Clyde. Not after the Cringle carnage, not after the brutal killing of a little boy, not after reading that snippet. I simply don't understand Dudley's thinking on the matter."

"Have you been keeping up on the broadsheet that's passed around town? The one called *FYI*?"

"I don't think I've seen it. What is it?"

Peabody dug around under the counter for a moment or two, coming up with the latest edition. "Somebody, and we don't know who, is hand writing these and making them available around town. Have another cup of coffee and read this. You're prominently mentioned many times."

Hoagland sat on a wooden crate in front of the hot pot-belly stove with a fresh tin-cup of hot coffee and took the broadsheet. Luke laughed, pointing at the steam rising from Hoagland and Clyde Peabody pointed at the boy, too, taking a quick little poke at Luke's shoulder. Sitting as close as they were to the red-hot stove and the rain on their clothes was evaporating in waves.

Hoagland saw that the penmanship was excellent, easily read, and he found himself chuckling at descriptions of what took place at the town's park. *I've seen this writing before. Where? It's distinct in its lettering. Cursive is hard to read sometimes, but this is not.*

"Somebody has a wonderful sense of humor and a delightful way of telling a story. You say you don't know who is doing this?"

"No one seems to know. I want to meet the man." Peabody looked around. "Or woman. I've also heard another rumor that is being gently passed around, that Amos Dudley is more than upset with Tobias Kennedy because Kennedy has been seeing Irene Creighton."

"Why would that bother Dudley? Even be any of his concern?"

"Because, the word is, Dudley wants to be seen with Irene Creighton," Peabody laughed. "I can't imagine that, but the word behind the wood shed is that Dudley is trying to get Kennedy out of town so he can pursue the lovely widow Creighton."

"I doubt that will surface in tomorrow's meeting," Hoagland chuckled. He motioned for Luke to head to the wagon. "Wouldn't have another copy of that *FYI* would you?"

"Oh, here, take this one, Jacob. For your box of keepsakes?"

Hoagland folded and tucked the missive inside his buffalo robe, laughing all the way to the wagon. "I'll bring you an apple in the morning, Clyde." Jacob had a smile as he drove off through the rain. *With Peabody and I voting in favor of hiring extra deputies in the constable's office, the idea is sure to pass, two in favor, one against. You're going to lose on this one, Amos Dudley.*

CHAPTER 21

I t was early morning and still raining softly as Amos Dudley made his way to the barn to feed his horse. The banker had one horse and one small carriage meticulously cared for. He had the means to have hired help but the idea of paying someone to do what he could do himself grated deeply. He knew the meeting of the county commission would be contentious at best and wanted to get his personal business taken care of early. He needed to get the horse fed, make his breakfast and still have time for a chat with Ben Thorndyke before the county commissioners' meeting, scheduled for ten o'clock.

All of this nonsense about immigrants bringing crime to the territory is just that. We need these people, we need the extra economic punch they bring, and we need stability. There has always been crime, there will always be crime. It's Kennedy's lack of ability and I'll pound on that. Get that man out of town, get him far away from Irene Creighton.

Thoughts of the lovely widow flooded the old man's attention. His thoughts were more ugly than beautiful. He wanted her in his bed and that was all there was to it.

No thoughts of a lovely marriage, of long conversations in front of a warm fire, no thoughts of raising young Carrie or helping get Irene's son straightened out. Only as much carnal knowledge as possible. And it was Constable Kennedy who stood in the way of all that.

He was planning on spending a great deal of time pontificating at the meeting and was enjoying putting together just what would be said. "I'll see to it that Tobias Kennedy looks like a fool, completely unable to control the crime in the valley. Mrs. Creighton will be glad to see me, spend wonderful days and nights with me, not that lug."

It wasn't immigrants, crime, or lack of ability that was behind his desire to eliminate Tobias Kennedy. It was his desire to be with Irene Creighton, the lovely widow whose smile was enchanting. Her seeming desire to be seen with Kennedy rather than Dudley was at the heart of the matter. He was also in the midst of planning how to court the lady once Kennedy was out of the picture as he approached the large doors to his barn.

Frightening her with foreclosure will make her want to be with me. I'll save her home and property and she'll be thankful. He had papers that looked official, made out in Irene's late husband's name, and if she'll spend a night or two with the lecherous old fool, he'll see to it that those papers disappear.

His mind was far from the falling rain or the deep mud, he never saw the foot prints leading to the doors. His thoughts were on the lovely widow Creighton and what it would be like to have her in his bed. He was surprised to find the doors to the barn partially open and swore softly, pushing them fully open. *I must be more careful. Why, anyone could walk right in and take anything they wanted. With all these newcomers milling about, who knows what might happen?*

The thought that someone could enter the barn didn't include the thought that someone might actually be in the barn, and Amos Dudley stepped into the dimly lit building, saw movement, and fell to the ground, unconscious and bleeding. The intruder slammed the cudgel twice more for effect, then went through Dudley's pockets. He fondled the pocket watch with gold chain and slipped it into his pockets, accepted the gift of two cigars and four gold double eagles, and stood up with a smile on his scarred face.

"Thank you, you rich dog. Been needing some good money to spend." He slipped out of the barn, hurried to the back door of Dudley's house, looking about to make sure he wasn't seen, and tore the place apart, coming up with more gold coins, a fine shotgun, and a humidor filled with cigars. *Again, you fat old pig, thank you.*

In less than ten minutes the intruder was back behind the barn, stepped up into the saddle of his waiting horse, and trotted off cross country to the north. His only thoughts were on what he'd put in his pockets, never saw the tendrils of fog and low clouds moving gently through tall timber in the early morning light, nor the sparkling light from rain drops hanging precariously from branches and bushes. Only other people's gold interested the man.

Would Dudley have asked how long the man had been in Oregon? Would the grocer, Thaddeus Younger have asked? In fact, did it really matter? Kennedy, on the other hand will know how long the criminal had been around if he can track him down and put him in irons.

About ten minutes later, as Hammerhead Povolny was making his way through the rain and mud, movement off to his right caught his attention. He walked that way and spotted Amos Dudley crawling through the mud on his hands and knees toward his kitchen door.

Dudley's head was covered in blood, his face badly bruised from falling into the corral fence while trying to get to his feet, and his clothing, ripped and covered in mud. "Mr. Dudley, my God, man, what happened? Here, let me help." Povolny gathered the robust man up, half dragged him into the kitchen, and got him in a chair. "Sit right there, Dudley. I'm running for the doctor."

Dudley didn't respond to any of it. He wasn't fully unconscious nor was he understanding of what happened. His eyes wouldn't focus, he had a hard time hearing what Hammerhead was saying, and just sat slumped in the kitchen chair, not even aware of the blood dripping from open wounds on his head.

Doctor Ralph Winslow's home and office was less than two blocks away and Povolny made the run in record time, found the doctor having breakfast and escorted him back to Dudley's. "Ain't seen a man beat that badly in a long time, Doctor. His head is really mashed up bad."

"You did good, coming to get me, Hammerhead. I might need some help here. Let's get him moved into his bedroom and then if you'd kindly stoke the fires and get me a pan of warm water, maybe you could try and fetch the constable."

"Right away, Doctor," Hammerhead said. "Kennedy should be at the café about this time of the morning."

Dudley was trying to say something as they laid him out on the bed, not worrying about the mud that went with him. "Don't try to talk, Amos. This is Doc Winslow and I'll get you fixed up." Dudley reached out and grasped Winslow's arm in a vice grip then slowly let his hand fall to the bed. It took both men to get the wet and muddy clothing off the banker after Hammerhead got the fires stoked.

Winslow took the pan of water and towels and started cleaning up the bloody head, wagging his head slowly back and forth. *Brutal. Man's going to have a hard time pulling through this. This level of violence comes from someone who hates anything and everything.* It was the level of brute force that worried the doctor. Fractured skulls, broken jaw bones, teeth missing all pointed to an early death.

Winslow knew there were broken ribs, probably broken limbs as well. Dudley was whipped with a heavy club and would not be out of bed for days if not weeks.

Povolny made the quick walk through driving rain to the café and found Kennedy having breakfast with Claude Atkins and the Boyington family. Hammerhead spilled out the story in rapid-fire half sentences. He saw Sandra Boyington become even more frightened than she already was.

"We'll talk later, Boyington," Kennedy said. "Eat your breakfast and go home. I'll come see you." He motioned for Hammerhead to lead and hurried out the door for the run to Dudley's.

"He gonna live?"

Povolny hunched his shoulders. "Don't know, Toby. Never seen a man's head that badly beat up. Must have been hit three or four times with something big and heavy. He was crawling in the mud when I found him."

"The mean ones like him usually do live," Kennedy snickered as they made their way into Dudley's home. Doctor Winslow was washing his hands at the kitchen pump.

"He's a mess, Constable but you aren't gonna learn

anything. His head is smashed bad and he's only about half way with us right now. I'm not sure he'll come out of this. Multiple fractures of the skull are deadly."

"Looks like his house was searched, too," Kennedy said. He walked around the living room seeing where books were flung from shelves, drawers at desks opened and emptied out, even cushions from chairs and couches thrown about. *Did the fiend know what he was looking for or just looking? Hammerhead said he was crawling from the barn? Was the encounter at the barn?*

"You said he was crawling from the barn, Hammerhead? I better look out there, too." He took the kitchen doorway out and saw where Dudley had been dragged into the house. He also saw where someone had walked or run around the side of the barn.

"Mud can be your friend once in a while," Kennedy muttered, following the splash prints to the back side of the barn. *So, our thief had a horse tethered back here, did he.* He followed the trail leading off north and knew it would connect with the north road in just a few hundred feet meaning he would not be able to track the man. *And it can be your enemy.*

He walked back around and into the barn and found the cedar post that the intruder used to whack Dudley. It was covered in blood, there was blood on the dirt floor where the banker had fallen, and blood stains leading out into the mud where Dudley had crawled. Kennedy found boot prints from Dudley and the assailant but nothing that stood out as something he could use for identification.

Already wet, and on a whim, Kennedy went back around to the back side of the barn to look at where the horse was tied. "That's called the luck of the Irish," he said to Murphy an hour later standing at the bar warming up with a coffee laced with some fine brandy. "That horse was missing a shoe, Murphy. How many horses in Brookside at this moment are missing a shoe? Not many, I'd think."

He downed the hot coffee and motioned for more. "In two days I've found crime scenes in which a horse missing a shoe was involved. If the streets weren't covered in mud I'd be able to follow that horse, Murphy. Ach!"

———

"We can't wait any longer," Clyde Peabody said. He and Jacob Hoagland sat at the county commission table waiting for Amos Dudley and Constable Tobias Kennedy to arrive. "It's ten fifteen now."

Claude Atkins. as county attorney sat at his own little table, and the county clerk, papers and pen at the ready, sat off to the side. He glanced at the large clock on the wall and made a note on his sheet of paper.

"Let's give them another ten minutes, Clyde, and then we'll make a decision on what to do. It's most unusual for Amos to be late for anything, and Kennedy was determined to make a stand when you talked to him yesterday."

It was five minutes later that Constable Kennedy arrived with the bad news. "I'm afraid Mr. Dudley will not be joining us," he said. "His home was broken into and he's been seriously injured. I won't be staying either as I might yet be able to follow whoever did this."

Kennedy tracked mud into and out of the meeting room and nobody noticed. The news that Commissioner Dudley had been attacked was dominant in every mind.

Jacob Hoagland looked over at Atkins. "Should we post-pone this meeting, Claude? What's the legal word?"

"You have a quorum, Jacob, so you could go on with the meeting. If Dudley is as seriously injured as Kennedy said, it might be some time before he would be back at the table. Maybe weeks or even more. County business must continue."

Hoagland looked at Peabody, then into the faces of the few citizens who braved the wet and mud to attend the meeting. "You have the gavel, Mr. Peabody," he said. "I guess it's your decision."

"The agenda, other than normal county business, has just the one item, hiring two deputies to work with the constable. With what's happened in just the last several days, I believe it is of utmost importance to hold this meeting." He banged the gavel lightly on the table. "This meeting shall come to order, please."

In less than an hour the commissioners, officials, and visitors filed out of the meeting, smiles on all faces, and walked out into wind and rain. "Storm's picking up, Peabody. I've got to get back to my farm," Jacob said. "Luke is alone out there and we've had enough rain that the irrigation ditches and impoundments will need lots of attention."

"Well," Clyde said, "We know we're going to be safer now. Giving Kennedy two full time deputies won't put any kind of strain on our budget and I'm sure the general public will approve. I'll swing by Murphy's and get the word out. There are no secrets when Murphy knows something."

CHAPTER 22

K ennedy was on the north/south road, riding slowly through the increasing wind and rain, his eyes searching back and forth, from one side of the road to the other. *Somewhere soon I'm going to find where somebody rode off from the main road, and he'll be riding a horse that's missing a shoe.*

The great fir tree's branches, draped in moss, hung low, the rain slowly dripping to the ground, but exploding in waves of wet when attacked by the wind, all of which made the ride difficult. "It makes things grow, Laddie-buck. Never forget that," he chuckled. "Every farmer and rancher in the valley is cheering, and everyone in town is cussing."

Two thoughts occupied more of his time than the current weather. The banker was out to run him out of town and he had a murder to solve. A third thought kept intruding, that of Thaddeus Younger and the people who are following his constant drumming on how evil the immigrants are. He was aware that all three thoughts might be connected.

Were the men who killed little Spike newcomers? If so, that would add fuel to Younger's complaints and, he quickly remembered, *I've not heard of someone named Torch, Amos Dudley supports immigration, it's good for business, he says, but says the increase in crime is my fault. That I'm not capable of keeping the county safe.*

His thoughts on the storekeeper kept interfering in the other two problems. *Younger is building a coalition of people with similar ideas and I have to put a stop to that before it explodes into violence. Small minds can wreak havoc in a community like ours and people will be hurt if I let it continue. Damn but I need help.*

He brushed a hand across his face wiping rain away. The cold rain was driven by a strong wind and even this early in the season, it could turn to snow, which would end the search. The rain was making it hard enough. It was about five miles from Brookside to Jasper and when the little village came into sight Kennedy knew he would not find his man today.

He hadn't seen another person on the ride out, never saw prints leading off west or east, but knew the assailant had ridden north from Dudley's place. "He had to come this way. The mud is not my friend today." The ride back was a little faster but Kennedy still kept his eyes open for indications of someone moving off the main road. *Even the people whose homes are off this road aren't moving today.*

On the best day Kennedy would have had a hard time spotting where Hawk Spivey rode off the main road. A stand of fir surrounded by brush and ferns was where Spivey turned off onto scattered rock and pebbles that led into a swale. Spivey would have ridden up and out on the other side and into the forest. The trail back into the canyon followed a stream that was storm driven and running over its banks. The stream emptied into the larger river that drained the Brookside valley. The trail was just wide enough for one horse and was difficult to see.

———

Spivey was on that trail not hours before Kennedy passed. His mind, unlike Kennedy's, whose thoughts were on killing Spivey, was busy calculating how many visits he might make to the Bird Cage, how many pleasures he would enjoy. He wanted to dig into his pockets and feel all that gold, all those coins, one more time.

"Ain't gonna split this with Torch, neither," he muttered. "Asked him to come along but he was too busy staying warm and dry to gather in the gold." Spivey was wearing an oil skin poncho and his wool pants and jacket kept him warm despite the bitter wind that was blowing. "He better have a fire going when I get there. Lazy, that's what he is. One thing I hate the most is a lazy man. Won't get off his butt even to get the gold."

———

Irene Creighton was in the Thorndyke office working on his books when Ben and Kennedy walked in. "My goodness, Tobias, you're soaked. Here, give me your coat and stand near the fire."

Kennedy struggled out of the wet bear-skin coat and doffed his wool cap. "It's going to snow tonight, I'll put a coin to it," he said. The fire made the Franklyn stove red hot and he stood as near as he dared. Mrs. Creighton's little office was warm but with three people in it, the air was stuffy.

Thorndyke left the door open and slipped into a

chair in front of Irene's desk. "Mr. Kennedy has brought us some terrible news, I'm afraid. Amos Dudley was attacked this morning and is in serious condition. He's been on the road trying to locate the criminal."

"Oh, dear," Irene said. She sat behind her desk and brought a hand to her face. She looked to the constable then to Ben, and didn't say anything else. Irene didn't like Amos Dudley, was afraid of him, but he was a member of the community. It was Kennedy and Thorndyke who told her that Dudley was going to try and take her home from her, but he was a neighbor of sorts, did live in her same town, and it would be wrong to say something against the man after he was attacked. She said nothing but her thoughts were alive with interesting things she wanted to say. Instead, she just sat looking back and forth at the two men. Her eyes, however, said considerable.

I'm not sure right now who I dislike the most, Ed Creighton or Amos Dudley. What a horrible man and to think he's a banker, someone we're supposed to trust with our money, and finances. He would not foreclose if I spent time with him? Never, on his best day, would I spend time in his bed or anywhere else. The anger in her eyes, the turn of her mouth was obvious to both men.

"The constable also brought us some good news," Thorndyke said. "He's going to be able to hire two deputies for the department. Maybe he can get a handle on these crimes."

"That's wonderful, Mr. Kennedy," Irene said.

Thorndyke picked up on that with the slightest grin. *When he came in all wet and cold it was 'Tobias,' but now all at once, it's 'Mr. Kennedy.'* He listened as Irene continued.

"Do you have any idea who it was that attacked Mr.

Dudley? So sad, and just after the attack on the Boyington family. Are those attacks related?"

"Interesting you should ask," Kennedy said. "I believe they are. Some things I found at the two sites indicate the attacks may have been made by the same men." He didn't go into detail, certainly would never have mentioned the horse missing a shoe or the fact the attacker rode north. That information was for him, and as he said before, not for Murphy or anyone else to spread it about. "I'd best be getting back to the office. Need to find two rugged young men to work with me. I'll be offering thirty-five cents a day, so it won't be hard to find them."

Getting back into his wet gear was a struggle and the big man strode from the office, that walking stick pounding just a bit with each step. "He's a happy man right now," Ben Thorndyke said. "I talked with Doctor Winslow before running into Kennedy and he said Dudley isn't expected to live through the beating he took."

"That's terrible, Ben. I don't like the man, don't trust him, really, but nobody deserves to die that way. Was theft involved or just someone angry at the banker?"

"Kennedy said there was considerable missing from the home and Dudley's pockets were ripped open as well." He stood up, paced around a bit. "Your eyes are telling me more than you are, Mrs. Creighton. Have you heard anything more about Dudley trying to foreclose on your late husband's loan?"

She sank back in her chair, grimaced some before speaking. "I'm afraid I have," Irene said. Tears welled quickly and she grabbed for her hanky. "I received notification of foreclosure yesterday. Hand delivered by Mr. Dudley. Mr. Atkins has the papers now."

"Dudley served the papers himself? Most unusual." Thorndyke looked into Irene's eyes, saw grief and fear. *I've known Amos Dudley for five years or more. In the bank he's the king but out on the street, he's afraid of his own shadow. I can't picture him delivering a foreclosure notice.* "Did the fool say anything? So cruel."

"Yes, he did," she said and he saw her mouth tighten up, saw anger flare up in her eyes, and waited for her to continue. "He said that I should join him for supper one evening soon and we could discuss the problem with the loan. I've never been so humiliated in my life, nor so angry. Ben, do you understand what he was suggesting? I'm not a tart! I've never been so humiliated in my life."

"I'm afraid I do, Irene. I'm afraid I do." Ben Thorndyke had a wicked sense of humor that surfaced at inopportune times, and this was one of them. *Our Mr. Dudley is one lucky man. Irene Creighton killed her husband with one swing of a cast iron frying pan. Dudley had best mind his manners if he's talking to her in her own kitchen or we'll be burying him, too.* He held in his chuckles and looked at Irene before speaking.

"Did you say anything about that to Claude Atkins? What you just told me is highly irregular, probably illegal. Did anyone else hear what was said?"

"No. I was alone at the doorway. Carrie was upstairs. I was so taken aback, I just stepped back and shut the door on the man. I did tell Mr. Atkins what Mr. Dudley said. What happens now?" She dabbed at her eyes some more, shook her head in despair. "Humiliated," she whispered.

"I'm not sure what will happen," Ben Thorndyke said. "I'll have a talk with Claude. Did you look at the papers Dudley handed you?"

"No. Mr. Dudley handed me the folded and sealed

package and said, 'You're served, Mrs. Creighton.' That's all he said until he started talking about making things right by me spending certain times with him. It was so ugly," Irene said. She tried but couldn't hold the tears back and she had to grab for her hanky again.

"With Dudley seriously injured, there's doubt that anything will happen for a while. That gives us time to find out just how far he really planned to go. It may all have been a ruse to get you to submit to him. He is that kind of ugly man. You can finish this work tomorrow. Go on home and be with Carrie. I'll see what Claude Atkins has to say."

Irene thanked him as he helped her into her storm coat and she left for home. Ben Thorndyke paced around the little office for a few minutes letting his anger at the situation calm a bit. *She'll be fine. One tough little lady. I don't blame Dudley for wanting to enjoy her company but he isn't man enough to take her on. Kennedy is her man, but I doubt she or he knows it.*

He had to chuckle getting his heavy winter coat buckled up. *Maybe a visit with the clerk at the bank before I see Claude Atkins. If foreclosure papers were drawn up Charles Nixon would have been the man to do so.*

CHAPTER 23

Ben Thorndyke was a big man, near the six foot mark in height and near the two hundred figure in weight. Put that man in a big and heavy buffalo robe coat that draped well below his knees and a wide, floppy brimmed hat, and people moved to the other side of the street when he walked toward them. Hammerhead Povolny, the hunter, has said often it's amazing that no one has shot Thorndyke thinking it was a black bear wandering the streets.

"My god, Ben, it's you. I thought we had a bear loose in town," Claude Atkins laughed when Thorndyke walked into the courthouse. "I see the rain is still coming down."

"By the buckets full," Ben said. "I just left the bank. Have you had a chance to look at those papers Mrs. Creighton dropped off? Charles Nixon doesn't remember writing up any kind of foreclosure notice on any property in Brookside."

"It's a farce, Ben. Designed to frighten the widow into spending time with the lecherous old bastard. He could

159

be held accountable for what he's attempting to do here. She could hire an attorney and scare the hell out of that old man." Claude Atkins was angry as he led Thorndyke into his office. "He's been known to harass and bully some who have borrowed from that bank, but this kind of personal intimidation is not just out of line, it is illegal." Atkins started to sit down and changed his mind.

"Kennedy has a stove in his office, but this one doesn't. To hell with it, Ben. Let's go down to Murphy's and have a brandy. The weather alone calls for that kind of action. Besides, as angry as I am I might just break something if I sit still here. The walk will do me good."

"You're feeling better, I take it," Thorndyke said. Atkins suffering from lung problems was well known and Ben almost laughed at the thought of the man trying to break something.

They were a wet but happy couple plowing through the door to Murphy's Inn, letting the wind help with the heavy door. "There isn't a farmer in the valley that isn't saying thank you for this rain, Ben, and there isn't a logger sitting by the fire cussing it out." Atkins knew that about fifty loggers in his employ were doing exactly that.

"Creeks will be going over their banks soon, irrigation ditches will overflow, and we'll be hearing some outlandish exclamations coming from those fighting the mud soon, I'm afraid," Thorndyke said.

The two men shucked their heavy coats and hung them on hooks near the fireplace. They started steaming right away. The two men stood at the bar, waiting for Murphy to come out from the kitchen. The open beam construction coupled with a large stone fireplace gave a homey feeling to the thirst parlor, and the men moved to stand in front of a blazing fire. "Winter will be with us soon, Ben. Several of my loggers have already quit, going into the hills to hunt. Remnants of the mountain man days when they lived off the land. Some men just can't put that aside." He coughed hard and Ben Thorndyke moved him to a chair on the side of the great fireplace.

"I'm fine Ben. It'll kill me, I know, but I will not move from these magnificent forests. I won't. Maybe I'm a bit like some of my loggers, eh?" The man's lungs were giving out, consumption taking a heavy toll, but Claude Atkins loved the Oregon forests and vowed to never leave.

"Those old mountain men I've hired have moved into these modern times, though. Instead of caching their smoked meats for winter, barrels will be filled with salted and corned venison soon." Atkins spotted Murphy coming out from the kitchen.

"Thought you'd taken leave of the place," Atkins said. "We poor and cold, tax-paying citizens of Brookside would most enjoy a draught of rum or brandy. That is, if you have time?"

"Ah, laddies, time I have and rum, too. What's the word on Amos Dudley? That bank is a big part of the economic life of this community. Will it survive if the old lecher dies?"

"He has it structured such that it will survive," Ben Thorndyke said. "The doctor doesn't think his chances are very good. Took several heavy blows to the head. He isn't a fine physical specimen to start with."

"Speaking of fine, Mrs. O'Reilly has a fine kettle of lamb stew boiling, gentlemen. She made fresh crusted bread for dipping, too."

Both men said a large bowl and half a loaf would do them well. "We've got a few things to discuss, Murph,"

Thorndyke said. "We'll take a table by the fire, a bottle of rum, and keep the stew bowls full."

———————

FOR THE NEXT HOUR CLAUDE ATKINS AND BEN Thorndyke talked about the foreclosure notice that Dudley served on Irene Creighton and what possibly could be done for her. Atkins brought the paperwork with him and Ben read it twice, shaking his head, glaring his anger at the sheets, and using language unfit for the ladies.

"I really must question whether Ed Creighton actually took out a loan on the property. This is wrong in so many ways. You noticed, I'm sure," Atkins said, "that there are no signatures, no witnesses claiming knowledge of such a deal. There isn't a court in the territory that would accept this as evidence. Dudley was only after Irene Creighton."

"The man has no respect for anyone. He had to know that Mrs. Creighton would go to someone for help. Had to know just how phony this document looks. The way he treats women, it's understandable why he's never married." Thorndyke said.

"He knows that Mrs. Creighton has few options, Ben. Women, as far as the law is concerned, are second class citizens. Were he to attempt something like this with a man, he could lose his bank in a lawsuit, if not his jaw," Atkins chuckled. "He knows that won't happen with Mrs. Creighton. As far as her home and that property, it is safe. I told her so."

"I don't think the bank is safe, though," Ben said. "I've a large interest in that bank, enough, I believe, that I could take it over." Thorndyke sat back, took a sip of

162

rum, and looked into the fire. "When Amos came to town and tried to get that bank started, he needed help, not so much monetary as legal from a long time citizen. I own forty percent of that bank."

"I knew you were involved but not that deep," Atkins said. "Dudley's illegal activity here might make the Territory want to close the bank entirely. You might lose your investment."

"I'll fight that to the end," Thorndyke said and Atkins saw the fire in his eyes. "I think we can assume that everything is settled as far as the widow Creighton is concerned. We need to help Constable Kennedy get these outlaws taken care of. The slaughter of the Cringle family, the attack on the Boyington family, and now the attack on Amos Dudley has left its mark on the people of the village. They're scared, Claude," Thorndyke said.

"Don't blame 'em, either. I'm not sure I'd go for a walk after dark," Atkins chuckled. "Thaddeus Younger wants a law passed to make immigration to Oregon Territory illegal. That won't happen but he is getting people riled up. What can we do?"

"We've got two big fights, I'm afraid. Let Dudley swim or drown, but save the bank, and help Kennedy get a handle on the criminal element. The criminal element will keep people from wanting to settle in this fertile little valley." He stopped long enough to take another quaff of rum. Ben Thorndyke was a big, robust man who was also a deep thinker, and Atkins was sure he could almost hear the gears turning in the business man's head.

"Kennedy now has the means to hire a couple of deputies, I have men who aren't that good at being metal workers but are strong and smart, and you have loggers who are looking to get out of the weather. I think we can find him a deputy or two, eh?"

"Let's work on that, Ben." Claude Atkins sat back in his chair and chuckled. You know, it's interesting when you think about it. There isn't much difference between what that thief did at Dudley's house and what Dudley is trying to do with Irene Creighton. Stealing something valuable from someone. No wonder he didn't want to hire extra deputies." The laughter from the two men could be heard out on the street were someone to be out there.

————

HAWK SPIVEY LED HIS HORSE SLOWLY THROUGH THE WET willows, deep mud, and wind driven rain toward the camp he shared with Torch McGhan. He saw the empty rope corral, saw there was no smoke coming from the small cabin they shared and cussed right out loud. "I'll kill that snake. Kill him dead."

Spivey didn't have to spend much time inside the cabin to know that Torch had run off with all the money and goods they had stolen from Ken Boyington. "He even took my shotgun. That's why he wasn't going with me to rob the banker. He had this all planned."

Spivey stuck his hand in his pocket and rustled the coins around. "I've still got more than he does," he chuckled. Spivey stirred the fire back to life and added a couple of logs to it. *Where would that bastard go? Did he just follow me out or did he wait some? Jasper? Maybe but there is more opportunity right here in Brookside.*

Spivey figured that trying to make a living robbing those who had money and goods would not be healthy in Jasper. Those loggers and mill workers were a tough bunch, he knew, but the families in Brookside would be easier to deal with. *He's got a set-up somewhere much closer to Brookside than this place. He's been planning this for some time.*

Spivey sat down at the rough table after the coffee boiled, and tried to think where he would go if he were Torch and came to the conclusion that he would not go to either Jasper or Brookside, but go north to Oregon City, or maybe just clear out of this country completely. "I'm going to stay right here in this little cabin and make a fine living off those farmers. They'll feed me from their fields and I'll rob them blind."

He let his mind work on that idea. *Rob the farmers, rob the businesses, and most of all, rob the people moving into the valley. Sam Bassett was wrong in having so many people in his gang. It only takes one. A big gun and knife, an angry face, and intimidation, and I'll be rolling in money.* His almost mad laughter rang through the cabin.

As with so many who ride the outlaw trail, Hawk Spivey thought he was among the smartest of men. Was sure that he could outsmart just about anyone, and was sure he would never be caught. *I've got a good haul from that old banker but it's Thorndyke I want. He's got more money in his little vault than that bank.*

His plan included spending enough time around the Thorndyke complex to know when it would be safe to make a move on the vault, and maybe even how to open it. "Surely it isn't locked up all day. Maybe all night, but not all day." He packed some smoked meat and a few camp essentials and left for Brookside in a pouring wind driven rain.

Need to find a cabin first then work on Thorndyke. This place is too far out. Good for an emergency but not convenient.

Torch McGhan had to chuckle watching Spivey ride off to rob the banker. "He ain't got brain one, only thinking of a few gold pieces. We could have done some serious talking and planning, and robbed the bank, not the banker. I'm sticking with my plan."

Torch's plan was almost identical to the one used by Sam Bassett. He would find wagons coming into the valley, catch them off-guard, and take what money and valuables they had. Bassett put together a gang but Torch planned to go it alone. In his mind, these immigrants were coming into the valley knowing they could not possibly have produce or meat to sell for at least a year, maybe more.

"Just like that couple with the screaming kid, they'll have a pouch or box full of money. That's all I want," he murmured. He had his kit put together and was on the trail to Jasper within the hour, all the money from the Hoagland family safely tucked away in his saddlebags. "Just set up a neat camp near the main road out of Jasper and follow a wagon out."

His was a snicker, thinking, *Maybe I'll just ride right up and offer to guide them to their new homestead.* The more he thought about it the more plausible the idea became. *Don't take nothing but their money. Maybe a fine horse or two, but nothing that has to be sold. Old Sam Bassett weren't nowhere as smart as I am, and he's dead to prove it,* he laughed, riding down the canyon and out to the main road.

On the outskirts of the little community, along a meandering creek, stood a tumble-down shack left over from the fur trade. It was back in heavy timber and brush, and Torch rode up, seeing a drift of smoke from the tin chimney. "Somebody got here before me," he murmured. He stepped down from his horse, about ten feet or so from the front of the building. He was tying his horse off when the door opened and a tall, heavy man with a flintlock shotgun stepped onto the porch.

"Private property, mister, and you ain't welcome." The man stood very close to six feet and had shoulders that told the world he could swing an ax all day and not even get tired. Torch got half a smile on his face.

"I thought this was the Sorensen place," he lied. "Who are you?" The smile stayed in place as he took a step forward.

"Ain't no Sorensen here. Like I said," the big man started, but the words quit coming as the knife drove deep into his belly, over and over. His legs failed, he let go of the shotgun and it clattered to the porch, and Torch stood back to let the man fall, dead.

"Hope he has food in there." Torch untied his horse, tied a rope to the man's feet and, using the horse, dragged him several hundred yards up stream. "Have a nice sleep, mister," he said, rolling him into the rapidly flowing creek, just off the seldom used trail.

The cabin was fitted out with a rope bed and straw mattress, wood-fired cook stove, table, and two chairs. The logger had two lamps, one hanging over the table and one on a wooden box next to the bed. There was considerable food stacked against one wall, and outside, he found two barrels, one with salted and brined meat, and one empty. There was plenty of powder, shot, and flint for a scattergun, and a set of knives that had been made from excellent steel.

"My kind of day," Torch said, piling the man's clothing off into the creek. He watched as they floated off in the roiling water. "I can see the road but it's hard to see the cabin from the trail."

The cabin was in the trees, slightly above the creek

and Torch figured he was close enough to the main road to Brookside that he would know of the passing of immigrant wagons. He never once thought the dead man would have friends come asking about him. Really, he didn't care.

CHAPTER 24

Tobias Kennedy was making his way through the muddy street from Amos Dudley's barn to Murphy's when he was hailed by Sonny Kniessel, riding into town, "Sonny. Ain't any kind of weather for a man to be out and about. You look anxious. Something wrong?"

"Maybe," Kniessel said. "Let's have some coffee and brandy and I'll tell you all about it. Rain isn't going to let up, I'm afraid. Must be gettin' old, Toby. I can actually feel the cold."

It was the third day and the rain was not letting up, seemed to be getting heavier and the wind had an icy edge to it. Older trees were downed, some falling on roofs, creeks and rivers were reaching their brim, and tempers were short.

"Be a happy man if I don't never see mud again. Ain't no good use for it, neither," the man said. He tried to laugh it off but that didn't work either.

"Well, Sonny, we can wash away the evil thoughts of mud with a crock full of brandy, now, can't we." Kennedy walked and Kniessel rode the two blocks to Murphy's and found several people with the same idea as theirs. "This weather is Murphy's best friend," Kennedy said. "Turn me into a sot if I'm not careful," he joshed. "What's the problem, Sonny?"

They settled in at the bar and got mugs of hot coffee laced liberally with brandy before Kniessel started talking. "Know that old log and sod cabin up the creek from my place?" Kennedy nodded. "Ain't nobody been in that old place for some time, but I'm sure I saw smoke coming from the tin chimney this morning. There was a horse in the old corral, too, when I checked."

"I don't know if that's on someone's land or just that someone built the place a few years ago, Sonny. Some of the old mountain men used it from time to time, I'm told. Don't remember but I don't recall that area being homesteaded," Kennedy sat back and looked into the fire before continuing. "Might be a hunter setting up for winter or a drifter finding it empty. I really don't think that land has ever been filed on."

"Maybe I'm just being a bit jumpy, Toby. These killings got me tense. Guess you think I'm silly riding all the way in to tell you about that." Sonny Kniessel wasn't the kind of man Kennedy would ever consider silly. He was hard headed from time to time, ready to help anyone who was trying to help themselves, and had never been known to back away from a fight that needed to be fought. His reaction to the recent savage killings was filled with the kind of thoughts Kennedy needed to know.

If Sonny Kniessel felt this way, as tough and hard as he was, the rest of the community must be going to bed at night in fear and anguish. "No, I don't," Kennedy said. He said it with a firmness that caught the attention of others standing near. "It's because of the killings that I don't." Kennedy noticed that he had others' attention and continued. "I'll ride out that way and take a look." He was going to say more but was interrupted by Joe Clausen tapping him on the shoulder.

"What do you want, Joe?"

"Wife's worried about all these killings, constable. Want to know what you plan to do about them. Seems like you been spendin' some time here at Murphy's."

Kennedy spun around, almost spilling his coffee, and grabbed Clausen by the front of his jacket. shoved him across the floor, banging him up against the rocks on the front of the fireplace. Kennedy got right up in Clausen's face. "You listen to me, you sorry example of a man. You haven't had a job in a year, your wife works her fingers to the bone, and you challenge me? I'll have a drink when I want one, and if you or anyone like you doesn't like it, too damn bad."

He thumped his walking stick a couple of times on the rough wood floor for emphasis and saw the fear in Clausen's face. If he had looked around he would have seen a number of faces carrying half smiles. That Clausen had had this coming for a long time was apparently on many minds.

The man was rude, ungracious, and demanding of others that of which he was incapable of. Some were anticipating that walking stick to come into play but Kennedy held himself in check. "You ever talk to me like that again and you'll be going home bloody and bruised. Your best bet at this moment is to go home before I change my mind."

Clausen almost ran for the door amidst laughter from the crowd and Kennedy squared his shoulders just a bit before he walked back to his chair. "A foolish man, Murphy. Foolish." He took a quick drink. "Now, Sonny

Kniessel, let's talk about what you saw. Just one horse?"
Sonny nodded. "Did you see anyone at all?"

"No, just the horse in the corral and some smoke
from the chimney," Kniessel said. "Weren't there yesterday, Toby. I rode up that way chasing some deer and
would have seen it."

"All right then. I'll take it from here. And thank you
for letting me know. I'm also looking to hire two good
men to work with me full time. You and Hammerhead
have worked with me several times. Want a full time
job?"

"No, no, Toby. I'll join a chase with you, but I don't
want a job. Between my place and my hunting, I've got
enough to do. I wish you well, though."

Kennedy chuckled knowing the man would refuse,
thumped that old cudgel and struggled into his heavy
coat. "Back into the maelstrom, Sonny, and again,
thank you." It took just a few minutes' walk to the
stables to saddle up and ride out into the rain and
wind.

*Sam Bassett and his gang of thieves and murderers have
been put away, but what am I going to do about the Kinsey
twins? Seamus O'Leary needs a good thumping, too, and that
man whose horse is missing a shoe. Those are the ones I know
about. Are there others?* His mind was churning out
thoughts as he rode through the driving rain, his horse
slopping through mud that sometimes was at least a foot
deep.

He let his mind drift to what Joe Clausen said and the
anger rippled up and down his spine. Who was that fool
to question whether Tobias Kennedy could have a drink?
When was the last time the man had offered his help
when Kennedy was facing more than one armed man?
I'll not be talked to that way. I won't. I bring murderers into

town, dead or roped up tight and all Clausen sees is me having a wee tad? Bah!

Seamus O'Leary was a hard case drunk who took his frustrations out on businesses after hours. He couldn't hold a job because of his love of liquor and then blamed his miseries on local businesses. He threw rocks through windows late at night, lit fires in trash cans, or worse, in doorways. He had not been a threat to any individuals, yet, but Kennedy was sure that wasn't going to last through the winter. It was another case of the unknown. Would someone like O'Leary change from breaking windows and starting fires to killing?

All right, now, Toby old boy, put Mr. Clausen aside and do your duty to the best of your ability. To hell with Joe Clause. to hell with the banker. Ah, now, that feels better.

Kennedy took Apple Street east and it became Creek Road as it left the village. The ride up the creek past several homesteads would have been most pleasant on a pleasant day, but today was windy, rainy, and cold, and Kennedy found himself in a foul mood by the time he rode into the wide and deep canyon that lead into some magnificent forests higher up the mountain.

Even the sight of a prime buck deer bounding through the fast waters of the creek didn't lift his mood. He hadn't been able to shake the visions he had of little Spike Boyington's slashed throat, of the Cringle couple, even of Amos Dudley's smashed head. *Why? Money, of course, is at the heart of it all and each life is worth thousands of times more than was stolen.* He chuckled briefly thinking that each criminal act had to be harder than simply doing a day's labor. *They've never learned how to do an honest day's work. Such terrible losses, lovely lives ended, all for a few pennies to spend.*

Each crossing of the creek was a little more difficult

as the water was rushing, deep, and the rocks were slick. He moved under an almost umbrella of trees and stopped, out of the rain for a moment. "Such beautiful country," he murmured standing up in the stirrups, stretching, then settling back down. "That little cabin was built by one of the old fur crews. These creeks were alive with beaver just a few years ago."

Remnants of the dams still held wat back and in some of those deep pools the trout grew large and strong. *Should have brought my old bamboo rod. I'd at least have something to go home with.* He chuckled, catching himself in full conversation, and nudged the horse. "Let's get it on, old boy."

The creek made its way through a mostly open meadow, with the run-down log and brush cabin off to the north side. There were stands of fir and pine, a copse of cottonwood near the cabin, and some aspen standing in review, in full autumn glory but sagging in the weight of the rain. branches would break if this storm turned cold with snow and ice. The little trail Kennedy was on rode up close to the cabin and as he got closer he could see smoke coming from the chimney.

I think I'll just ride right on past the place and try to see everything possible. The rain was coming down in sheets, the wind could be heard above the hissing of the rain as it shook the trees with a vengeance. Kennedy kept his head down but with the horse at a slow walk he was able to take in everything. One horse was standing alone in the corral but then he spotted a mule taking cover in a brush covered stall at the back of the corral.

He was within ten yards or so of the cabin, following the trail, when the door was flung open and a man walked out onto the covered porch. "Hey," he hollered out. "You must be drenched. I've got hot coffee if you'd like to make a quick stop?"

"Interesting," Kennedy murmured. "Thank you," he yelled back and turned the horse toward a tree that stood near the front of the cabin. "Yup, a wee bit wet, I am," he said. When he was able to see the man through the pouring rain he had to catch his breath.

"Is that you, Jack McGee?"

CHAPTER 25

McGee was Joe Clausen's cousin but that was as close as the two men would ever be to being alike. McGee was heavy, full muscled, and enjoyed hard work. He sailed on Boston whalers before entering the timber field and came west for the simple thought of opportunity. He was twenty-six, single, and willing.

"I thought you were staying with your cousin," Kennedy said, stepping down from the wet horse. "How'd you end up out here?"

"Come in and get warm and I'll tell you all about it." He stepped back into the two room cabin and Kennedy followed, closing the door. A wood fired cook stove dominated the front room and made the room exceptionally welcoming. The spitting and hissing of the fire was a welcome sound after the long ride in the storm.

There was a table with three bent cane chairs, and slabs of wood laid across boxes served as shelves along one wall. A window next to the door was covered by a cut-to-fit deer hide curtain.

"Comfy," Kennedy said, trying to shake himself out of that heavy bear skin coat. "Smells good, too."

"I have some biscuits in the oven and there's a pot of honey I filled from a hive yesterday, so settle in, Constable and get dry." Jack McGee was a different man than who Kennedy met at Murphy's just a few days before. Outgoing, personable, full of life. "Me and cousin Joe had a bit of a falling out after we met the other day. I packed up, heard about this place from a store keeper and checked it out. A man at the courthouse said no one had filed on it, so I did."

"Quick work, Jack. Good for you. Hope your problem with Clausen isn't too deep."

"Man's a lazy and fat piece of dung, Constable. Won't even bring in wood for the stoves, makes his wife do it. A few days at that place was enough for me." He half chuckled and poured coffee for the two of them. "Half that meadow out there," and he pointed toward the door, "and half the hillside behind me is mine. Welcome to McGee's one-sixty, that's what I'm calling the place. The One-Sixty Ranch. Fruit trees, cattle, and sheep, coming your way soon," he said through hearty laughter.

The man was alive and Kennedy couldn't help but join the gayety and took a long drink of coffee. *I like this fellow. What a difference between he and Joe. He's affable, appears strong as an ox, and sure isn't afraid of taking on a big chore. I wonder ...* and his thoughts drifted off.

McGee opened the oven and pulled a sheet of biscuits out, nicely browned and smelling perfect for a cold rainy day. "I might even have to look for a lovely lass from the homeland to join me."

"There aren't many, Jack, but you might just attract one or two." Kennedy looked around the tidy but cramped room and made his decision. "It's a long winter we're looking at and I'm in a position to make it a little better for you. Doubt you can do much along the lines of planting fruit trees or bringing in cattle or sheep during the winter."

"No, I was planning on surviving on game and buying a few other necessities. I'll get to making this a ranch next spring and summer. What are you thinking?"

"I'm ready to hire two full-time deputies, Jack. Ever thought of being a copper?"

"Well now. That 'ere's a thought." He smiled as he put a basket of hot biscuits on the table along with a pot of honey. "Wouldn't that flap Joe Clausen's sails. Ha!"

It was quiet as each man prepared a couple of biscuits each. "You know how to make bread, Jack. Best I've had in some time," Kennedy said. It was just a small fib, Kennedy thought, knowing those made by Irene Creighton were quite a bit better. *Interesting,* he thought. *How did Irene creep into these thoughts?* He shook his head, just slightly, to hear what Jack McGee was saying.

"My father's brother had two boys. Joe, who you've met, and Peter, two years older than Joe. He's a policeman in Boston. Completely opposite of his brother. A hard worker and one who won't tolerate sloth. He's my favorite cousin," McGee said.

"Did you learn anything from him about police work?"

"He loves it, I can tell you that. He said I would, too, but I was going to sea in those days. In answer to your question, yes, I learned a lot from him about trust, defensive moves, weapons." McGee sat back and stared at the rough board ceiling, thinking about the offer. "Tell me what I'd be doing, Constable. This place is several miles from town as you know."

"The job would mean you coming to town just about daily. It would mean working closely with me, learning this country so you could ride on a chase at midnight with no moon showing, and be safe doing it. It would mean facing down men larger than you, more well-armed, and every once in a while taking sass from one of our fine citizens."

McGee cocked his head and smiled. "You sound like cousin Pete, Constable. You've also got me more than interested. I don't much care for fighting, I know that sounds strange what with being Irish and all, but if there is a good reason for a fight, I can hold my own."

"I'll just bet you can," Kennedy laughed. "Some of the men I've had to deal with carry big knives, some carry shotguns, and a few have come to the table with rifles. What say you to that?"

"I met a man on the wagon train while making the crossing that only carried a short club, something like that stick you carry, only shorter and heavier. Toughest man on the train. Nobody messed with him. He showed me some moves with that thing that would take out two men with knives."

Jack McGee got up and walked back into the other room coming out with a short, maybe eighteen inches long, length of maple wood, highly polished and the end, carved and fitted as a handle. "His name was Cecil and he helped me carve this. It's all one piece." He worked it around, swung it across, up, and down, and twirled it a time or two.

"That's what I was talking about," Kennedy said. "That, for daily use, a good knife for the needed times, and a shotgun, and you would be in business."

"Can't work once spring gets here, Constable. Gotta tell you that."

"Oh, I'm afraid I know that, Jack." Kennedy didn't try to hide the smile, knew immediately that he had the right man. He downed his coffee and grabbed his big coat. "I'd best be getting back. Be in the office tomorrow morning and we'll get your training started. You'll do fine. Just fine." The ride back to town, despite the wind and rain seemed much shorter, even a bit warmer.

HAWK SPIVEY'S ANGER AT TORCH RUNNING OFF WITH THE Boyington money hadn't cooled as he rode off down the canyon, cussing under his breath. As he crossed the creek in a stand of trees, rode up the other side, and turned sharply around a rockslide, he came face to face with Skinny Doten, apparently riding up the creek trail.

"What do you think you're doing out here?" Spivey said. He reached to his side to make sure his knife was ready but saw that Doten had his flint-lock rifle in hand.

"No need to talk like that," Doten said. "It's a free country and I'll hunt where I wish." Doten saw an angry man reaching for his knife, and simply moved the rifle a few inches so it was aimed at the man. He kept the striker down, protecting the black powder from the rain. It was Spivey's his eyes that gave Skinny a start. Blazing hatred, the man's mouth turned down into a snarl, and no fear in his stance.

This man's a killer if I've ever seen one. Ain't gonna rile him if I can help it, but ain't gonna take none of his clabber neither. Bein' pushy don't go over well with me.

"Don't like people coming into my country. That's my cabin back there. You got no business there."

Skinny Doten knew there was the remains of an old lean-to, didn't know anyone would call it a cabin. "Ain't caring none about your cabin, mister. I'm hunting, this is open country, the trail goes on past your cabin, and I'll go where I want. You just ride on around me and be on your way. I'll go up the canyon when I please."

Doten moved his horse off to the side, watched carefully as Spivey walked his horse around and moved on down the trail. Skinny watched him for some time, got his breathing slowed down, and found his hand holding the reins was shaking some. *That man's eyes were the eyes of a madman, a killer. Ain't seen the likes of him around, neither.* Thoughts of the recent killings and vicious attacks moved though his mind. The Clingers were killed by Sam Bassett and his gang, but who killed the Boyington boy? Who beat the hell out of Amos Dudley?

———

KENNEDY WAS HALF WAY BACK TO TOWN WHEN HE realized Jack McGee hadn't even asked about pay, hours, days of the week. "My kind of man," he chuckled. The rain seemed to be letting up some, the wind slackening, and he was sure he got a glimpse of the sun once or twice on the ride in. "This is a good day."

Irene Creighton and her daughter were just leaving the Thorndyke complex and waved at the constable. "Good day to you," Kennedy said. "Looks like our storm is finally going to leave us."

"I'm never sure whether or not I like the storms. They bring much needed rain and they make life much more difficult," she said and laughed. "It's a bit of a toss-up. You're soaked to the skin, Tobias. You'll catch your death if you don't get dried off and warmed up." She hesitated, and then went on.

"I spoke with the doctor earlier and he said that Amos Dudley seems to be getting better. That was a terrible beating he took. I still don't know what is going to happen with my property. Have you heard anything?" There was considerable expectancy in her voice and looked down quickly, afraid she'd gone too far.

"Only what we've already discussed, I'm afraid." Kennedy smiled. "I did hear one good thing, though. The clerk at the bank doesn't remember any foreclosure notices being written up. Dudley may have been trying to pull a fast one on you. He's a lecherous old fool. Atkins is certain that there's no validity to what you were served."

Kennedy didn't go any further, didn't mention the fact that generally speaking, women had little if any voice in such matters. If push came to shove, even if there weren't signatures or such, a court would probably lean toward the man's point of view.

"We had best be getting home," Irene said. "You get yourself dried off and into warm clothes."

They smiled their goodbyes and Kennedy turned his horse toward the courthouse. *I wanted to say 'yes, dear,' and almost did.* He chuckled at the thought. *I would like to spend more time with that woman. Smart, warm, attractive. My god, man, just do it. Invite her and Carrie for a picnic, or something. I'm a coward, I admit it. She scares me.*

Skinny Doten was waiting for him in his office. "Thanks for keeping the fire going, Skinny. You look worried, what's the problem?"

"I stumbled on a man late yesterday, Tobias, who actually put the fright to me. He's got himself a ragged lean-to set up about half way between here and Jasper. It's deep in a canyon. There was hate, death, in his eyes when we come up on each other."

Doten stuffed another log in the wood stove and sat down next to it. "I let him go on down the canyon a spell, then turned and followed. I was supposed to be hunting.

He's setting up camp, in the rain, about half way between here and Hoagland's farm."

"That was quite a ride," Kennedy said. "Back into and through town, and then out south a ways." Kennedy hadn't seen Skinny Doten this upset by anything and stood next to the fire for a minute, giving himself time to think about what the man said. *He was set up north of town and is now south of town? And old Skinny is frightened? That's a new one. When I last saw the hoof prints of the horse missing a shoe it was heading north.* "You sure it's one man, not two?" Kennedy was thinking of the two men who attacked the Boyington family.

"Just one man that I saw. I'd sure like you to check him out."

"Want to ride with me, Skinny? Might want to talk to you about something." *Will my luck last?*

CHAPTER 26

The rolling hills spread out as a frame to the valley, their rocky spires softened over thousands of years of rain and wind, mellowed by time into ground that would grow just about anything planted. To the south of the east bound trail, those hillsides and swales were filled with tilled ground, stands of orchard trees, and as one moved more into the hills, herds of cattle and sheep.

Most of that wasn't seen by the lone rider making his way through the mid-day cold. "Sure don't want to be here," Spivey almost snarled. "People what runs places like this shoot first. Gotta find a place much closer to town but where I'll be ignored." Self-preservation is at the heart of the man while at the same time looking for easy pickings.

He rode down from near the Hoagland property, connected with Third Creek Road and followed it back toward Brookside, coming up on Eagle Street, just a half block east of the river. He saw several docks with small buildings connected and thought how convenient one of those buildings would be.

He was frustrated in what he wanted compared to what seemed to be available. He needed to be close to his bounty, that is, close to what he would be stealing and pilfering. But he needed to be unseen, too. Where he had been, up te canyon at the lean-to he was unseen but not close. At one of these shacks along the river he would close but definitely seen.

Spivey was a thief, had no qualms about hurting someone, had killed many a man in his pursuit of gold and knew the town was ripe. The River Road was the main road north and south out of Brookside, which had three main roads off it. Eagle Street, Apple Street, and Main Street, south to north. Each of those started at the river and turned into mountain trails as they left town to the east.

The north/south streets were First, Second, and Third, from the west, and they, too, simply trailed off into the forest at the edges of the village. *These town people and their little stores will be easy pickin's,* Spivey thought as he sat his horse near the river. *Hunker down in one of those river shacks for a few weeks, until I have a goodly filled poke, and ride off to the north.*

Spivey was remembering how easy it had been to knock that fat old man down and take everything he could get. He had deep thoughts of killing Torch for taking all that gold from that farmer's family from him. Anger at just about everything drove the man. Anger at a partner. Anger at the weather. Anger when his horse tripped and ripped a shoe off.

Often whatever was closest was smashed, injured, or destroyed to appease that anger. Sometimes furniture, sometimes his horse, sometimes just an innocent who happened by. Spivey's rage had no bounds, and in his current state, Torch was lucky to be miles away.

He rode slowly along River Road, taking in each of the riverside properties, saw areas where men stood along the banks fishing or shooting ducks and geese, and saw more than one of the buildings fully occupied. *Only that one with the broken door seems empty. Can't look at it now, though. Too many eyes.*

Spivey rode into town along Apple Street and stopped at the café for hot coffee and something to eat. *I'll check that place out tonight. Have to have a place to hide my horse, too. Maybe I'm wrong. Maybe that lean-to up that canyon would be best. Maybe just go back there.* He had a full meal of roast elk, mashed potatoes, and even a piece of apple pie, not saying five words to the woman trying to serve him.

Where did Torch go? Oregon City? He said they knew him up there? Across the Columbia into British country? Maybe I should just drift south. They say there are easy pickins in San Francisco. It was getting late in the day, he had a full meal, but nowhere to spread his bedroll.

He was about to leave and got a start spotting Skinny Doten riding by with that big constable, Kennedy. *They're riding south. That old man followed me yesterday. Can't go back to the canyon now. That old man's gonna die.*

"Rain's about ended," Kennedy said as he and Skinny walked out from the courthouse. "Do you remember what the man's horse looked like?" Kennedy was thinking of the horse with a shoe missing, but didn't have a good description of the horse. The second man involved in the Boyington boy's death also rode a horse and Kennedy didn't know what it looked like either.

"It was a dark, maybe reddish color. Hard to tell it

was so wet. White blaze, don't know about sox because of the mud. Call it reddish mud, Toby," he chuckled.

They took First Street south through town to connect with Third Creek Road on the edge of town. Only one set of eyes paid attention to the two.

There's that big copper that Torch was afraid of. That man with him is the one I met on the trail by my lean-to. Is he a copper, too? He had a nasty way about him and had that rifle pointed at me the whole time. Spivey watched them ride south and made up his mind that the old canyon lean-to was not going to be his best bet. The shack by the river would give him better access to businesses and homes to rob, but it would be safer up the canyon. *At least the rain has stopped,* he thought, leaving the café.

He got on the north/south road, saw several shacks as he rode north, but it was when he was passing the Thorndyke complex, across the road from the river, that he spotted what looked like an abandoned building in a stand of cottonwood trees, right at river's edge. *I almost missed that.*

He walked his horse to the river side of the road and trying not to be obvious took a long look down at the well-hidden wreck of a building. He nudged his horse into a trot and knew he couldn't just ride down to the building. *Gotta come back tonight.* He crossed the creek that runs behind the Thorndyke property and a few hundred yards past, turned into the deep forest. He found a spot surrounded by trees, made up a quick camp and crawled into his bedroll. The rain had ended, there was no wind, and Spivey had dreams of gold. He'd sleep until it was late, then find his new hide-out.

"Too damn close to town to have a fire," he muttered, pulling the wool blanket and canvas wrap closer. His thought on a fire changed as the temperature dipped and he crawled out to light one. "Someone comes looking, they won't be going back to tell about it." He could look across the open field and see the tops of the Thorndyke complex way off. "He's gonna be the first to lose things," Spivey chuckled. His bedroll was almost too close to the fire.

————

"THAT FELLER YOU FOLLOWED MUST NOT HAVE LIKED THIS area," Kennedy said. "He wasn't here long and pulled out. Looks like he rode back into town. Tell me how to get to that canyon where you ran into him. Would it be that narrow one with the creek running down the middle?"

"That's the one, Toby. Widens out into broad meadows up a mile or two. There's a couple of rock slides but easy to negotiate. What was it you wanted to talk to me about?"

"I got the word from the commissioners that I can hire two deputies full time. I'd like you to be one of them."

"No, Toby. No. I enjoy making a ride with you every once in a while, but full time? Ain't in me to work full time. Too busy hunting, drinking some, even cutting wood for the winter. No, you need a young man looking to settle in."

"It would be thirty-five cents a day, Skinny. Think about that."

"More than I've had in a long time, but it ain't in me, Toby, to work for someone. I got a nice cabin, grow lots of food, hunt whenever I want or need to, catch fish, pick apples. I just couldn't do it. Don't be mad at me, Toby, it's just the kind of man I am."

"It's the kind of man I want working for me,"

Kennedy laughed. "Think you can come up with someone who would work with me? Somebody I could trust with my life? Some one very much like you, Skinny Doten?"

Skinny chuckled. "I'll work on that, Toby. Yes, sir, I'll work on that." They passed through the village and were a mile or so north when Kennedy pulled his horse to a stop and climbed down from the saddle.

"What's up?"

"Come look," Kennedy said. He walked off the road a few paces and got down on his haunches. "What does that look like?"

Skinny got down next to the big constable and smiled. "Man might come up with a lame horse is what it looks like to me. Shoe pulled off, but a nail or two is still stuck. Man needs a whuppin' if you ask me."

The two stood up and Kennedy looked off in the direction the shoeless horse was heading. "Somebody riding off cross-country, this close to town? Hunting? Doubt it." He walked back to his horse. "When I was at the Boyington's after their boy was killed, I followed a horse with a missing shoe, Skinny. What's the chance of two horses in Brookside with a missing shoe on the front left hoof?"

"I'll ride with you today, maybe even tomorrow, Toby, but you ain't hired me."

Kennedy chuckled stepping back in the saddle. "We'd best be nice and quiet, Skinny. You got some kind of weapon?"

"Never go nowhere without my shotgun, Toby. And my knife."

CHAPTER 27

The rain was gone, there was no wind, and Kennedy figured they were less than an hour from sunset. "These prints are fresh, Skinny. I'm gonna be a lot more comfortable following this trail on foot. Let's move these critters into the trees and walk in." They tied their horses off and started the search on foot.

They could see the outline of buildings even though they appeared to be in deep forest. Open patches that had been logged off in past years were now meadows, and Kennedy could see where some of the locals had marked off sections that they might want to make a claim on. "Whoever we're following doesn't seem to know where he's going, Skinny. Looking for something?"

Maybe. Maybe looking for a spot to spread his blanket."

The trail left by Spivey was as obvious as if he had dropped bread crumbs but Kennedy was aware that a man on a horse can make a lot more ground in an hour than a man on foot. Did this killer keep riding? Or was he holed up somewhere close, waiting for two men walking toward him. After several days of rain, Spivey's and his horse's prints were the only ones to see.

"You're right, Toby. He's looking for something," Skinny almost whispered.

Kennedy nodded and motioned for Skinny to stop. *That's smoke I smell or I'm the queen.* The air was fresh from rain and wind and there was just the hint of smoke. Kennedy moved around a stand of large fir trees and stopped, flagging Skinny to move to the other side of the trees, maybe thirty yards or so over. Spivey's horse was tethered to some low branches and was feeding on fresh grass. Spivey was spread out on a tarp and under wool blankets, oblivious to visitors and the remnants of a fire smoldered nearby. The sun was down and the failing light was not in Kennedy's favor.

Why is he here, asleep this time of day? This close to town? He was at the Boyington's and this is where his problems are about to begin. He has that boy's blood on his hands. Kennedy was in the cover of trees, a mean and angry look on his face.

Kennedy could still see that boy's blood drenched body lying in the dirt, could still feel the wrench in his stomach. Could still feel the desire to kill the varmint. Skinny was on the other side of Spivey, waiting for Kennedy to make a move. *Sloppy camp set up, but why? Is he waiting for that other man, Torch? Or someone else?*

Kennedy smiled as he moved slowly toward the sleeping man, getting within five feet of him. Skinny Doten was less than ten feet on the other side and neither man had made a sound. Kennedy nodded to Skinny and yelled, "Wake up!"

Spivey jumped from the covers, a big, shiny knife flashing in the late afterlight. He was in his underwear whipping that knife back and forth, first at Kennedy, then at Skinny. The constable never took his eyes off the man and waited for his chance. It was quick when Kennedy's cudgel slammed him across the side of the head, knocking him unconscious and flinging the blade out and away.

"Let's get him tied up, Skinny, before he wakes up. He's killed one, is probably the one who beat the hell out of Amos Dudley, and we don't need someone else hurt. Wonder where his partner is?" He knew he was only following the one man, but was Spivey waiting for his partner? Is that other man going to all at once appear, rifle in hand?

"Was he with anyone when you ran into him?"

"He was alone." Skinny picked up the knife and checked the edge. "Keeps better account of his knife than he does his horse, Toby."

They packed up Spivey's kit, tied him across his horse, walked out to their horses, and made the quick ride into Brookside. "Mind running for the doc, Skinny? I'll get this fool into a cell, but he'll need looking at. I knocked him hard, I did. Need to get Ken Boyington in to identify him, too. Think you could make that run for me?"

"Yup, Toby, I'll do that but just remember, I don't work for you." He was laughing as he helped get Spivey off the horse. The man's head was still bleeding, his eyes wouldn't focus, and Kennedy had to help him with his balance as he walked him into the courthouse. Skinny Doten was still chuckling as he rode off to find the doctor.

You don't work for me, Skinny, but I sure wish to hell you did.

THERE WERE TWO WAGONS MAKING THEIR WAY SOUTH OUT of Jasper, along the river. It was a miserable road, muddy but passable, and the man leading the first wagon spotted a fair place to spend the night. "Let's move into those trees yonder," he yelled at the man leading the second wagon. "Good grass and water."

"How much more to Brookside?" The second man called out.

"That little village was Jasper that we just passed through. In the morning we'll have about five miles and be in Brookside probably about the middle of the day. Just a few miles between the two but with all this mud it'll be slow going. Been on this road many times," he said. He led the two oxen off the road, across some open grass, and into a stand of tall timber. "One thing we want to be wary of is strangers showing up and offering to help. They would likely be thieves and killers, Owen. Seen it more than once."

Owen Hardy and his wife Susan were moving west from the Ohio Valley where Hardy's family had moved to a hundred years ago. They were in their twenties, no children yet, and Owen had farming knowledge from five generations back. "We're almost there, Susan. I can smell good ground, good water, crops ready to harvest." He swept his head back and forth, pretending to pick up the generous aroma of good earth.

Susan was laughing, poking him in the shoulder with her prodding stick, the one she used on the mules and oxen. "Go on with you," she said. He skipped away and kept dancing and laughing.

The second wagon was led by Bobby Valentine. His wife Mary-Louise was sitting up high with her prod stick. The two wagons had been part of a larger group that made the crossing and broke up in Oregon City where they met their guide David Macintosh. Unlike Owen Hardy, Bobby Valentine was thin, slightly with-drawn, and was fearful of being a failure at just about everything he faced. The fear almost guaranteed that failure.

His wife, Mary-Louise was more like Susan Hardy, full of life, looking forward to the challenges from this emigration. Valentine depended on her far more than she depended on him. She was, however, madly in love with the man despite his being a pessimist. It was her idea to make the dramatic move to Oregon Territory. She had to get him away from the family that spent so much time telling him he would never amount to anything.

He was told that so often he knew it had to be true. What drew Bobby to Mary-Louise? She couldn't say, but he did say often. "She's so strong, so positive. I feel good just being around her. We'll make it, in Oregon, I know we will."

Hardy and Mackintosh took care of the animals while Valentine and the women set up the camp. Wood was gathered all along the trail and they found more than an ample supply on the ground anyway. "Not like out on the plains," Valentine laughed. "And better than buffalo chips, for sure."

It was just after supper when Mackintosh spotted the stranger moving toward their camp. He casually stood up, gathered his flintlock rifle, and stepped out of the campfire light. "Don't be moving another step, mister or it'll be your last."

"Didn't mean to frighten you," Torch McGhan said, holding his arms out from his sides. "Just thought I'd come say howdy. My camp is just over the rise there. Need any help with something, just ask. They call me

Torch and I've been in these parts for some time, could even guide you to your homestead, if you need me."

Mackintosh saw Torch for what he was, a thief and killer, and wasn't going to let him get anywhere near the women. Hardy saw Mackintosh's move and retrieved his rifle to stand off to the side. Valentine stayed near the fire all but unaware of the danger.

"We've said our howdies, now go on back to your camp," Mackintosh said.

Torch shrugged his shoulders, had the slightest grin on his face, and turned to leave. He took a half step and turned back. "I didn't mean to ruffle your feathers, old-timer, just trying to be trail-friendly. It's hard living in this Oregon country and a man always needs a willing and helpful friend. You needn't be so quick to turn down friendly help."

"Got no reason to be friendly to a man who creeps up on a camp after the sun goes down. Your camp is over the rise, you say? Best get back to it, then. We got plenty enough friends." Mackintosh was only forty, didn't care much for being called old-timer, and knew Torch for what he was. "You ready to shoot this varmint, Mr. Hardy?"

"Indeed I am, Mr. Mackintosh. Cocked and primed," Owen Hardy said as he lifted his long rifle to his shoulder.

"Ain't nice to turn away friendly help," Torch said. He turned and walked off into the gloom and over the rise to his own camp. Hardy eased the rifle down and joined David Mackintosh for the few steps back to their fire.

"Think he was one of those bad men you were talking about?" Hardy asked. He had his rifle by his side as he sat next to Susan.

"I could see it in his eyes," Mackintosh said. "We have

four mules, four oxen, and three riding horses out there in good grass, gentlemen. You just made the crossing and I'm sure you remember how them redskins would try and steal the stock every night. Those animals out there would bring good money in any farming community."

"I'll take first watch," Owen Hardy said, almost before Mackintosh had finished his statement. "No, sir, ain't nobody taking my stock, not when I can smell just how good this ground is."

Susan couldn't help but chuckle even though once again the fear of a night-time attack gripped her. "You be careful, Owen. Remember what happened before."

Owen and two others had been night-guard some- where on the plains of Nebraska when they were attacked by a group of Sioux Indians. The fight was hand-to-hand, Owen was slashed by one man, almost knocked out by another, and fought like the devil himself to save the stock. One night-guard had been killed, three Indians lay dead, and none of the stock was lost.

Hardy rubbed his chest, where scabs had worn off and scars remained. "Ain't something a man would forget, Susan," he said, giving her a big smile. "Ain't nobody gonna kill this pilgrim, you got my word on that." Mackintosh noticed that Bobby Valentine hadn't said a word.

"I'll take second watch," Mackintosh said, "and we should be prepared to move out as early as possible. We don't know just how many men this man might have with him."

"Oh," Susan said. "I never thought about that. You think he's part of a gang?" She looked about quickly, from Macintosh to Owen, to Valentine.

"That would be my guess," Mackintosh said. "There

are three men with rifles, two women who can probably shoot as well as a man." He looked at the two women and they gave him smiles back. "It wouldn't be up to one man to attack us." *That Valentine boy ain't offered to help with one single thing. It must have been a hard crossing for those with him. He ain't gonna be any help if that fool neighbor of ours gets it in his head to take our stock.*

CHAPTER 28

Torch McGhan let the fire burn down while he made his plans for how best to get his hands on all those animals. "I'm looking at making more than fifty dollars there, getting those mules and ox to Jasper. Sure could use old Hawk Spivey right about now."

Stealing all of Spivey's money from the Boyington murder and running off with other possessions never entered the man's thoughts. As with most carrying the outlaw brand, thinking only of himself was the way of life. Torch was shaking his head trying to come up with an answer and couldn't. *Damn fool with that rifle just aching to shoot me. Old guide had his gun ready, too. I need to find me a partner. Hawk would know what to do, but I can't do nothing alone.*

Torch stuffed wood onto the fire and poured some whiskey in his tin cup and sat, dejected, in the dirt. His level of frustration was growing, he knew there was no way he could pull this off alone and finally wrapped himself in a blanket near the fire and went to sleep. He never saw nor heard David Mackintosh move back from the brush and trot over the rise back to his own camp.

Torch tossed and turned through a fitful night, visions of all those animals playing about in his head.

A brisk sunrise found the wagon party having breakfast around a warm fire, all the animals accounted for. "He was alone," Mackintosh said. "If this was just one wagon, and just a couple, he would have attacked, killed the couple, plundered the valuables, and made off with the stock."

"Glad we're all together, eh Valentine?" Hardy said. Bobby Valentine just nodded, still feeling as fearful as he had all night. He was wakened at every sound and scratch, at every bird-call, and every cough or sneeze. It had been a long crossing for the man. He just sat there, warming his hands at the fire. His family had done a fine job convincing him he wasn't worth much.

"Let's get those animals, Owen," Mackintosh said.

———

Torch rode out before sunrise to make his way to where the immigrants had their stock. *Took a while to make my plans. Thinking too big. Ain't no way I could take all that stock but I sure as hell can take the mules and horses. Them ox would bring good money but can't run them off like I can the others.*

He sat his horse just a few hundred yards from the stock, watched David Mackintosh ride back to camp after the sun came up, and slowly moved down the slope's side and around the herd. It took a little time, but he cut the horse and four mules from the oxen, and was about to get them moving out, back across the rise, down a long swale, and onto the trail back to Jasper.

"Look," Owen Hardy pointed and Mackintosh turned and ran back to camp, Hardy on his heels. they had their rifles and were racing back up the hill. "He waited till dawn," Owen said. "Indians did, too. Should have remembered that." He was reprimanding himself, but was the guide included?

"We'll get him." They crossed the top of the rise, saw Torch trying to get the animals to herd up and they weren't in any mood to do so. Owen Hardy knelt down on one knee, brought that Tennessee long-rifle up and took aim. The flint stuck, and the charge went off, sending the fifty-eight caliber chunk of hot lead deep into Torch's back, severing his spinal column, and sending the man, already dead, face first into the mud.

"You are one hell of a shot, Mister Owens," Mackintosh said as they walked across the lush meadow.

"I used to shoot the heads off the turkeys instead of ruining too much meat," Hardy said with a laugh. "Susan is as good a shot as I am."

"Wish I'd made the crossing with you folks. I betcha ate good."

The gunshot brought Susan, carrying a shotgun, and Mary-Louise running. Bobby Valentine was not with them. "Everybody all right? Nobody hurt? What happened?" Susan said, almost as one continuous question.

"Man from last night tried to run off with our stock," Owen Hardy said. "We got him."

"You got him," David Mackintosh said. "Man's a crack shot with that long Tom. Everybody except the thief is safe. The thief is dead for sure."

They got the stock, all together, left them to their grazing, and went back to camp for packing up. After getting the wagons ready for the day's ride they roped Torch McGhan's body to his horse to be led behind the Valentine wagon. "We'll have to ask somebody where to take the body," Mackintosh said. "They do have a town constable, though. I'm sure he'll want to know about all this."

———

TOBIAS KENNEDY WAS IN A FINE HUMOR WALKING BACK TO the courthouse after a visit to Irene Creighton's office at the Thorndyke complex for a mid-day snack of sweet rolls and coffee. She had a note delivered inviting him for home-made sweet rolls. They spent time discussing Amos Dudley, but underneath all the talk, they both needed to talk about themselves. It was a wonderful time with her, he reminisced.

"I've wanted to invite you for a picnic, Irene, but it isn't the right time of year. Can't picnic in the mud, eh?"

She laughed and blushed slightly. "I would say yes, Tobias. I would. Would I be out of line inviting you to have supper with Carrie and me? I would enjoy that more than a picnic in the mud."

They both were laughing when Ben Thorndyke walked in. "I hope I'm not intruding but I have some news for both of you. I just got the word that Amos Dudley is probably going to live." Thorndyke looked at Irene, then Kennedy. "It might not be proper to say, but this is probably good news for you, Mrs. Creighton. There is no record of any loan being made by Ed Creighton at the Brookside Bank, nor any foreclosure on your property. I've just come from a meeting of those of us who have a financial interest in the bank."

"Oh, dear," Irene said. "I'm sorry the man suffered such a dreadful beating, but he is a horrible man. But... the loan..." Her voice just trailed off. Kennedy moved to her side quickly and put his arm around her shoulder. It was such a natural move, but both felt a distinct tremble.

She dared to look up into his eyes and found his looking deep into hers. The tremble was real, the urge to do more than look was felt by both, and it took great strength for Irene to drop her head, hopefully before Ben Thorndyke saw all of that.

"It's difficult, yes, but wonderful news about your property. There was no loan, no foreclosure," Thorndyke said. He didn't try to hid the smile, seeing the two of them so close, so happy.

Kennedy lifted her face, smiled, and simply said, "Yes, tonight would be fine." Before she or Ben Thorndyke could say anything, he grabbed his coat and walked out the door, still smiling. Ben Thorndyke couldn't help notice the smile that lit up Irene's face as well.

Those two need to spend a lot of time together. "It will take some time for Amos Dudley to fully recover from that beating he took and we have decided that young Charles Nixon will be the interim bank manager until we can find someone for the position. Dudley will not be coming back. You will not hear another word about an Ed Creighton loan or the possibility of a foreclosure on your home"

"That's wonderful, Ben, just wonderful." *I wish Tobias hadn't rushed out of here like he did. I'll fix him a supper he'll never forget.*

Kennedy, a smile on his face, walking toward the courthouse had his thoughts interrupted. *What have we here?* He was watching a lone rider leading two wagons into town and the trailing wagon had a horse tied to the back with a body strapped to it. "Hold up there, folks." Kennedy said, stepping out onto the muddy street. "I think we need to have a little talk."

"We do," David Mackintosh said. "You must be the town marshal."

"Constable is what we call it here." He walked to the back of Valentine's wagon, saw that the man was shot through the back, and told Mackintosh to take the wagons to the courthouse, just a block north. "Name's Kennedy, Tobias Kennedy, and we got some talking to do."

Any gunplay had to be investigated but when the dead man was shot in the back, there were usually charges of some kind filed. Often, if someone was shot in the back, the perpetrator simply left the scene as fast as possible. They seldom wrapped the body across the back of a horse and delivered it to the constable.

He directed the little train to the courthouse, sent a youngster to find the undertaker, and invited the party to his office. "Tell you what, let's go up to the courtroom. Surely isn't room for all of us in my little hole in the wall." He tried to keep his demeanor as light as possible, but immigrants hauling a body? The body shot in the back? It took just moments for everyone to get settled and Kennedy nodded to the group. Now was the time for business.

"Who's first?"

Owen Hardy stood up and introduced himself, his wife, Bobby Valentine and his wife, and their guide, David Macintosh. "Mr. Macintosh was guiding us to our holdings here in this little valley when the man you saw strapped across his horse tried to steal our stock. I'm the one who shot him."

"It was only because we're a large party that the fool didn't kill before stealing the stock. Seen his kind before," Mackintosh said. "These are fine folks who made the crossing, fighting off Indians and outlaws

203

along the way, and now again, being attacked before reaching their new home."

Kennedy took an immediate like to the guide, liked the way he defended Hardy's actions, liked his attitude. No one, he saw right away, was trying to hide anything.

"The man said he's been in this area a long time and helps people find their homesteads," Susan Hardy said.

"He didn't give up his name by chance, did he?" Kennedy asked. "I don't think I've seen him before."

"Yeah," Mackintosh said. "Yeah, he did. Said folks around here call him Torch. Seemed like a strange name but that's what he said." Mackintosh looked around and both Hardy and Valentine nodded.

Kennedy got a grim look on his face. "I know the man, just not. by sight. Been looking for him. Don't mind telling you, Mr. Hardy, you have done this valley a good deed, indeed. Torch killed a young boy not too long ago. He and a partner robbed an immigrant family and killed their boy. I brought his partner's in. He's in one of the cells back there," and he pointed to a door behind him. "Thank you, Mr. Hardy."

Kennedy had all the names and facts written down and ushered the group back downstairs. "Welcome to Brookside. Mr. Mackintosh, when you get these people onto their properties, why don't you stop by the office. Got a few things we might enjoy discussing. You've brought more than one family into our valley."

"I keep my operation in Oregon City and help get people across that pass and into these beautiful valleys regularly. Brookside is one of my favorite little villages to visit. In fact, I'll be staying at Murphy's Inn tonight. Maybe we could meet there."

"Couldn't have come up with a better plan," Kennedy said. He had a wide smile watching the group get things put together in order to head out. *I might have to talk fast and sweet but I would sure like that man to be my deputy. With young Jack McGee and David Macintosh alongside, we'll put a stop to these criminal shenanigans.*

Kennedy started to say something when reality struck. *No, I can't meet you at Murphy's What was I thinking?* He looked at Macintosh and shook his head. "I'm afraid I spoke too soon. I've got another appointment tonight. Come into the office in the morning. that would be much better."

Macintosh nodded, and the group made their way out of town. Kennedy made his way to his cabin for a hot bath and change of clothes. *I don't know if she invited me or if I invited myself, but I'm going to enjoy this dinner.*

CHAPTER 29

Kennedy was still half a block from Irene Creighton's home when he remembered his manners. "My god, man," he mumbled, turned around and walked to Annabelle Winthrop's long white picket fence, looked around as a furtive thief might, and picked two roses from a bush that ran up and over a trellis. "I've spent so much time with the criminal element I've forgotten how to be a gentleman."

The thought bothered the big man and he couldn't get it out of his head. He remembered how, as a youth so many years ago, he cringed at the thought of being in a fight, yet he was so big and so strong that few ever wanted to fight him. He almost ran for home the first time he saw a dead man. *Now, Tobias, just look at yourself. You'll fight at the mere mention of the word, and what's worse, Laddie Buck, you enjoy the hell out of it.* He didn't even try to hold back the chuckle.

"Oh my, the dead men." He muttered. *Just how many have there been?* "Ach. Away with these thoughts." But they wouldn't go away. "The problem is people," he snickered at the thought. "It isn't the newcomers, it isn't the old timers. It isn't even the crooks, gamblers, whore-mongers, or murderers. It's people in general. Dogs, deer, lions, and elephants don't act this way, don't have need of constables and commissioners.

"There, I've solved the world's biggest problem. Oh, my, what do I smell?" When he turned up the short walkway to Irene's the rich aroma of something roasting filled the air and when Irene Creighton opened the front door, just a second after he knocked, Kennedy found himself speechless. "Oh, my," is all he was able to get out. Irene stood, framed by the doorway, in a green taffeta gown, glowing in the lamp light. "Oh, my," Kennedy said again. The world's problems evaporated in a blink.

"Come in out of the cold, Toby. Don't you look just fine. I love that jacket." He was wearing a soft kid skin jacket over a deep burgundy colored wool shirt, black wool trousers were tucked into high laced calf skin moccasins. She almost blurted out something along the lines of, "You're beautiful," but simply said, "So handsome."

A blazing fire warmed the living room and lamps added a soft glow to the atmosphere. "I wanted to make these into a bouquet," he said. "But I don't know how." He handed the two rose blossoms to Irene.

"They're beautiful," she said. "Here, Carrie, put these in a bowl of water and make them the centerpiece for out dining table." She turned a smiling face to the constable. "Would you like a glass of sherry before supper?"

"Splendid," Kennedy said. He couldn't take his eyes off the woman. In his mind she was glowing, seemed to float across the living room rug to pour the sherry, and her smile weakened his knees to the point he had to sit down or topple to the floor. "That's a right smart dress, Irene. You're beautiful."

Now I've done it. That's not what you say to a lady. Remember your manners, Tobias Finnegan Kennedy. He sat, muted, as she brought his drink across the room and sat beside him. *I've not been alone with a lady for so many years. It's like I'm fourteen again, sitting with Edith and her proper grandmother.*

"I wonder when the next storm will hit?" he said. He didn't know what else to say. *I want to say something smart, clever. Why did I say that?*

"Oh, I'm sure we'll have one soon," he said, answering his own question. Before he made a complete fool of himself, he took a sip of his sherry. "Very good," he said.

Carrie came back from taking care of the rose blossoms and sat down on the other side of the constable. "Mama's really nervous, Mr. Kennedy. She likes you, you know."

"Carrie," Irene said. She reddened and noticed that Tobias's cheeks seemed to be a little more colored than normal. "Oh, my," she said.

"It's all right, mama. The constable told me that he likes you, too. Didn't you, constable."

"Um, uh," he stammered, saw Irene's flushed face, and got to his feet. "I'm acting like a school boy at his first dance, Irene." He stood with his back to the fire and let a genuine smile cross his rugged face. "Yes, I like you very much. There. I've said it, I meant it, and I hope I get a chance to say it again."

"You will," Irene all but whispered. The blush was a deeper color, the eyes fully averted came back to rest on Kennedy's frame. "I'm sure our dinner is ready. Shall we move to the kitchen?" She was ready to run, full out, and maybe then she wouldn't blurt out something else that would be out of line for a proper lady.

With a platter of sliced roast elk, oven roasted potatoes, and carrots, conversation became a little more relaxed and by the time Carrie brought a freshly baked apple pie to the table, Irene and Toby were talking back and forth like the friends they had been.

"This has been a most enjoyable supper, Irene. I haven't eaten this well in some time."

"Thank you, Toby."

"Mama makes the best chicken, too. And the wild turkey is the best." Carrie looked at her mother with a big smile splashed across her young face. "We should have the Constable over for turkey supper next week, mama."

"Carrie, you must stop," Irene said.

"I think it's a splendid idea," Kennedy said, then realized what he said, and just sat shaking his head back and forth. He took a quick look at Irene and found her taking a quick look back at him, and they broke out in gales of laughter. They laughed for several moments, looking at each other, back and forth.

"I think, with Carrie's continued help, that we're going to be good friends for a long time, Irene." He chuckled some more, gave Carrie a little nudge with his elbow. "The fire boys are having a dance this next week, Irene. Ladies will be bringing food and there's sure to be a fat calf on the fire. I'm not very good at it, but I would most enjoy dancing with you."

"That's wonderful. I haven't danced for years but I would be charmed to be with you." *Oh, to be held by this man, to dance and be close.* "Yes, Toby, I would like that very much."

CHAPTER 30

S unrise came with icy temperatures but bright sunshine as well. The storm was over but the warm sunlight turned the streets to muddy pathways, which in turn brought continued short tempers among the people. Among them was Doctor Winslow, storming his way into Constable Kennedy's office.

"I simply don't understand why everyone you arrest is either dead or terribly injured. This man Spivey that you have in a cell back there was brutally beaten, Constable. Another man brought into your care was dead. Why?"

Kennedy sat quiet behind his desk still relishing the night before and gave the doctor a long jaded look. "You live in a haze of golden light, eh doc? All things beautiful and warm, cozy in fact. It ain't the way in the real world. Ever had a man with a knife attack you, Doctor? Answer me, have you?"

"There are ways to stop a man with a knife other than beating him half to death," Winslow said. "Violent behavior is the work of criminals, sir. It shouldn't be the work of the man upholding the law."

"That's what I thought," Kennedy said. He got up and grabbed a log and rammed it into the already hot stove. "You've never faced a man with a weapon who was looking to kill you. You've never faced real danger but you're willing to tell me I shouldn't hurt someone trying his best to kill me? You're the one out of line, Doctor. Yes, I whupped pretty hard on Mr. Spivey."

Kennedy walked over to his desk and opened the bottom right drawer and came up with a knife with a blade at least ten inches long. It was shiny bright, the edge as keen as anything Doctor Winslow had seen other than his scalpels. "This is Mr. Spivey's knife, doc. Here, hold it, test that blade, and tell me what you would do if a man came at you with this in his hand, his eyes narrowed for the kill. What would you do, doc?" He was louder than he wanted to be and eased himself out of his anger.

"You don't know, do you? You don't know because it is your position in life to help people, not hurt them. It's my position to help keep people safe, doc. Sometimes I have to face people who want to kill me because I'm good at keeping people safe. You don't have to face a man with a knife like this one because I did, and that man is behind bars, and he won't hurt anyone ever again."

Kennedy eased the knife back in the drawer and sat back in his chair. "As to the dead man who the immigrants had brought in, he was a wanted man, doc. His name was Torch." Kennedy saw the recognition in Doctor Winslow's face. "That's right, Torch. The man who viciously killed little Spike Boyington."

Kennedy let it remain quiet in the little room for several long moments, waiting for the good doctor to say something. When it became obvious the doc wasn't going to, he coughed, and stood up. "I guess our conversation is over, then. You have no idea what my job entails but you're willing to criticize how I do my job. Keep your criticism to yourself, Doctor, I'm a busy man keeping you safe. Have a good day, and goodbye, sir."

It wasn't Doctor Winslow who walked out of the office, it was the constable and he headed for Murphy's for a morning brace of brandy, smiling at his comments as he walked.

———

JACK MCGEE WAS NOT AMONG THOSE WITH SHORT tempers as he made his way into Brookside for his meeting with Constable Kennedy. His good humor changed when two young men stepped out from a stand of trees signaling him to stop. They were mirror images of each other, their heads covered in bright red hair that flew in every direction, light and ruddy faces glaring and mean, topping off large bodies in ill-fitting clothing.

McGee had seen the two the day before, he remembered. How could anyone not remember those two? They rode past his cabin and he thought it strange how they had slowed, giving the place a full looking over. That they were twins was obvious to the most jaded of observers, but it was the shocking red hair that caught most eyes. "That's far enough," one of them said. "Let's have your poke and nobody gets hurt."

"Ah," McGee said. "You're highly mistaken." He held the horse's reins in his left hand and slipped his right hand inside his coat. One of the thieves rode up too close, pulled a knife and flashed it back and forth, threatening him. McGee's short, iron-hard club came out from under his coat and knocked the knife away in a wild swing. On the return swing, he knocked the young man right off his horse and into the mud.

McGee jumped from his horse and slammed the cudgel across the man's head knocking him senseless. "You next?" he said to the second man whose astonished face turned even more angry and mean.

"I'll kill you," the man was in a rage, kicked his horse into a run right at McGee, catching him by surprise. He simply didn't expect the man to use his horse as a weapon and stepped aside quickly, swung his club hard for the rider. He misjudged the speed of the attack and clobbered the horse. The horse was hit hard enough that it threw a fit, throwing the outlaw to the ground. McGee jumped on his back, slipped the club under the man's chin, grabbed the other end, and pulled back hard, snapping the outlaw's neck.

The melee all over in less than three minutes and Jack McGee stood up, breathing hard, looking at the damage. One dazed horse, one unconscious thief, and one dead one. He found the knife in the mud, wiped it clean and shoved it in a saddle bag, tucked the club back in his belt and got the live one to his feet. "First, we lay your friend across his horse and tie him tight. One wrong move and you join him. Move it now," McGee said. *A most interesting way to start my new job, Jack McGee. These must be the twins that the constable said needed taking down. Job accomplished.* The irony of his conversation with himself brought the slightest grin to his face.

They had the body tied onto the slightly spooky horse and with the outlaw's hands tied behind his back, McGee helped the outlaw onto his horse. McGee then tied his legs to the stirrups. The dead outlaw's lead rope was then tied to the other outlaw's saddle horn, and McGee got on his horse. "Not gonna be a nice ride, mister. You try something stupid and you'll be a dead man, just like your friend. You lead off and ride to the courthouse."

"I can't ride with my hands tied behind my back," the man whimpered.

"You can or die. Move it."

Only a fool would not be amazed that one man, armed only with a stick of wood, took out two large men out to rob and possibly kill him. To Jack McGee it happened so fast that he had no time to think past his actions. On the long ride into town he didn't even try.

———

CONSTABLE KENNEDY WAS TALKING WITH JACOB Hoagland in front of the courthouse when Jack McGee brought the little caravan to a stop. "What's this?" Kennedy said. "The Kinsey twins? All trussed up?" Kennedy looked over to Jacob Hoagland. "This is my first new deputy, Jacob. Your decision to back my need has already paid off."

Kennedy yelled at a couple of kids playing catch to run for the undertaker and the doctor. "Tell me what brought all this on, Jack."

"I was riding in to meet up with you when these two jumped me, wanted my money, and at the threat of a knife. You called them by name. Well known, eh?"

"Indeed they are. These are the Kinsey twins we talked about. Been raising hell around here for too long. Sneak thieves, usually. Open armed robbery and assault hasn't been their game. I'll need you to write a full report on this and then I'll deliver it to the county attorney. You haven't been properly sworn in yet, so your actions were those of a citizen. In my opinion, fully justified."

Hoagland nodded his feelings as well. "Looks like you have things under control, Constable. I heard from Murphy this morning that Amos Dudley is expected to live and that there are what he called discrepancies at the bank. Know anything about that?"

"Only that Murphy talks too much," the constable chuckled. "Dudley is a lecher, Jacob, and he was using the bank to take advantage of a lovely lady. From what I understand, it's all taken care of and Dudley will probably lose his interests in the bank. It's for sure he will not return as manager."

"You have a good day, Constable. By the way, I understand the men at the fire house are planning a Harvest Ball for next week. Martha's already promised that we're going. The women love these things. Lots of food and dancing is on the menu."

"A good day to you, too," Kennedy said. *Now there's something I will enjoy. Food and dancing and I'll probably even sing a ditty or two.* He laughed, thinking about it. His slightly ribald offerings met with pleasure by groups of men standing at the bar at Murphy's. His smile was wiped clean with the arrival of the doctor.

"The Kinsey twins?" the doctor said. "Looks like you've put a stop to their shenanigans."

"Not I, doctor. The work of my new deputy. Have you met Jack McGee? He's one of the newcomers that have caused so much grief recently. He's Joe Clausen's cousin."

Shorty Salinski, the long-time undertaker in Brookside brought his small one-horse wagon to a stop. "A lot of killing going on, constable. Got to put a stop to it. Got to. What happened this time?"

"Sometimes the dead ones are the bad ones, Shorty." Kennedy chuckled. "Doc, bring the wounded one up to my office to work on him in a cell. Shorty, Evan Kinsey is all yours. Mr. McGee, let's move into my office and let these gentlemen do their jobs."

Before they could move off David Mackintosh arrived. "Looks like it's been a busy morning, constable."

"Has indeed. Good morning. David Mackintosh say hello to Jack McGee. You two might be working together a lot in the coming days. Let's get up to the office and get this all put together."

Kennedy got Travis Kinsey in a cell and untied so the doctor could work on him after he helped Shorty Salinski load Evan Kinsey's body in the undertaker's wagon. "Paperwork first, gentlemen. Always paperwork in this business. I need a written report on what happened to you this morning, Jack McGee, and while you're doing that, Mr. Mackintosh and I will slip into the courtroom before it opens and have our discussion."

———

THE COURT CLERK HAD THE POT-BELLY STOVE NICE AND hot and Kennedy motioned for Mackintosh to bring a chair up close to the fire and join him. "That was a fine job yesterday. We've been overwhelmed by criminal activity these last few months with all the new people coming into the valley."

"All those immigrants can't be criminals," Mackintosh said. He had a grin on his face and wagged his head back and forth.

"Not likely," Kennedy said. "Some are, but with so many new people, some of those who have been with us for a while have found it's easier to steal from the newcomers than it is to make a decent living. Opportunity, David. The newcomers have given some the opportunity they needed to become criminal. Those two this morning fit that category. Evan and Travis Kinsey have been on the fringes of decent society for several years, but now, the newcomers have become easy pickings."

"Looks like they picked on the wrong man this morning."

"Indeed, and that brings us to you, my friend. Torch McGhan picked on the wrong man, too, and I'd like you to consider taking up a new profession. Have you ever considered being a lawman?"

"Whoa," Mackintosh muttered. He rocked back in his bent cane chair and let out his breath. "No, I don't think I have ever given it a thought. Whew!"

Kennedy chuckled, got up and walked around the free-standing stove, sat back down. He gave the guide a good look. "I liked what I saw in you yesterday, I need another man in my office, and I would like you to give it some serious consideration. It would be a busy job, and not always pleasant."

"I understand that part," Mackintosh said, "after what I saw outside." David Mackintosh got up and walked to the second floor window, looked out over the bright green of the Brookside valley. *Me, a lawman? Ain't that far from what I've been doing as a guide. Helping people get from here to there and keeping them safe. That fella this morning took on those two men single handed. Hell, I've done that.*

"Tell me all about this, constable. I've got a cabin in Oregon City, all my stuff is there."

Kennedy smiled, could almost see the man saying yes, and spent the next ten minutes describing what Mackintosh would be doing. "You, McGee, and I would be working very close."

"I want to say yes but I have to know it would be permanent. My guiding, if I stayed at it, would be work that will last for many years, what with all the people wanting to move to Oregon Territory."

"Your staying on as a deputy would be determined by how well you do your job. The job will last a long time because, as you said, all the people moving here. I see you being in Brookside a long time."

"I am good with people, I believe we need laws to have decent lives, I'm just not sure I'm up to the task."

"You're more than up to it, David. That I'm sure."

"I'll find a place and leave for Oregon City to gather my stuff. Might take a bit of time before I could start," Mackintosh said. He had a tentative smile and a shake of his head. *Now I've done it. A lawman? Uncle Percy would roll over in his grave three times.*

Sitting at the bar at Murphy's that afternoon, Kennedy had his own smile going. *Neither one of them ever asked how much money they'd be making.* "I am one lucky man, Murphy. Let's have some brandy, eh?"

CHAPTER 31

J acob Hoagland left the courthouse for a short stroll to Murphy's. He wasn't a drinking man but did enjoy a touch of brandy in his coffee on brisk mornings like this one. He found Ben Thorndyke sitting near the roaring fireplace and joined him. "Do you remember us discussing this broadsheet that's distributed around town?"

"You're talking about what's called *FYI?*" Hoagland nodded. "Yes, I remember you saying you thought you recognized the handwriting." He cocked his head all but asking why.

"I got some papers out last night, papers from the bank, and recognized the handwriting right away. I know who the person is who writes *FYI.*"

"Well, don't just stop talking now. Don't leave me in the dark here," Thorndyke laughed. "Have a sip of your coffee and tell me." He hollered at Murphy to join them. "Better hurry, Murph, before Jacob decides not to."

Hoagland laughed and drank some coffee. "Our editor is none other than Charles Nixon, the bank clerk.

He has an immaculate hand. Interesting no one else has figured it out."

Murphy harrumphed a couple of time and walked back to the bar not interested at all. Thorndyke on the other hand sat right up. "I am leaving here in just a short time for a meeting with the young man. He asked for it but didn't say why. I wonder..." He let his voice fade off.

"Being the bank's clerk he knows a lot of what goes on around the village," Hoagland said. "That's why the little broadsheet is good, so filled with the news of the town."

Thorndyke walked into the bank and caught Nixon's eye. The two moved into Amos Dudley's old office and found seats. "I'm not sure what you wanted to talk about, Charles, but I certainly have something to talk to you about. I just spent a short time with Commissioner Hoagland and he told me he believes you are the person behind the broadsheet that's delivered around town. True?"

"It is and that's why I asked to have this meeting." He had an amazed look on his face, was almost blushing, before continuing. "I can't take the offer you made about me helping to run this bank. My father will scream when he hears that, but what I've always wanted was to run a real newspaper. That's what's behind *FYI.*"

"Without a printing press you hand write your news-paper," Ben Thorndyke said. "And you can't afford a printing press, eh?"

"About the size of it, sir. My thoughts and efforts would not be on the bank I'm afraid."

"How much is a printing press?"

"There's more than just the press, there's boxes of type, boxes of wood cuts, ink, and of course, paper.

There's all of that available right now in Oregon City. A man was going to set up in the city and died of the flu. His whole operation is sitting at the courthouse and is available for nine hundred dollars."

"That's a lot of money. How would you make a living, Charles?"

"That's the question my father always asked but never understood my answer. A newspaper is a business, Mr. Thorndyke. It must make money to survive, and that money comes from two sources, purchases of the editions and advertising from the community."

Thorndyke was a successful business man and fully grasped what the young man was saying. "And you believe that a newspaper in Brookside would make enough money to support itself and you?"

"Brookside County has many people who would buy the paper if it was available, and there are many businesses that would advertise." Young Nixon smiled as he looked at Ben Thorndyke. "I believe sir that I would be calling on you to advertise your many operations."

Thorndyke laughed and nodded his head. "I'm sure you would. And you could do this? You could make this a successful operation?" Thorndyke asked. "Sounds a little iffy to me. Have you done any research on the idea of a newspaper in the county?"

"I have indeed," Charles Nixon said. He got up and walked out of the office saying he'd be right back. He came back with a sheaf of papers. "Some of the answers are here. The number of businesses that might advertise, and number of homes and businesses that might subscribe. Turned into dollars, it would pay for the press and for ink and paper, and make a decent living for me."

He spread the papers in front of Ben Thorndyke who

started reading through the jumble. He read, looked at Nixon, read some more, and got up to walk around the room. "Want a silent partner, Mr. Nixon?"

———

AMOS DUDLEY MADE HIS WAY SLOWLY TOWARD THE kitchen of his large home, still covered in bandages, still hurting in every joint. So many blows to the head, so many kicks to the ribs, and an equal number of bruises on his back and legs have the man whimpering in pain with every step. He never hired help around the house, called such expenses nonsense and desperately wished there was someone around to light the fires on a cold morning like this one.

There was no kindling in the box, no firewood stacked by the fireplace, and the kitchen was equally ill-prepared for a cold morning. He had a wool bathrobe wrapped tight as he made his way to the back porch for an armload of kindling. His balance was off, he dropped most of the little sticks before he made it to the fireplace. It was the second trip that ended his day. Coming back in with three heavy split cedar logs he tripped, falling against the rock fireplace and onto the floor amidst the logs and dropped kindling.

He was dazed by the fall, knew he had ripped several of the stitches on his head, and found he was unable to get to his feet. *I'll kill the man next time I see him.* In Dudley's mind the man who attacked him was Constable Tobias Kennedy. He spent hours in bed thinking the attack through, over and over, and it was so logical.

Kennedy knew that Irene Creighton would rather spend her time with the banker than someone who was unable to perform his duties. It had to be Kennedy who waited for Dudley in the barn. But what could he do about it? *I must get word to Claude Atkins. Kennedy was desperate for the widow Creighton and tried to kill me because of her deep feeling for me.*

Dudley's mind had been severely affected by the many blows his head took. The cold seeped its way through the wool bathrobe and nightshirt underneath, and Amos Dudley lay in a heap, softly crying himself into a deep sleep.

Just before the shades of dark fell, the banker had another thought. *If that woman has eyes for the man who tried to kill me, I'll see to it that she has no home to live in. I'll see to it that her children will never see her again. I'll show her who she should spend time with.*

It was several hours later that Doctor Winslow made a stop to see his patient. "My God, Amos, what have you done?" A few cedar logs scattered on the floor, and Dudley sprawled amongst them, his head a bloody mess. He wasn't dead, the doctor determined immediately, but might not be that far from it either.

His breathing was labored, the doctor tried to listen to his heartbeat but it was weak and sporadic. The doctor eased an eyelid open and found a blank stare and was unable to revive the man.

Winslow got the fire started first and then attempted to get Dudley awake enough that he could be moved to a couch near the fire. "I'm not a young man, Amos. You have to help me." Dudley was rotund and either unable to help or unwilling. Either way, the doctor could not move him onto the couch. He kept mumbling something about getting the word to Claude Atkins.

Winslow couldn't understand what was being said,

stoked the fire and left Dudley on the floor wrapped in a wool blanket. "I'll be back quick as I can, Amos. You'll not die, I'm sure." The doctor walked out onto the street hoping to find a young man or two to help get Dudley either on the couch or in bed, but there was no one around. It was a quick walk to Murphy's Inn and possible help.

There is more than one woman in this little village of ours who would suggest I leave him lie until he's dead. Lecherous old fool. It would serve him right, too. Winslow had a wonderful conversation with himself on the two-block walk to Murphy's.

"Ah, constable, am I glad to see you."

"Hello, doctor. You're a mess. What's wrong?" Kennedy said. "How can I help you?" Kennedy was standing with Jack McGee, each with mugs of well laced coffee.

"Amos Dudley took a terrible fall this morning and I can't get him off the floor and back in bed. The place was freezing cold when I got there, too." Doctor Winslow was breathing hard from the fast walk and Kennedy motioned for Murphy to get him some coffee.

"Better put some of the good stuff in it, too," he chuckled. "Let's go see what we can do about Mr. Dudley, Jack. You come along when you get your breath back, Doc."

Dudley was wrapped in a fetal position, he had a desperate grip on the edge of the blanket when Kennedy and McGee walked in. Jack McGee immediately stirred up the fire and added some wood while Kennedy bent to check on Dudley.

"Feeling bad are we? Let's get you up on that couch, Dudley." Kennedy eased the man into a sitting position, motioned McGee to take one shoulder, he had the other, and they stood the man up and moved him the two steps to the couch. "Easy now, Dudley. Let's get you stretched out, eh. It might make you feel better to know I caught the rascal who beat you up"

"Let go of me. You," he said, his eyes wild with fright. "You. You tried to kill me. Stay away. Stay back."

Dudley's eyes wildly swung back and forth between Kennedy and McGee, and he kept saying something about his attacker. He wasn't aware that the two men moved him from the floor to the couch, made him comfortable. He wasn't the type of man to give his thanks for something that was already expected. After all, it was Kennedy's job to catch perpetrators of violence.

His mind was flawed and neither Kennedy nor McGee could understand what he was rattling on about. "Killer. You catch killers. You're a killer. Tell Atkins," he mumbled over and over.

"I'd like you to meet our new deputy, Dudley. This is Jack McGee, one of our newcomers and an upstanding citizen of Brookside. In your absence the county authorized two full time deputies for the department, and McGee has already made his first arrest." Kennedy wanted to prod the banker, not aware that the man fully believed that it was Kennedy who had attacked him.

The only reaction from Dudley was a scowl and a quick look at McGee. "Jack, why don't you get a fire lit in the kitchen and get some coffee boiling. I think Mr. Dudley will feel better about things with a cup of hot coffee."

"He doesn't seem pleased with me being here," Jack said. "Not even about us getting him up off the floor.

"He's a difficult man to please, Jack." Kennedy was going to say more but Doctor Winslow made his arrival known.

"Ah, good, you got him off the floor. If one of you gentlemen would fill a bowl with warm water, I'll see what I can do about that mess he's made of his head. I see he's still talking some kind of nonsense about Claude Atkins knowing who it was who attacked him. In juries to the head do alter one's thinking, I believe."

"I was just about to get the fire going in the kitchen, Doctor. I'll get your water and get a pot of coffee boiling as well." Jack McGee said.

"Thank you," Winslow said. Turning to Kennedy, the doctor's demeanor changed somewhat. "Seems some of these men accused of wrong-doing are being killed rather than arrested, constable. Is that really necessary?" His eyes were narrowed and his mouth was turned down showing his anger.

Kennedy sat back on his haunches next to the couch and gave the doctor a stern look. "It would be best if all those accused of a crime had their chance before a judge, doc, but life isn't always laid out in perfect patterns like that. You really need to wake up to that. When a man comes at you with a knife, his intentions are obvious. One can't say, 'now, now, sir, I want to arrest you, not hurt you'. No, doc, one defends one's self."

Kennedy wanted to say something along the lines of, I won't tell you how to doctor someone, don't tell me how to stop a killer, but he used his wits and humor to make the point. "We don't have criminals with good manners here, I'm afraid. Quick and brutal response is often required."

Doctor Winslow didn't respond and Kennedy stood up and walked to the kitchen. *He spends his time trying to help the sick and injured so, in a way, I understand his feelings. He'll never understand mine, though. I help people, too, but he doesn't see that part of the job, trying to keep people safe, only the violence.*

"How's that coffee coming, Jack?"

CHAPTER 32

I rene Creighton and her daughter Carrie walked into Thaddeus Younger's market late in the afternoon following her day at the Thorndyke office. It was cold and blustery with leaves from the few trees along the walkway doing their wild and invigorating dance as they sashayed their way to the ground.

"I see you have some fresh venison, Mr. Younger. Makes for a fine stew." Irene said.

"Skinny Doten brought in a beautiful black tail buck this morning, Mrs. Creighton. Hello Carrie. My but you're growing as fast as a morning glory runner." Younger actually smiled. "How much would you like Mrs. Creighton?"

"I think two pounds and we'll need a few vegetables, too," Irene said. She and Carrie walked through the displays and put up potatoes, carrots, and onions in their basket. "That should do us," she said.

"Thank you," Younger said, taking Irene's money. "Saw the constable and his deputy put those Kinsey twins out of business. We need to get all these horrible criminal immigrants out of Oregon."

"I just met Owen Hardy and his wife this afternoon, Mr. Younger. They're awfully nice people. And the Boyingtons are delightful. Certainly not criminals. Well, we must be on our way. Say hello to the missus," she said, urging Carrie out the door.

"He doesn't like people, does he?" Carrie said. "I like people."

Irene laughed. "So do I, honey. It's cold. Let's hurry home and get the fires lit."

"Mr. Kennedy is a nice man," Carrie said. "I like the way he talks and he's always smiling. He makes me laugh."

"He's a true gentleman, sweetie," Irene said. *He makes me laugh, too. Last night was wonderful in so many ways. My father would approve of me seeing Tobias. Where were you ten or twelve years ago, Tobias Kennedy?*

"Can he have supper with us again, mama? When you played the piano he and I danced. that was really fun. He whirled me around, and then sang what he called a lullaby."

"The man has a beautiful voice," Irene said. "I'm glad you like him, and maybe I'll just invite him over again."

"Do it soon, mama," Carrie said.

Soon, yes. Very soon, Irene thought, a beautiful smile splashed across her lovely face. *And we'll be going to the Fireman's Social, too.* "I'm not sure we have any apple pie left," Irene said.

"Mr. Kennedy ate the last piece, mama," Carrie laughed, "but we have apples. Luke Hoagland and his father dropped off a basket, remember? I'll peel some if you'll make another pie."

"One apple pie coming up," Irene laughed. Memories of the night before were playing some fine music as they made their way through the muddy streets. *Toby said that*

Amos Dudley was going to live but Ben Thorndyke said he would not be the manager of the bank. Ed Creighton never did make a loan. Toby said that Dudley made all that up just so he could be with me. That's despicable.

As they passed near the courthouse Kennedy walked out. "Two of my favorite people. Good evening," the big lawman said. "I want to thank you for the most delightful evening I've had in years, Irene. We must do that again."

"Indeed we must," she said, realized what she'd said, and blushed, trying to duck her head from his view. "You look tired, sir,"

"Ah, yes. Seems that Amos Dudley had a fall and Jack McGee and I, along with the good doctor have been trying to get him nursed back into bed. Hit his head again and is talking in riddles."

"Riddles?" Carrie asked. "I love riddles."

"Probably not these," Kennedy laughed. "When we got him calmed down, it became obvious that the man thinks I'm the one who attacked him last week. Utter nonsense."

"I would think so," Irene said. "You've helped the man more than anyone in town and I think he should be a little more thankful of that."

Kennedy didn't say anything about what Dudley also rambled on about. Could he take her home? Could he take Carrie from her? The constable didn't have those kinds of answers. "He is still certain that Ed Creighton had a loan. You must get with Claude Atkins again, and soon. Tomorrow morning at the latest."

KENNEDY STOOD ON THE STEPS OF THE COURTHOUSE watching Irene and Carrie head for home, saw Ben Thorndyke coming his way and walked toward him. "Evening, Ben. How has your day been?"

"From what I can gather, immensely better than yours," he said. "I think we need to have a chat with Claude Atkins, if you'd be kind enough to lead the way." Ben Thorndyke was normally effusive, bright, and cheerful, but Kennedy saw dark clouds storming across the man's face.

"Trouble, Ben?" Kennedy turned and led the two back into the courthouse and to the County Attorney's office. Atkins was seated at his desk, a stern and clouded look aimed at Kennedy as the two walked in.

"Glad you're here, Toby. You, too, Ben. Take seats, please. You just missed Doctor Winslow."

"He was at my place earlier, Claude," Thorndyke said. "That's why we're here."

"You two seem to be riled about something," Kennedy said. "What's going on to get you so excited?"

"Doc Winslow said that Amos Dudley is accusing you, Constable, of being the man who attacked him in his barn. The doctor believes him and wants me to file charges. The doctor says you have a mean history of killing people so they won't have a chance to defend themselves."

"That's just pure nonsense," Kennedy said. "I'm the one who caught the attacker."

"And killed him," Atkins said. "Calm down, Toby. I don't for a minute agree with the doctor or Amos, but it definitely looks bad. I'm of the opinion that Dudley knows he can't get you out of office as he planned, and is taking this road to victory. Destroy your reputation, credibility, your good name."

"The good doctor is a fool," Ben Thorndyke said. "I told him so when he came to me with that story." Thorndyke got up and literally paced around the tiny office. "The doctor also said that Dudley plans to file charges claiming that Irene Creighton is a bad mother, wants Carrie removed from the home, and Irene jailed, thereby losing her property."

"My God." Kennedy exploded from his chair, glared at Thorndyke and Atkins, walked around the room and sat back down. "I'll not let that happen. Amos Dudley has lost his mind, is taking out his frustrations on those who can't fight back. He'll not hurt Irene. He won't."

Thorndyke looked at Claude Atkins. "So, what is it we do?"

"One thing at a time, Ben. First we exonerate our constable, then we put a stop to having the widow Creighton's life destroyed, and then we have a long sobering talk with the doctor. Always, gentlemen, it's best to fight these kinds of fires one item at a time." He saw that the two men were able to see his point. "Put them all in the same pot and your stew won't be edible. Take them one problem at a time, and you have a better platter." All three were shaking their heads in agreement.

"Amos said you attacked him, constable. What do you say in your defense?" Atkins had sheets of paper, pen and kink at the ready.

Kennedy looked around the room and realized that Atkins planned follow through with the possibility of charges being filed. This was not the time for glib commentary, but rather, straight from the shoulder truth.

"I was having breakfast when Hammerhead found me and brought me to Dudley's. My investigation found footprints leading around behind the barn where I found that a horse had been tethered. Now listen, Hammerhead was with me. He'll verify my words." Kennedy looked at the two men and continued.

"Just days before, while investigating the brutal murder of the Boyington child I found horse prints indicating the horse was missing a shoe. The undertaker was with me. He'll verify those words. The prints behind Dudley's barn were the same."

"Is that why you attempted to arrest the man you say attacked Dudley?" Atkins asked.

"Exactly why," Kennedy said. "In resisting, he attacked me with a knife and I killed him. Any man in this room would have done the same." He looked back and forth to Thorndyke and Atkins, and continued. "There was a second man at the Boyington murder and he's now sitting in a cell, badly wounded, again for resisting by way of attacking me. In both instances, I had a witness with me, who will be more than happy to testify on my behalf."

Atkins was more than pleased hearing the word 'witness' and looked at Ben who nodded with a grim smile. "As far as I'm concerned, constable, that's good enough for me. I'll not file charges of any kind. You were simply doing your duty and did not attack Amos Dudley."

"Good," Ben Thorndyke said. "Now, let's get on with the real problem. How do we save Irene Creighton from Dudley's wild accusations?" He almost said, how do we keep Irene Creighton from the man's bed. "I think, Constable, that you might have a lot to say in this matter. You and the lady are quite the centerpiece in back fence gossip." He chuckled but Kennedy frowned.

"Among the women in our little village, who knows Mrs. Creighton the best?" Atkins asked.

"My wife," Thorndyke said. "They're together almost

every day. And, she visits with Jacob Hoagland's wife as well."

"Can't ask for better," Atkins said. "Now, let's pay a little visit with our doctor, shall we?" He saw the two others look at each other. "Yes, gentlemen, all three of us."

CHAPTER 33

"I need to get out of the house, Jacob. Can we take a carriage ride around the valley?" Martha Hoagland was seven months pregnant and it was one of those wonderful late autumn days with plenty of sunshine, a nip in the air, and no wind to make it bitter cold. "Maybe we could visit some of the newcomers. You've met them all and I've only heard names."

"The way the wind was blowing last night I would have bet on a storm coming in," Jacob said. "You'd never know it looking out the window right now." He turned to Luke, just coming in the door. "Why don't you harness the horses to the carriage, Luke, saddle your mule, and we'll leave for a little ride shortly."

Lucas shot back out the door, hooraying all the way to the barn. Martha smiled. "Never had that kind of energy when I was a child," she said. "Seemed that sometimes all we children ever had was work and more work." She was aware that her childhood had deprived her of so much. She looked at Jacob and knew their life was completely different from her earlier one.

Luke runs free but does so much around here. Just coming

eleven and works as hard as any man in the valley, yet is happier than I ever was as a child. All because I married the right man.

"Luke does more work around this old farm than any kid in the valley, Martha." Jacob echoed her thoughts. "He's born to the land I think. The difference is, you weren't raised to think that work around a farm is good. It was always a difficult and hard chore in your mind. As hard as it is, Luke looks on his work as a good thing to do."

She looked at Jacob and smiled. *He's right. Luke and Jacob have fun all the time they're working harder than I've ever had to. Because of attitude.* She let her thoughts drift around about attitude and couldn't keep the smile away.

"You're right, Jacob. Lucas helped me all summer with our kitchen garden. I never once had to ask or tell him. We've got dried beans for the winter, potatoes and onions for the winter, and he spent hours working with you out in the fields, too." She had a tired smile on her face and Hoagland walked to where she was sitting and ran his fingers through her hair and down across her neck.

"It's all in the attitude, Jacob. I look at you two in the barn or out in the fields, laughing, sometimes cussing, and getting so dirty, so covered in sweat, and having so much fun, too. I'm like that in my kitchen, Jacob. It's attitude."

Hoagland took her in his arms, stroked her hair, kissed her a little longer than maybe he should have. "Is this going to be a Christmas baby, Martha?"

"Maybe a little after, Jacob. Middle of January I think. He's squirming around some."

"We'll need to get you help," he said. "From the weather standpoint, it's a terrible time to have a baby, but from the farm side of things, it's just right." Jacob saw her give him a questioning look and continued. "There's very little that Luke and I can do out in the fields. You'll have to put up with us being your help around here."

"That's frightening," she chuckled, reaching for his hand. "Why did you suggest Lucas ride his mule while we're in the carriage?"

"I have plans on being very close to you, us wrapped in wool blankets, while I drive us around the valley. That's why."

"That's why I love you, Jacob. I hope this is a boy baby I'm lugging around. He'll be Jacob Junior whether you like it or not. That's what I wanted Lucas to be, but this one will be."

"Yes Ma'am," is all Jacob said. He couldn't hide his smile and helped get Martha wrapped in a great coat and gathered up wool blankets. Martha pointed to a basket on the table and Jacob grabbed it up and walked them out the kitchen door. Luke had the team and carriage ready for them. "All right, buster, let's get your mama in the carriage and wrapped tight."

Martha handed Luke a small package. "Put these in your saddle bag. Fresh oatmeal cookies, son. We'll stop and have some cold fried chicken, a little later, too."

"Amazing," Jacob said. "You fried chicken and made cookies while Luke and I did our chores this morning? No wonder you're tired. How did I get lucky enough to marry you before all those other sad men found you? Lead us out to the road Luke. You're our guide. We want to meet some of our new neighbors."

———

KEN BOYINGTON WAS DRAGGING A LIFT OF LOGS DOWN the side of the hill to where he was building their cabin. He usually chained three logs of lodge pole pine to drag down, but today, had four. The two mules knew their job and Ken walked along with their lead rope, talking to them the whole way.

It was dangerous work, dragging the heavy logs downhill. If one got loose, or the hill was too steep and the logs ran up on the mules, men and animals could die. It was Boyington's eyes and ears and the mules knowing their job that kept things moving along safely.

"This is the kind of morning I love," he called out to the mules. The sky was clear, there was no wind, and the air had a chill to it. "Just look at that little homesite down there, boys," he called out. "Those walls you're looking at are the ones we built. And these logs here will become stringers and rafters. Ain't it a beaut?"

Boyington was strong when they arrived in Oregon Territory, particularly after making the crossing, but with all the work he's done clearing the land, leveling it, and cutting and dragging timber for their cabin, he's bulked up considerably. Sandra, pregnant, does most of the skinning of the logs, helps as much as she can with the long two-man buck saw, and works with the mules as Ken levers the heavy logs into position.

"Time to take a break, big boy," she called out as he pulled the mules to a stop. "Sonja and I need something to eat and so do you. Put the mules in the grass and join us at the fire." They were still living in and around the lean-to they made from their wagon and its canvas. They had an open fire and also the iron wood-fired cook stove they bought from Ben Thorndyke. It stood out in the open, its shortened chimney often belching smoke. It would eventually be the central piece in their kitchen.

"Looks like we've got company coming, Sandra. Get your shotgun." There was never a time, since the death of little Spike that one or the other of them had a gun nearby. Boyington swore they would never be caught with their guard down again. For the last several days they had seen a lone man riding in the neighborhood. It was unusual since they were almost at the end of the little dirt trail the led up higher.

"Is it that same man?" Sandra called out. "He scars me, Ken."

"No I don't think so. This is a small buggy and there's someone on the back of a mule, too."

Sandra stepped out of the lean-to with the scatter gun and looked out where Ken was pointing. "That's Jacob Hoagland," she said. "What a nice surprise."

"Perfect," Ken said. "I've been wanting to talk to him about a bull for the girls we bought. His herd is one of the best I've seen in these parts." He acquired several heifers from around the valley and needed a bull. "We'll be late with calves this year even if I got one today."

Hoagland waved as he brought the buggy to a stop. Luke jumped down from his mule and took the lead rope from his father. "Nice to see you, Ken. Hello, Sandra," Hoagland said. Beautiful day, eh?"

He helped Martha down from the buggy and Luke led the carriage and his mule to a tree where they could have grass and shade. He didn't miss seeing Sandra holding a shotgun when they drove in. "Thought for sure we were getting another storm, but looks like it took another track," Hoagland said.

"Wind blew things around last night is about all," Ken said. There were several recently built chairs around the fire and Boyington motioned for everyone to sit. "Got a fresh pot of coffee boiling and I'm sure we can find a platter of biscuits if we look around some."

"Grab that big basket, Luke," Martha said. "I brought some fried chicken that might just go well with biscuits. How are you folks getting along? That cabin's going up fast."

"It is," Ken said.

"What's with the shotgun?" Jacob asked.

"Had a man lurking around the place the last couple of days," Ken said. "After losing Spike, we ain't taking no chances."

"I take it you didn't recognize this stranger. Have you said anything to the constable? Kennedy's got help now and is putting a stop to a lot of the mischief that was taking place."

"I was planning on riding in later today. Didn't recognize the man at all. Tall and skinny is about the best I can come up with. Long beard and hair, and he wore a buckskin shirt."

"Sounds like Seamus O'Leary," Jacob said. "Trouble maker but he has been accused more than once of stealing from people and businesses. Kennedy needs to know about this."

Sandra stood still for just a minute, remembering their time in Virginia. *Weren't nobody come to visit us and surely nobody never brought us fried chicken. They were so cold to us because we had to farm that other man's land. Weren't ours to farm and we 'bout starved cuz of it.*

"That's most wonderful, Mrs. Hoagland. Thank you."

"Please, call me Martha. We're neighbors." She looked at the two, so brown from working every day and all day in the sun, and so strong doing so much heavy work on the cabin and the land. "Your place is going to be comfortable and warm. It's the hardest work, building a home, and the end result is so wonderful," she said.

Sandra stepped into the lean-to and put the shotgun down, turned, and came back out with a basket of biscuits wrapped in a cotton towel. "I made these this morning, but they'll need to be warmed by the fire. Don't have a milk cow yet so don't have any fresh butter but there is some good peach jam."

"I love peach jam," Luke cried out. "And fried chicken."

Sitting around the fire, plates on their laps, brought memories to both families of their crossing. In Hoagland's mind, it was several years ago, but for Ken Boyington it was like yesterday. "Caught myself looking around for Indian trouble," he chuckled, flipping a chicken bone into the hot coals. "Our crossing was troubled most of the way. Trouble from some of those in our group and trouble from both Indians and white marauders. Feels good to have you folks visiting with us. Next year we'll be sitting at our kitchen table for a repast like this."

"Ben Thorndyke said you're looking for a bull or two to get your herd started." Jacob said. "Come around tomorrow and we'll take a look at a couple of nice young ones I've got. They get along well in this hilly country and are looking to make friends with some heifers."

"I'll be there," Ken said. *Just like that he offers to sell me a bull or two. I would have had to pry one loose back in Virginia, even if the old farmer didn't want the bull anyway.* He looked over to Sandra and smiled. *We made the right decision.*

The conversation continued for some time, the fried chicken and basket of biscuits disappeared, and the fire had been stoked several times. "It's a good feeling knowing that the constable found the men who killed our little boy," Ken said, "but he'll be missed forever. We have a new baby coming but I'll just have to keep Spike locked in my heart."

Sandra wrapped her arms around the big man and tried to hold back the tears. "We're lucky to have a man like Mr. Kennedy around. Could have used him back in Virginia." She looked over to Luke. "You're a good boy, Luke."

"What brought that on?" Ken asked.

"Luke said that if we wanted some he'd be glad to bring a basket of apples for us." She smiled and winked at the boy. "I think he wants some apple pie."

"I love apple pie," he said, stepping up and onto the mule.

CHAPTER 34

"It was a long afternoon but I'm glad we visited them," Martha said. "It felt good to be in the fresh air, to watch you and Mr. Boyington wrestle those logs. He's one brute isn't he?"

"He is that. Doing the work that Luke and I do keeps me in pretty good shape but Ken Boyington is probably the strongest man I've ever met. He don't need those mules to do his plowing come spring."

Martha laughed and poked Jacob in the ribs. "You're the strongest man I've ever met."

It wasn't a long ride back to their place and it was Lucas who spotted the tracks leading up their pathway. "Somebody's been here, dad. Might still be here. Prints going in and none coming out."

"Come here and take over the buggy," Jacob said. "Give me your mule." He reached behind the buggy seat and grabbed his shotgun and mounted the mule. "Stay well back, Luke and protect your mama." Luke jumped in the buggy and grabbed the reins. His eyes were roving all over the property.

Luke, coming eleven, was big and strong for his age,

and never questioned what his father just said. Was it the times? Was it the way he had been raised? Still almost a baby in some eyes, almost a grown man in others, Luke took on the responsibility as if it was not only expected of him, but something he knew he had to. "Be careful, papa," he said.

Luke looked over at his mother and smiled and Sandra saw Jacob writ large in the boy's face. *The spittin' image of his father in so many ways and yet he's just a boy.* She turned and watched as Jacob rode the mule toward their now large home. *We're in our fourth year here in the territory, our ranch has doubled in size, and the community is in a fearful state. Is it the newcomers, as that mean Mr. Younger swears it is? Is the fear because Mr. Kennedy is doing his job as the banker says? Or is it opportunity as Jacob insists it is?*

Hoagland rode at a trot toward the big house, still about a quarter mile up the trail. The visitor's prints stood out and when the Hoagland home came into view he saw a horse tied off to a cottonwood tree near the kitchen porch. He stepped down from the mule and left it ground tied, walking slowly, off to the side, not straight in toward the house.

Hoagland was in a stand of brush and small trees, across the yard from the kitchen porch when a man ran from the back door to the horse. "Stop right there!" Hoagland yelled it out, bringing the shotgun up to his shoulder. The man turned and Hoagland immediately recognized Seamus O'Leary. "Don 't make this worse than it is, O'Leary."

O'Leary pulled an ancient one-shot flintlock pistol from his belt, cocked it, dropped the striker, and aimed it at Hoagland. "Don't do that, O'Leary. My shotgun will cut you in half. Drop the gun."

O'Leary pulled the trigger and the slug tore a hole in Jacob Hoagland's lower leg. Kneeling now, Jacob unloaded the first barrel, driving Seamus O'Leary back several steps, but not knocking him down. O'Leary, bleeding and crying out in pain, mounted his horse and sunk his heels hard, trying to turn the horse toward the driveway.

Hoagland fired off the second barrel, knowing full well he hit the man hard, but the gunshot gave O'Leary's horse a bigger command to run than the heels to its sides. Jacob opened the gun and slid two more rounds in but O'Leary was already out of range by then.

Luke brought the buggy right up to where Jacob was kneeling in the dirt and jumped down. "No, son. Take care of your mother and the horses first. I'm hurt but not that bad. Skedaddle, now, and take care of your mother." Hoagland pulled a handkerchief from his jacket pocket and tied off the leg wound, limped to Luke's mule and stepped into the saddle.

"Keep your mama safe, Luke," he yelled swinging the mule around and headed down the path, following O'Leary. It wasn't hard to follow the man as the horse had slowed considerably about a mile down the trail. Third Creek Road ran right into Brookside along the river, and Hoagland found it strange that a wounded man would ride right into town.

He's hurt bad and the horse is just wandering its way home. I'll find the man sprawled in the mud soon. O'Leary lived in a small cabin tucked away behind Thaddeus Younger's grocery, and as Hoagland thought, he found the thief face down in the mud in front of Younger's store, his left foot tangled in a stirrup.

Two men ran from the store to help get O'Leary free of the leather before the horse threw a fit. "He's been shot," Hammerhead Povolny said. "My God, man, look at his face."

"What happened here?" Jack McGee, wearing his brand new badge of office, said as he continued to try to get O'Leary out of the saddle.

"I shot him," Hoagland said as he rode up. McGee saw the blood on Jacob's leg and helped him down from the mule. "Caught the fool robbing my house. I'm shot as well. One of you needs to run for the doctor and for the constable. Hurry, please. Both of us have lost a lot of blood." Hoagland tried to walk over toward O'Leary and almost fell down, catching hold of the saddle skirt just in time. "Let's get him untangled and then both of us need to sit down," Jacob said, weaving, tripping, as he tried to walk up to O'Leary's horse.

"I'm Jack McGee, Constable's deputy. Let's get the two of you inside. Hammerhead, run for the doctor and then find Kennedy."

Hoagland was weak from loss of blood but was able to help get O'Leary's leg free and McGee dragged the thief inside Younger's store, followed by a limping county commissioner. McGee plopped the bleeding and unconscious O'Leary in a chair near the pot-belly stove and saw to it that Jacob Hoagland was seated as well.

"Tell me all about it, commissioner," McGee said. He stuffed a log in the stove and poured coffee for the two of them.

"Wife, Luke, and I came home from a visit with neighbors and found O'Leary coming out of our house. I demanded he stop and instead, he shot me. I shot him back with the shotgun but he was able to get on his horse and run off. I trailed him here." Jacob was slurring some of his words, his eyes weren't fully open, and blood was dripping from his leg wound.

"You're one tough feller," Jack McGee said. "If you'd had a slug in that shotgun old Seamus O'Leary would be dead right about now. As it is, you peppered him pretty good with your bird load. He'll live, I think. Let me see what I can do about you."

Jack McGee knelt down in front of Jacob Hoagland and undid the rag tied around the wound. "Nasty," he said, "but I don't think it hit any bones. Doc'll be able to get this fixed up, I'm sure. I'll clean it up some before he gets here."

"Just what's going on here?" Thaddeus Younger said, coming out into the store from his living quarters behind. "They're bleeding all over the store. Get these men out of here. They're making a mess of my store. Get 'em out I say." He tried to get Seamus O'Leary out of the chair, but O'Leary's dead weight was more than the storekeeper could handle.

"Take it easy, Mr. Younger. These men are seriously wounded. The doctor will be here shortly," McGee said. "You're hurting that man. Leave him be." Younger was trying to jerk O'Leary out of his chair and McGee had to physically restrain him. "That's enough now. This man is in my custody and I'm not going to tell you again to leave him alone."

He took Younger by the arm and made him step back several feet from O'Leary. "You put your hands on me again and I'll have you charged," Younger said. "There's blood all over the floor, on the chairs. Get these men out of here. Where's the constable when we need him. You get these men out of my store."

"I'm the constable's deputy, Mr. Younger, as you well know. These two men are wounded, one of them is in my custody, and when the doctor gets here, we'll get them moved. Not one minute before. Now, stand back."

McGee's big body stood between O'Leary's and Hoagland's, and Younger spun around and walked back toward his living quarters just as the doctor and Hammerhead Povolny arrived.

"As deputy, I suppose you shot these men instead of just arresting them?" Doctor Winslow said.

"No, he didn't," Jacob Hoagland said. "Seamus shot me and I shot him. You're awfully quick to throw blame at people, Doc." Jacob turned to Hammerhead. "Find Kennedy?"

"I left word where we are for him. He'll be along."

"Probably drinking at Murphy's," Doc Winslow said. He bent down to look at Seamus O'Leary's torn up face. "Couldn't have made a worse mess if you'd tried, Hoagland. No need for this kind of violence and destruction of a human body."

"Hope you remember those words if you find your-self being shot someday, Doc," Jacob said. "How about treating this old leg of mine first. I'm the homeowner who shot a burglar. He's the burglar."

"All right, all right. Justify your violence any way you can. I brought the buggy so help me get these men in it and I'll get 'em fixed up at my place."

Jack McGee helped Hoagland out to the buggy and got him settled then went back in to help Hammerhead carry O'Leary out and lay him in the back. "They're all yours, Doc," McGee said.

"Oh, no. You two follow along and help get these men into my place."

Younger came out and stood on the porch of his store. "Who's going to clean up this mess? You can't just ride off and leave my store a bloody mess. You can't," he said again, but it was obvious they would. Younger stormed back in screaming for his wife.

248

"That will be a scene I don't want any part of," Jack McGee chuckled stepping into his saddle. "Might have more patients for you, doc, when the Youngers get through."

Doctor Winslow just humphed a bit and got his horse started. Constable Kennedy saw them as he turned the corner and followed along on foot. "Looks nasty, McGee. What happened?"

"Seamus O'Leary was caught robbing the Hoagland home. The commissioner shot him in the face with his shotgun." McGee looked back. "Mr. Younger is about to file a complaint, against me, I'm afraid."

"You?" Kennedy laughed. "What on earth did you do to him?"

"I let two men bleed all over his store."

Kennedy just looked at him as they stopped in front of Winslow's place.

CHAPTER 35

"**W**hen are you going to do something about these newcomers killing people, robbing and hurting people?" Thaddeus Younger was standing, his legs spread, in front of Constable Kennedy's desk. "A shooting right in front of my store. Blood everywhere. But you weren't there to stop any of it. These newcomers must be flushed from this valley. We're supposed to be civilized in Brookside."

Kennedy sat back with just the slightest grin on his ruddy face. *Not one single word of truth in what he just said. He's as bad as Doc Winslow is.* "Neither man was shot anywhere near your store, Thaddeus and you know it. Neither of those men are newcomers and you know it. And my deputy was right there taking command of the situation. You know that, too."

"Yes, and he's the one that forced those men inside my store and he let them bleed all over the place. These newcomers are ruining our lives."

"Seamus O'Leary has been living in that cabin behind your store for several years, Younger. Jacob Hoagland has been ranching and farming in this valley for years.

Quit stirring up this nonsense of yours about newcomers. My deputy is a newcomer. The Hardy family that spent almost ten dollars at your store yesterday are newcomers. These are good people moving into our valley. You're profiting from them."

"Well, you'd better start doing a better job keeping these newcomers in line. That's all I've got to say." Younger spun around and stormed out of the office, slamming the door as he left.

It does make one feel better to slam the door. Kennedy chuckled and reached for a tin cup just as the door reopened.

"Younger's got quite an anger built up," Jacob Hoagland said. He limped into the office, followed by his son, Lucas. "Word from the good doctor is that O'Leary is going to live, Constable. The reason no one was at the farm is, we were visiting with the Boyington family. I'd like to thank you for hiring Jack McGee. He cooled a hot situation well."

"Glad to hear it, Jacob. I'll pass the word along his way." Kennedy sat back in his chair thinking about what Younger had to say, how Hoagland is doing with the attack and all, and working on what to do about Doctor Winslow.

"If you need more from me, I'll be at the farm, Constable. Let's go home, Luke," Hoagland said, limping out the door.

Younger's bit off a large wad thinking everything that happens around Brookside is the fault of those moving into our community and Hoagland simply accepts the new people. The last two major crimes were committed by folks who have lived here for some time. There is a connection, and I know it.

Kennedy's thoughts were on those attacks. *The Kinsey twins attacked McGee and O'Leary robs the Hoagland family, and the perpetrators are not among those classified as newcomers.* "Opportunity," Kennedy mumbled right out. *Because of the constant complaining from the likes of Thaddeus Younger and others, those of a criminal mind are using the newcomers as the goats and stepping up their attacks. The general public will assume the crimes were committed by those just arriving.* "Opportunity," he said again, getting to his feet.

The fire needed new wood, the coffee cup was empty, and looking out the one window in the office he swore he could see snowflakes coming down. "Opportunity," he mumbled. "It's like an offering when you think about it."

He wasn't smiling despite the fact he considered what he just thought as being the truth. *Truth isn't at the heart of my problems right now. The opportunity goes both ways. The people doing the dirty are almost helped along the way. Those being robbed are helping the thieves in their work.* He was alone in the office, carrying on a full two-way conversation and had the feeling that an answer was right around the corner.

"So, Mr. Constable, sir, what do you plan to do about this?" The mumbling took over from just sitting in front of the fire thinking things along. "I may just have a solution to all this," he said. "Murphy can help me as can whoever it is who writes these *FYI* broadsheets."

———

"IF WE THOUGHT THERE WERE ONE HUNDRED MEN LIVING in Brookside, Murphy," Kennedy said after settling himself in a chair near the fireplace at Murphy's Tavern and Inn, "how many might be a visitor to this fine purveyor of fine liquor during any week of the year?"

"Well now, Toby," Murphy started to answer, shook

his head slowly back and forth. "It would be nice if I could say all of them." He chuckled. "Hard to judge what with the weather and all contributing to my answer."

"Just a wild guess will do."

"Then, I must say about three quarters of them would visit with this publican," Murphy said. "Is this leading somewhere?"

That's more than I would have guessed, but he might just be right. "Might just be, Murph. I'd like you to help me end these home and business burglaries that have cropped up since the influx of newcomers to our little valley."

"Any way I can." *I hope he's not taking Younger's position. I hope he remembers how averse to hurting another human being I am.* "I will always be at your beck and command, Toby." Murphy swelled up a bit, his eyes and face changing from mirthful to serious. "What is it you'd like me to do? Remember now, I'm not going to shoot anyone. Never have, never will."

"Don't want you shooting anyone, Murph," Kennedy laughed. "Most of our crimes are committed because too many of us invite the burglars in."

"Really? How, Toby?"

"We leave our doors unlocked when we leave home or business. We let others see or hear about our money and other resources. We don't pay attention to what those around us are doing."

"Up to that last point I understand," Murphy said.

"Do you ever look around your windows from the outside, Murph? Like looking for footprints?" Murphy's eyes lit up and Kennedy continued. "Have you ever wondered why there was someone watching when you lock up at night?"

"I see where you're going," Murphy said. "I'm guilty of

all of that. Why, for heaven's sake, even more so. So, Mr. Constable, what is it you want me to do?"

"Just talk about what we've just talked about. Talk about protecting what we have, keeping our families safe, not believing that such a thing as a burglar would never be in our house. You get the idea?"

"Sure, and I will do just that." Murphy filled Kennedy's porcelain cup with brandy. "How much snow is coming in with this storm?"

"The wind's blowing it horizontal, Murph. There will be some serious drifting if it keeps up the same as it started. Not sure what's worse, rain and mud or snow and ice. Well, the snow is more enjoyable to look at," he chuckled. "Got to make my rounds."

"Do those rounds include a stop at the widow Creighton's, bucko?"

"That is a possibility, Murphy, and, it's none of your business." The heavy oak walking stick was heard thumping the floor as Kennedy made his way to the door.

————

KENNEDY'S FIRST STOP WAS AT THE THORNDYKE COMPLEX for a chat. "Nice storm coming in, Ben. You ready for winter?"

"Ah, Constable Kennedy. Good evening. Your new man Jack McGee kept that fracas at Younger's from getting out of hand. Looks like you picked a winner. Younger is in a huff, though. Blames every single problem on those moving into our valley. For a man being in business and not recognizing just how much these people are spending is insane. You have any ideas on how to cool him off?"

"Wish I did, Ben, but it isn't part of my job description either. He'll talk long and loud for a long time simply because he isn't a thinking man. Just a few minutes of contemplation and a thinking person would know the immigrants aren't the problem."

"What is the problem? We have thieves breaking into homes and businesses, we have attacks on citizens, but they aren't the work of those new to Brookside. Why now, Constable?"

"I just had this conversation with Murphy, Ben. I think it's opportunity. We leave our doors unlocked. We don't even check to see if someone might have been around while we were gone. We've become complacent. And those like the Kinsey twins, Seamus O'Leary, and several others are taking advantage of it."

"That's one fine answer. Think Younger would agree? I don't, but I think you're right." He paused for just a moment. "I may even have some help for you. You've read the broadsheet *FYI*." Kennedy nodded. "Young Charles Nixon has been putting that out and he and I have just formed a partnership to create a real newspaper for Brookside. He's on his way to Oregon City to purchase a press and all that goes with it."

Kennedy had a smile cross his face. "What a splendid idea. So, Nixon is the one, eh? He's done a good job with pen and ink." Kennedy walked around the room and came back to stand in front of Thorndyke.

"The one thing I'm concerned about is Doctor Winslow thinking I'm to blame for Dudley's attack. He's actually believing what Amos Dudley is saying. Doc actually believes that I'm the one who attacked Dudley."

"He's been here twice ranting about that," Ben Thorndyke said. "What you just said about leaving doors and windows unlocked, even open, fits Dudley's attack perfectly. His barn doors were unlocked as was his house." Thorndyke chuckled. "My barn doors were open to the world when my horse was stolen. Doc Winslow is getting old, Constable. He's having to do a lot more as far as doctoring goes since the influx of new people and the increase in crime."

Thorndyke had to chuckle. "You know, my own barn wasn't locked when that fool stole my horse. Dudley's place was open to a visitor, but we know it wasn't you. Doctor Winslow is wrong."

"He's going to say the wrong thing to the wrong person, Ben. He's the one who will need doctoring I'm afraid. His remarks cut all the way to the bone sometimes and there are those who won't take that kind of talk." Kennedy said. The constable was thinking of himself as well as others. "He's said some really mean things to me and about me, and they do hurt."

"How many people do you have locked up, Toby?"

Kennedy chuckled. "Maybe that's why Doc is angry at me. Travis Kinsey and Seamus O'Leary are both wounded and Doc has to come to the jail twice a day to take care of them. Territorial judge will be here next week and hopefully they'll be found guilty and transferred to the Oregon City prison. Don't have much room here."

"Have a good night, Constable. Keep us safe," Ben Thorndyke said. Kennedy's next stop was going to be quick visit with Irene Creighton, then a good supper at Murphy's, and a long night alone in his cabin.

"It's been a long day," he muttered, walking through strong winds and heavy snowfall. The warm light shining from the Creighton home brought a smile to his face. *I've never had a real relationship with a woman. This is an interesting feeling, standing out here, the wind whistling through the trees, and the warmth of a loving home inviting me in. A man could get used to this kind of feeling.*

"Just look at you, Tobias Kennedy," Irene said beckoning him in. "You're all but encased in ice. How long have you been standing out here?"

He had a sheepish, almost little-boy look on his face. "Just enjoying the light from your windows, Irene. So warm. Lovely, actually. Where's that little scamp of a Carrie girl?"

Carrie came rushing down the stairs and almost leaped in Kennedy's arms. "There you are," he said, getting a wonderful hug from the girl. "I just wanted to stop and make sure you were all right. Part of my duties, you know."

I hope it's more than that, Irene thought, seeing the big man holding her daughter and smiling at her. *No, I know it's more than that. Someday he'll hold me like that. Stop it now. Stop.* Irene smiled, her cheeks rosy from her thoughts, and led them into a warm kitchen. "You're just in time for supper, Toby. I have some venison in the pot with potatoes, onions, and carrots."

"And mama baked an apple pie, too," Carrie said. "She had to because you ate the rest of the other one."

"Carrie. Oh, my, Toby, she didn't mean anything by that."

"She's right, you know. I did finish that pie and it was delicious." He gave Carrie a big smile and a wink. "If I'm not— Well, yes, Irene, I'd love to have supper with my two favorite ladies."

CHAPTER 36

"Just exactly what are we going to do about this, Mr. Atkins?" Doctor Winslow was in the county attorney's office first thing in the morning. He had shaken off most of the snow and ice and settled down in a chair opposite Claude Atkins. Winslow was in his fifties and had come west with a fur trade company following his medical training. Never married, there are some who believe coming west may have been the result of a broken promise many years ago.

His compassion for the wounded and sick is well known in Oregon Territory, which extends from the western slope of the Rocky Mountains to the Pacific Ocean. His cantankerous personality is just as well known. As Murphy likes to say, "Old Doc Winslow calls 'em as he sees 'em and it's a poor man who wishes to contradict him."

"We have a vicious criminal posing as our county constable." Winslow said. His bushy eyebrows were drawn tight, his mouth grim, and his chin and jaw jutted straight out.

"I've known Tobias Kennedy for five years, Winslow.

You are, to put it in simple terms, wrong, sir. Amos Dudley is lying about being attacked by Kennedy and you are wrong in foisting off Dudley's story. You're an educated man, Doctor, but you're not acting like one. You're upset with the constable because he's a little rough on those he has to bring in. You're forgetting the fact that many of those people have tried to injure or kill the man."

Claude Atkins was well aware of how the doctor felt about violence of any kind, knew that the doctor was seriously opposed to Kennedy's rough ways with criminals, and was not going to allow Winslow to railroad him into any kind of legal actions against the constable.

"You and I are also aware of Dudley's recent attempts at getting Constable Kennedy removed from office. He has even attempted to have Irene Creighton thrown out of her home because of her and Kennedy's friendship. You're playing right into Dudley's hands, Winslow. I'll not be a part of it."

"You must file charges against the man. I demand it," Doctor Winslow said.

"Demands don't work on me, Doc. You are coming very close to abuse here, and Kennedy could well file some charges of his own. Go have a sip of brandy and think about what you're trying to do. Ruining a good man's reputation is a serious charge, sir."

The two men sat across the desk almost glaring at each other. Winslow was most caring of those injured, wounded, or ill, while at the same time had no truck with those committing violence. He and Kennedy had been at odds over Kennedy's ways with criminals for several years but other than voicing his disapproval had never sat and talked with the constable, never understood Kennedy's point of view, only knew some men died and other men were injured coming into official contact with the constable.

"I'll go over your head, Atkins. The man must be held accountable," Doctor Winslow said. He gathered his coat, hat, and scarf, and left the office, not bothering to close the door.

Claude Atkins didn't get up, there was no good byes, and he sat shaking his head, watching the old man walk toward the big courthouse doors. "You're a hard man yourself, Doc, but you don't see that part," he mumbled. Atkins was aware that Winslow could possibly go to the Territorial Governor but doubted he would.

I think I'll have a long talk with Kennedy and invite Ben Thorndyke and Jacob Hoagland to sit in on it. I'll bring out the big guns, he snickered, standing up and reaching for his winter's jacket and hat.

Atkins wasn't aware of it, but the idea of going over his head, as voiced by Doctor Winslow included calling on Ben Thorndyke and Jacob Hoagland to put their combined efforts to keep from getting Kennedy put out of office and behind bars.

———

"In my opinion, Doctor, you could not be more wrong," Ben Thorndyke said. "I've had many discussions with the constable about that morning at Amos Dudley's. I'm fully aware of the procedure Kennedy used to find the man responsible."

"Bah," Winslow said. "Hoagland will back me up. This man needs to be out of office and charged with attempted murder. I'll see to that."

"I'll tell you what, Doc," Thorndyke said. "You bring Jacob Hoagland and Amos Dudley to Murphy's Tavern tomorrow morning and I'll bring Claude Atkins and Tobias Kennedy, and we'll sit at the large family table and have this out. Be prepared to be embarrassed, Doctor. What you're doing is attempting to ruin a good man. I'll not hold anything back."

————

"YOU AGREED TO THAT? WHY?" MARTHA HOAGLAND SAT at the kitchen table with Jacob and Lucas, enjoying an oven roasted rack of pork ribs and boiled cabbage. "Constable Kennedy is our friend, Jacob. He's been an immense help to us. Why would you agree to testify against him at Murphy's?"

"I'm afraid you didn't fully understand what I said, Martha. Yes, I agreed to meet with Claude Atkins, Doctor Winslow, Amos Dudley, and the constable to discuss the charge of Kennedy attacking Dudley. I never said I was going to testify against the constable, and I'm not saying that right now. I'm saying, I'll be there. I'm more than sure that Dudley is lying, that Winslow has a grievance with Kennedy, and that the air needs to be freshened. All of this needs to come out in public."

"Is it true that Mr. Dudley's saying these things because Irene Creighton won't see him, sees the constable instead? Rather childish if you ask me," Martha said. "Something a school-boy might do."

"I wouldn't," Luke said.

That lightened the atmosphere in the kitchen and Martha got up to bring a still warm apple pie to the table. "When is this so-called discussion going to take place, Jacob?"

"We're having an early lunch at Murphy's tomorrow. I'm sure there will be some nasty words flung about but

Ben Thorndyke has told everyone involved that rude behavior at the table will not be acceptable. I think even Winslow will behave himself. He has an acid tongue at times, as you know."

I certainly hope no one gets hurt," she said.

"Only feelings, I'm sure." Jacob tried to smile but was fearful of the outcome. "Kennedy has big shoulders, has taken a beating before, but is angry at these charges being flung about. There's nothing behind the ugly words, and they have stung the man deep. He's a proud man, Martha. He's the only one who might get physical if the wrong things are said."

———

THE WORD OF AN IMPENDING MEETING TO DISCUSS something about Amos Dudley's recent beating spread through the village and among those who planned on being at Murphy's the following morning was Thaddeus Younger.

"By god I'm going to be there. All this violence because of these criminal newcomers has to end. Constable Kennedy has not done enough, has not seen to it that our homes and businesses are safe. We need someone who will end these violent people being allowed to come and ruin our lives."

Hammerhead Povolny just shook his head, having heard the rant many times over. "I think I might attend as well, Mr. Younger. I've worked with Toby several times over the years, chasing criminals, trying to keep Brookside safe. He's a good man, does a hard job well, and will have my support. In fact, I think I'll bring Sonny Kniessel with me. We've both worked with Toby."

"You just go on, then, Hammerhead. If you feel that

way, I'd just as soon not have you as a customer. Go on, get out of my store." Younger's rotund belly was shaking with anger and Hammerhead had to chuckle as he slipped out the door.

He's a strange man, that storekeeper is. Don't know where he got all those weird ideas about the people coming into our valley. Afraid of the unknown is what I'd say. I wonder what it is that made him come across the great plains if he's afraid of the unknown?

"That's what they're saying, Sonny. That the constable attacked Amos Dudley and tried to kill him. There's a big meeting at Murphy's in the morning. Doc Winslow's got himself all in a twit."

"Doc needs to curb his tongue, Hammerhead. Ain't never heard of anything so uncalled for. Damn right, I'll come with you." Sonny Kniessel stuffed some wood in his stove, poured the two of them some coffee and sat back down. "Kennedy's a far better man than either Winslow or Dudley. I'll stand up and say so, I will. Such nonsense."

———

"That's what I heard, Sandra. That they're going to try and run the constable out of town. I don't know anything other than what I heard from Mr. Younger. There's one who should think about leaving town. He's simply not a nice man. You'd think he would try to say thank you or at least smile when we spend our money at his store."

"Are you planning on going to that meeting? Is it open to everyone?"

"I want to go. With this storm blowing things about I can't do any work on the cabin or cut wood. Constable

Kennedy has been very nice to us, found the man who killed Spike, seen to it that at least some of our money was returned. I think it's my responsibility to be there for him."

"You're a good man, Ken Boyington," Sandra smiled, inviting him to slip under the covers. "Yes, I think you should be there for him. Right now, I want you here for me."

CHAPTER 37

The day broke with screaming winds, flailing snow, and un-tempered tempers in the Brookside valley and surrounding mountains. Murphy's wife started her daily pot of stew early, planned on having roasted elk, and maybe even some roasted turkey if the crowd was to be as large as Murphy thought it would be. The meeting would break up just about dinner-time is what she was hoping and many attending would stay for a hot meal.

"We don't have meetings like this very often, Mrs. O'Reilly, so let's take advantage of the offering." The O'Reilly's never turned down an opportunity to make a nickel or two. They weren't skin flints at all, spent their money wisely among the Brookside business community, and went out of their way to help those in need.

"Murphy O'Reilly, you're a gem of a publican, you are. I'll have food for fifty and you'll have rum and brandy, too. Even the weather is on our side. Everyone will want to be inside, warm, and with fine victuals."

Mrs. O'Reilly was an ample woman, robust, still quite lovely to look at, with full cheeks, an open and genuinely smiling mouth, and eyes that seemed to dance to their own tunes. She and Murphy were never able to have the children that both wished for and have spent many years spreading their charms to their neighbors.

Murphy's Tavern and Inn was based on those in the old world as best as Murphy O'Reilly could remember. He was a wee lad when the family emigrated to Boston. He married young and the two fled to Oregon Territory before either family could put a stop to their foolishness. They knew nothing of frontier life, had only read about Lewis and Clarke, but youthful imaginations, no fear, and a great desire and ambition led them safely to the great green blanket known as Oregon Territory.

They've never had children and their life is based on the tavern and inn being open, warm, and inviting to all who come through the doors. They were born and bred Irish but Mrs. O'Reilly swore that Murphy was mostly Scot in his worshipping of species of the realm.

Murphy had a large fire burning in the rock fireplace, had most of the blown snow cleared from the doors, and sat near the end of his bar, an open earthen jug of fine rum near at hand when the first of the visitors arrived.

"Tobias," Murphy said. "A good morning to you."

"Well, we certainly hope it will remain as such," Kennedy said. The normally ebullient man had a frown frozen to is snow covered face and his eyes did not have the sparkle Murphy expected. His massive buffalo coat was covered in pounds of ice and snow, his wool hat the same even though he had tried to shake off as much as possible before entering. He worked his way out of the buffalo robe coat and sat near the fire, rubbing his hands to get circulation back.

"That wind got its start near the north pole, Murph. Cuts right down to the bone." He made sure that he and

Murphy were alone. "Think they'll all decide that I'm only good for hanging?"

"Not a chance," Murphy chuckled. "How did all this get started? I can't picture you attacking anyone who isn't attacking you first. And I surely can't imagine Amos Dudley attacking you."

"Preposterous," Mrs. O'Reilly said as she came out of the kitchen. "Oh, Tobias, give us a hug now."

Kennedy held the gracious lady tight and gave her a kiss on the cheek. He had been pondering that question Murphy asked most of the night and morning. It wasn't in his bones to hurt someone who wasn't trying to hurt him. He did what he could in his position of County Constable to rein in those who broke the rules and from time to time he had to use force, even to the point of killing a man.

Just how did this come about? He looked at the O'Reilly's, stared into the fire for a moment, and let his mind go back to that early morning. *Dudley was beat bad, the prints of the intruder were clear, even the horse's prints in the mud showed well. How, no, why does Dudley insist that I was the attacker? Ben Thorndyke is sure it has to do with Irene Creighton.*

"They won't be hanging me and they won't be chasing me out of town, either," he said with an angry look to his face. Murphy couldn't imagine anything like that, yet, here they were, waiting for people to come in and maybe even reach that type of conclusion.

"All of this uproar started because of these new people coming to our village and not one of them as has filed for their property has committed a crime yet." Kennedy took the cup of brandy Murphy offered and took a long sip. "Others of the newcomers have, I'll attest to that, but not a single homestead family member has committed a crime."

"They've been good for my business," Ben Thorndyke said coming in the doors. "They've been good for your business, Murphy, and they've been good for Younger's." He slipped out of his heavy buffalo robe and joined Kennedy at the fire. "I just left Amos Dudley. The man's not fit to be here, I'm afraid. He fell again last night and banged his head on a bed post. Doc thinks it might be that fatal blow this time."

"Sorry to hear that," Kennedy said. "The initial attack was severe enough to kill most men. I'm sure Doc Winslow will be here."

"That's all he can talk about." Ben Thorndyke found a chair and dragged it to the fire. "Do you have anything special that you're going to say or show, constable? Something that we can build on?"

"Nope," Kennedy said. "Just tell the truth. That's it. If they don't believe me, too bad for them. Ain't gonna put on no kind of show."

The doors opened and Jacob Hoagland and Claude Atkins made their way in. "Wind's ferocious this morning," Atkins said. "Bet we have half a foot of snow by sundown." His cough from irritated lungs that didn't work well anyway was deep and angry.

"It isn't even the end of November," Hoagland said. "If this keeps up we'll be facing some floods come spring. Best plan on it, I think." He looked around the bar area. "Thought there would be a big crowd by this time."

"They'll be coming," Ben Thorndyke said. The doors were opened and several people made their way in, shucking coats, scraping ice and snow, and trying to crowd close to the fireplace. "This is Dakota weather," Hammerhead said. "Even the wind is Dakota wind."

Over the next half hour or so, Murphy's Tavern and Inn filled, everyone commenting on the weather. Discussion about Constable Kennedy would have to wait its turn, the weather was far more important.

———

BEN THORNDYKE MANAGED TO USHER EVERYONE INTO THE dining area and called for quiet, which took a few moments. All the chairs at all the tables were filled and anticipated quiet settled on the room. "We'll give Doctor Winslow a few more minutes and then begin without him if necessary. He's late because Amos Dudley took another fall this morning and Winslow is with him."

"It don't matter none what the doctor has to say or what that lecher of a banker has to say," Hammerhead Povolny said. He stood up and gave a long look around the tables. "Doc's good at fixing people up but I ain't never heard a word about him capturing a killer or bringing a thief before a judge. The banker's only good at making women feel uncomfortable."

Some men needed to use fifty to a hundred words to make a point. Hammerhead Povolny used as few as possible and the points he made were sharp and sure. There were snickers, a guffaw or two, and Hammerhead continued.

"I've been on the trail with Constable Kennedy more than once, captured, sometimes killed, some mean and ugly varmints. Our little village is safer because of him. I helped him catch the fool what beat up on Amos Dudley."

"If we're going to talk about our constable I'd like to speak," Ken Boyington said. "My wife and I had only been in Brookside a day or two when two men robbed us and killed my little boy. Constable Kennedy never questioned whether or not we should have come to Oregon Territory, he only set out immediately to catch the killers. And he did catch them. Ain't no finer man in the territory in my opinion."

"He's a wanton killer himself," Doctor Winslow said striding into the large room, still in his ice and snow covered wool cape and felt hat. "Amos Dudley is dead," he said in a loud voice, "and that man killed him." He pointed his finger straight at Tobias Kennedy.

There were excited voices, mostly calling out no, or invectives aimed at the doctor. There were men standing and shaking their fists at Winslow, others howling in protest at the accusation.

"Sanctimonious old fool," one man yelled out. "Shut up about something you don't know nothing about."

Ben Thorndyke knew he couldn't let it go on and jumped to his feet. Another few seconds and the loud voices would have turned to outright violence, men would start throwing punches, and sure as hell guns and knives would appear. Murph wondered if the furniture would last.

"All right, gentlemen, knock it off," Thorndyke shouted, looking at Constable Kennedy. Kennedy stood up and thumped his walking stick hard onto the floor several times to no avail. He finally slapped it onto the table twice and there was immediate silence.

"Thank you," Thorndyke said, just a hint of a smile on his face. "Constable, what have you to say about all this?"

Kennedy, already standing, nodded, looked around the tables, and let his eyes fall on Doc Winslow before he began. "The story of Amos Dudley actually begins at Ken Boyington's homestead. Investigating the horrible death of young Spike Boyington, I discovered that the man who killed the boy rode a horse that was missing a shoe."

He looked around the room again, and again let his eyes settle on the doctor. "Investigating the attack on Amos Dudley, I discovered the man who attacked him rode a horse missing a shoe. How did we find that man? Anyone?"

Hammerhead chuckled, stood up, and glared at Doctor Winslow. "Me, Sonny Kniessel, and the Constable trailed a man riding a horse that was missing a shoe, that's how. The same man who killed little Spike Boyington beat the dickens out of Banker Dudley, and our constable caught him, that's how."

Thundering voices were yelling loud and strong, hands were beating on the tables, and Ben Thorndyke let it go on. Finally, things calmed down a bit on their own and Thorndyke looked at Doctor Winslow. "Do you want to know the real reason that lecherous old bastard Dudley blamed Kennedy for the beating? Do you?"

Winslow sat still, his eye glaring back and forth between Thorndyke and Kennedy. "I'll tell you why," Thorndyke said.

"No," Kennedy said, quietly. "The man is dead and his reasons for how he made his decisions should die with him."

"No, Constable," Claude Atkins said, standing up. He had both hands on the table, he was coughing, and it was obvious the man was in pain. "I really shouldn't be here, but what Amos Dudley was attempting needs to be made public. It might be somewhat embarrassing, Constable, but the truth is more important than your feelings."

It got quiet in the room, the only sounds were the labored breathing and continued coughing of the county attorney. Kennedy slowly sank back into his chair,

Doctor Winslow, his pugnacious chin stuck out half a mile or so, relented and sat down as well. Ben Thorndyke nodded to Atkins and sat down.

"We're all aware of what took place just about a year ago when Mrs. Creighton, after years of physical abuse took it upon herself to eliminate Mr. Creighton. Creighton, it was learned was involved in considerable illegal activities and those activities almost cost Mrs. Creighton her home and property.

"Amos Dudley had a fancy for Mrs. Creighton and it was not returned by the lady. She has a fancy for the constable, and that brought Dudley considerable pain." There was gentle laughter and many eyes were aimed at Kennedy. The constable just shook his head, slowly, back and forth, not wanting to hear any more. Atkins continued. "Enough personal pain that our once esteemed banker created a false set of papers indicating that the late Ed Creighton had an outstanding loan from the bank and unless Mrs. Creighton agreed to be his paramour, he was going to foreclose on her home and property."

The silence ended in an uproar of vindictive comments and it took Ben Thorndyke some time to regain control at the tables. "Please, Mr. Atkins, continue."

Atkins had a short coughing episode, took a long drink of brandy, which seemed to calm him down, and gave Doctor Winslow a hard look. "Dudley was a cruel man. He was a sadistic man. And he thought that if he could rid the community of Tobias Kennedy, that Mrs. Creighton would have to submit to him.

"That, gentlemen, is why he has spent months trying to ruin the good reputation of our constable. That is why he claimed that it was Kennedy who attacked him. What he didn't know was this." He paused for more coughing, wiped his mouth, and smiled at Kennedy. "Mr. Kennedy has forgotten where he was the morning Amos Dudley was beaten and robbed. Do you even remember, Tobias?"

Kennedy looked around the tables, filled with eyes eager to hear what he would say. "At your request, Mr. Atkins, Mrs. Creighton and I were having breakfast with you and your wife at Mr. Stevenson's bakery and café. We were interrupted by Hammerhead Povolny bringing us the news of Dudley's attack, and I left to begin my investigation."

Ben Thorndyke had to thump the table several times to get things quieted down. "So," Thorndyke said, "At the time Amos Dudley was getting the tar beat out of him, you had breakfast with these people sitting right here." He looked at Atkins and Hammerhead. "Do you vouch for that?"

"Damn right I do," Hammerhead said. "I ran into the café and found Mr. Atkins, Constable Kennedy, and Irene Creighton having breakfast. No question in my mind."

"Well, Doctor, it seems that Amos Dudley's charge is nothing but an old fool's lie. It's time for you to apologize to the constable for spreading it around."

"I'll apologize to no man," Winslow said, jumped to his feet, and stormed out of the dining room, shoving people around as he made his way out. Men were booing, yelling obscenities, and shaking their fists at the man.

Thorndyke looked at Kennedy and started to say something but was interrupted by Murphy O'Reilly. "Vindication is sweet, Constable. Now, just to prove what a fine upstanding man I am, the first drink is on Mrs. O'Reilly's tab. This meeting is adjourned."

Some say they could hear the howling of grateful men clear down at the river, and Kennedy swore his back and shoulders were bruised for a week. *I've been dealing with every sort of person for the last many years, but there are some I'll never understand.* Kennedy had a wistful smile on his face as the crowd led him into the barroom and shoved a mug of rum into his hands.

It's going to be a long day, I'm afraid, he thought and took a solid drink of Virginia's finest. "Thank you, Mrs. O'Reilly."

CHAPTER 38

"I 've never been that embarrassed, Irene." Tobias Kennedy was sitting with Mrs. Creighton at the fireman's dinner and dance. "Claude Atkins took such delight in telling how you and I enjoy each other's company."

"Well, Toby, we do, you know. I'm terribly sorry that Mr. Dudley had to die but I'm so grateful that all this nonsense of me losing my home is over. So grateful that those terrible things said about you were proved false." She gave him a big smile and took his hand, squeezing it some.

"Tell me about this new man you've hired. Is he really a mountain man, like the old-timers we know who were in the fur business?"

"He'll be returning in the next day or two from Oregon City. He's leading a small caravan over the mountains now. Yes, he even wears buckskins, carries an ax and knife at his belt, and swears he hasn't shaved once in five years."

Irene was laughing and Tobias Kennedy realized it was the first time he'd heard a real, sincerely honest laugh from the lady in several weeks. The heavy weight of possibly losing her home had been lifted.

The music for the fireman's party was provided by three young men who had never had much time to practice but nobody seemed to care. A banjo, a fiddle, and an accordion playing the music most of them remembered hearing many nights on the long road from the east. They were folk songs, not really meant for dancing, but they were being played by young men who weren't really musicians, either. Nobody cared. It was fun to dance, to sing the old songs, to enjoy the end of the harvest season.

Tobias Kennedy towered over Irene Creighton as they danced, and little Carrie, attending her first ever community hoe-down, giggled watching them. Food was provided by everyone attending, that is, it was a potluck supper. Roasted game meats, spit roasted young pigs, lambs, and beef spread a delightful aroma over the entire valley.

This wasn't a party for just the adults. Entire families were on hand for the festivities, and boys were involved in races, wrestling matches, and stone throwing. Many spent long minutes next to the table that was covered in pies of every taste, knowing they could eat every one of them.

Members of the fire department were dressed in their finest, displayed one of the new pumpers that had been brought to Portland after coming around the horn. It was a fine pumper, made in Boston, and the boys put a stream of water over the top of the two story county courthouse to prove its value. The ladder crew ran their ladders to a building and ascended the roof in style, accepting loud cheers from those on the ground.

"It was a wonderful evening, Toby. Thank you. I've

not danced since making the crossing. My feet will ache for a week."

Kennedy was standing in front of the fire in the Creighton living room, holding Irene close. "I'm afraid I'm more like an ox than a dancer but it was pure pleasure being with you. It's been an interesting time, these last few months. I'm glad everything is finally settled."

Irene reached up and pulled the big man's head down and gave him a full-on kiss that seemed to go on forever. "I'm glad many things are settled, Toby. Many things."

He wasn't entirely sure what many things had been settled but was positive that if she ever kissed him like that again, that he would never leave her side. She pulled her arms tight around his neck again and kissed him again.

TAKE A LOOK AT: BORDERTOWN TROUBLE

A SNAKE AND THE DOG-MAN CLASSIC WESTERN

It's the early 1870s, from the Rocky Mountains to northern Mexico a couple of drifters manage to discover their true purpose in life in this hard-hitting western adventure!

A pair of nomadic cowboys are 'asked' to leave Deadwood and travel south to what they think would be gold country. Along the way, the two vagabonds manage to get in trouble, help others, cause trouble, and find the gold they set out for.

Their adventures are rollicking fun some of the time, incredibly dangerous often, and they are able to maintain their dignity most of the time. One might call them searchers...always looking for something, not knowing what that something is.

AVAILABLE NOW

ABOUT THE AUTHOR

Novelist, Johnny Gunn, is retired from a long career in journalism. He has worked in print, broadcast, and Internet, including a stint as publisher and editor of the Virginia City Legend. These days, Gunn spends most of his time writing novel length fiction, concentrating on the western genre. Or, you can find him down by the Truckee River with a fly rod in hand.

Born in Santa Cruz, California, on the north shore of fabled Monterey Bay, Gunn now resides in Reno, Nevada